The Fall Again Series

Donna Figueroa

Fall Again: Beginnings

An Unrealized Romance

Fall Again: Lost Boy

Marc: The Interim Years 1989-2010

Coming Soon

Fall Again: California Girl

Lauren: The Interim Years 1989-2010

Fall Again: Reunion

A Romance Realized

www.fallagainseries.com

D1525416

Acknowledgements

I would like to thank Ed Robertson for his superb editing skills and phenomenal patience. Helen Allen and Dr. Stephen Sobel for your excellent proofreading skills. My back cover photo was taken by Beka of Pic-Chick Photography Chicago, IL. I owe a great deal of gratitude to Story Salon in Valley Village, CA for allowing me to grow as a writer and producer while giving me unlimited support. As always, I thank my wonderful husband and the love of my life, Tony Figueroa. Tony has designed another beautiful cover, and given me even more of a glimpse into the male psyche. I am forever grateful for your constant love and support.

Lost Boy

Marc: The Interim Years

1989-2010

There's some things I don't have now
Some things I don't talk about
These things are between myself and I
In my thick skull the joker hides

There's consequences I'm scared to taste
Cold hard truths I can't face
These days are different than the past
Reflections change in the looking glass

And everywhere I look there's something to learn
A sliver of truth from every bridge we burn...

Elton John

"Birds"

Chapter One

Montreal/New York City

December 28, 1989

"What the hell were you thinking?" This was the icy greeting that Marc Guiro received from his father, Charles, as he entered his family home in Montreal Quebec, Canada. It was nine o'clock in the morning.

Marc had just returned from the home of Miriam Lebel, his longtime girlfriend or, depending on who you spoke to, Marc's fiancée. But as of thirty-three minutes ago she was neither; Marc had just ended their relationship.

The romance of Marc and Miriam began when they were in high school. At one point they told their families that there would be a wedding in 1990 after both had completed their educations. But over the past several years the couple had grown apart. They were different people with different interests and had very little in common.

Marc had been sincere in his promise to marry Miriam, but that was years ago. He was older, wiser and at this point in his life he was having trouble seeing himself married to anyone. Unfortunately, Marc said nothing to indicate he was having second thoughts as 1990 loomed closer.

Miriam, on the other hand, was in the process of planning her huge springtime wedding despite the fact that there was no formal engagement-a minor detail that she hoped to remedy when Marc came home for Christmas.

She had hired a photographer to take engagement photographs, with one appearing beside the formal engagement announcement in the paper. They were to be the guests of honor at an intimate reception hosted by Miriam's aunt and uncle as the wedding date was announced to the couple's family and closest friends.

Most importantly, Miriam had selected a three-carat princess cut diamond ring in a platinum setting that she hoped to have sized and on her finger by the time Marc returned to New York.

But Marc had come home to Montreal with a different agenda. He had to break things off with Miriam, permanently. Many reasons factored into this decision, but only one mattered; Marc had fallen in love with someone else.

Marc knew that he would be unable to move forward with his life and new love while Miriam was still a part of his life. That's why he was at the Lebel home at eight o'clock this morning: to end things.

While there is no good time to end a long-term relationship, a breakup during the Christmas holiday season is especially awkward, in part due to busy social calendars and family affairs. Marc decided he could not end things until *after* Christmas Day, thinking that the last thing he would want to do would be potentially ruining the holiday for those around him. Over the next few days there just never seemed to be a good time to sit down privately with Miriam without festive distractions.

But, on the evening of December 27, Miriam informed Marc that a photographer would be at her home at nine the next morning to take engagement photographs. She instructed him to wear a jacket and tie. She then told him that immediately afterwards they had a second appointment at a jewelers to take care of the pressing matter of her engagement ring.

Marc realized he could no longer postpone the inevitable.

On December 28, less than an hour before the photographer was to arrive, Marc ended their relationship.

Miriam was hysterical. "How could you *do* this to me? You promised! You said when we were both through with school we'd have our wedding! I finally finished in December so I just assumed we'd go forward with our wedding in the spring-just like *we'd* always planned! Most of the details are already in place."

Marc observed that Miriam appeared to be more upset about the prospect of no wedding as opposed to no marriage. He struggled to keep calm. "When did *we* ever talk about a wedding, let alone a marriage? And how could you possibly start making plans without me?"

She tried using guilt to make him come around. "Remember when we had our scare? The pregnancy scare a very long time ago? "You *promised* to marry me! You swore you wanted me and didn't care whether there was a baby or not! I've planned *everything* based on your promise."

Marc tried to reason with her. "Miriam, do you even understand what's involved in a marriage? That it's more than a big party and an expensive white dress? There's responsibility, compromising and fully committing yourself to another person. You're demonstrating none of these things-and right now you're acting like a child!"

This last remark caused Miriam to release a guttural scream before she quickly turned and stormed out of the room. The conversation was over.

As Marc left the Lebel home he walked past Miriam's stunned parents who must have been listening to the entire heated discussion from just outside the room. They said nothing to Marc as he quickly made his way past them. Though he acknowledged them briefly with a nod of his head in a feeble gesture of civility, Marc would have given anything to have been invisible at that moment.

While Miriam Lebel was no longer Marc's girlfriend or fiancée, she unfortunately was still the only child of his father's business partner, Gerard Lebel. While Marc was driving home from the Lebel residence, his father had received an irate phone call from Gerard. This would explain Charles Guiro's less than warm greeting to his son when he arrived home.

Marc had never seen his father this angry.

"How can you do this to our families? Am I supposed to admit to her father, my business partner that you're a coward and you've reneged on promises that you made to his daughter and to his family? This is an embarrassment!"

Charles Guiro stopped yelling long enough to take a long look at his son, who seemed to have no answers to his questions. His words took on a deeper intensity. "How do you think this will affect my business, Marc? Did you even think about that? And what about all of the money that the Lebels have already poured out for this extravaganza? They've already put down thousands of dollars in deposits for the church and the hotel ballroom for your reception. They've hired musicians and bought a greenhouse worth of flowers! And then there's Miriam's wedding gown, which is costing a small fortune on its own!"

Marc felt ill. "Miriam said that she had been planning...but I had no idea that things had actually been booked-and paid for!"

His father snapped. "Dammit, Marc! These things take a lot of time, energy and money to facilitate... especially something on a major scale like Gerard Lebel's daughter's wedding! That girl has expensive taste and her father will refuse her nothing!"

Charles noticed his son's blank expression, which infuriated him even more. "You mean to tell me you knew *nothing* about the plans for your own wedding?"

There was no possible chance of Marc having a reasonable conversation with his father this morning. "Where's Mother?"

His father grew angrier. "Idiot! I want you to stay away from your mother! Don't you know how close she and Miriam have become over the years? We've both been thinking of her as family-as our daughter in-law! When I delivered this awful news to your mother she was so upset, she cried. You are a disgrace to this family! You've upset the Lebels, your own mother and me- and that poor girl! What are you going to do about this?"

Instead of answering his father Marc left the room knowing that any further discussion would be pointless. Marc had always regarded his father as cold and insensitive, with the sole purpose of his life being his business. Marc had often described himself as brooding; a characteristic he inherited from his father and a trait he did not care for despite the fact that it was imbedded into his personality.

Charles Guiro and his oldest son had always been at odds, rarely seeing eye to eye on anything. Charles was a shrewd businessman who saw life in terms of profit and loss, with money being the true measure of a man. He never understood how his eldest son chose the life of an artist instead of taking his place in the successful family business, as Charles had planned.

When Marc revealed his plans to stay in New York after his graduation from NYU, Charles had been incensed and cut him off financially, thinking Marc would return home within a year. Instead, Marc began working steadily as an actor with no plans to come home.

Thankfully Charles's youngest son, Phillippe, seemed to have an aptitude for business. But his youngest son was still in high school, so Charles would have to wait a few more years before a son joined him in the business. And, as evidenced by Marc, a lot of things could happen to steer Phillippe away from the family business.

For Charles, the only thing that Marc had done right was to become romantically involved with his business partner's daughter. Charles liked Miriam; she was a smart and determined girl who he assumed would finally bring Marc home to Montreal. But now it appeared that Marc had also ruined this opportunity.

Marc considered going against his father's wishes and finding his mother to explain why he had to end things with Miriam. He was sure his mother would understand. He felt his mother, Paulette, would at least listen to his reasons for ending his relationship with Miriam, and possibly give him her support. He was sure she would understand that it would be wrong for him to marry a woman he didn't love. But after careful reconsideration he decided it would be best to leave his mother alone. He loved and respected his mother too much to possibly upset her more and further enrage his father.

Normally, Paulette Guiro was warm and vivacious with a quick sharp wit. In Marc's eyes she was exactly the opposite of his father, possessing warmth, kindness and generosity. Marc sometimes questioned how a wonderful woman like his mother ended up with his cold and driven father. But for whatever reason his parents adored each other.

The only family member that Marc could talk to that morning was his little sister, Marie-Christine. When he had quietly knocked on her door the twenty-two-year-old told her brother to come in. She had been aware of Marc's breakup as soon as Miriam's father called her father and the screaming and yelling began. Marie-Christine sat calmly in her plaid flannel pajamas as she listened to her older brother. She had never seen him this upset.

"I don't understand how all of this happened! There was never an engagement-only a desperate promise made when we were teenagers. Chrissie, we were different people back then. I don't even know Miriam anymore! Not this Miriam."

Marie-Christine was hardly surprised at her brother's realization. "Remember, Miriam is used to getting whatever she wants, and right now she wants a big expensive wedding. I know the type; a girl's friends start to get married and then they want their own big party and princess dress. But mostly this type of girl wants the attention! That girl has always wanted to be at the center of everything." Marie-Christine was making a great deal of sense.

"Why didn't I see this before?" Marc was dumbfounded.

"Maybe you were blinded by her beauty or seduced by her charms. I've seen through her since we were children." She thought for a moment before she continued. "She's come to see Mother several times since she's been home. She's been talking as if she's been in contact with you regularly… and that you've been onboard with *all* of her wedding plans. She told us the two of you had decided to start planning the wedding after she visited you in New York last spring."

Now Marc was angry. "She's lying! That visit was a disaster. She ended up leaving a day early!"

Marie-Christine seemed relieved. "Things are starting to make sense now. I knew you'd never give her carte blanche on handling all of the details of something so important. You know, when she got home a few weeks ago she wanted to put an engagement announcement in the paper and almost succeeded."

Thankfully this had not happened. Marc was curious. "What stopped her?"

Marie-Christine smiled. "*I* stopped her. Miriam and her parents were here for dinner the day after she got back from Paris. She casually mentions that she was planning to send her announcement to the papers. I told her she couldn't possibly expect to post anything that important without a photograph."

Miriam had planned to have photographs taken this morning.

"Then I also reminded her she wasn't wearing a ring and people might talk. I thought Papa was going to kill me, but Mother and *her* father agreed with me. I had a feeling you weren't aware of certain details-or any details at all." She noticed her brother's bewildered expression. An alarming realization came over her. "Marc? You weren't aware that she was even planning a wedding, were you?"

Marc shook his head as he tried to make sense of his shambled life. "Not to this extent. She told me she knew what she wanted, but I didn't know she would take things to extremes and had actually starting making plans. Now everyone is angry. Mother is beside herself and is in tears… and Papa thinks I'm trying to sabotage his business! I can't believe all of this is based on a promise I made when I was a naive kid. I went along with it then because it seemed like the right thing to do. You have to believe me when I say I never wanted to hurt anyone, especially Miriam. But by trying to be a good dutiful son, I've managed to hurt everyone."

Marc closed his eyes as he unexpectedly remembered the pain he caused Lauren just days ago. The memory of his last few horrible moments with Lauren stirred a new set of intense emotions within him. Suddenly nobody else mattered.

Marie-Christine looked at her brother as he became lost in thought. "Marc, what is it?"

Marc was concerned about Lauren back home in New York. He desperately needed to get back to her and make things right between them. "Chrissie, I don't think I can do anything here now, other than creating more tension and anger. I need to let things calm down because right now nobody is thinking rationally, including me. I don't know how I could have let things get so out of control. I don't know what's what anymore!"

Marie Christine gave her brother a big hug. "Marc, what can I do to help?

He knew exactly what he had to do. He began pacing and hoping the physical action would help him think more clearly. "Chrissie, I need to get back to New York! What are you doing right now?"

She saw a plan formulating. "I'm taking you to the airport. Marc I'm here for whatever you need." Marie-Christine was more than happy to help her brother escape the hell Miriam had created. "I can be dressed and ready in less than ten minutes. How long do you need?"

Marc was already in motion. "I can be ready in fifteen." Marc started to head back to his room but stopped as he took a deep breath. "I suppose I should talk to the folks."

Marie-Christine thought this could only make a bad situation worse. "No Marc! Let me get you out of here. I'll talk to Mother and Papa... *later*, after things have cooled down and I'm sure that you're on your way back home."

She looked at her brother and noticed how sad and tired he looked. Marie-Christine had always had a special connection with Marc. There was more going on than he was admitting.

"Marc... is there somebody else in your life?"

Marc leaned heavily into the door frame. "Would you think less of me if there was?" He hoped he still had his sister's respect and understanding.

"No, of course not. I only want the best for you. And, to be honest, I don't think Miriam has ever been good for you." She hugged her brother. "Now hurry and get your things together so I can get you back to New York."

Less than fifteen minutes later Marc and Marie-Christine were on their way to the airport.

It was shortly after nine-thirty in the morning and Marc's day had already been very long. But this day was far from over and would only get longer.

Marc knew that trying to return home a day early during the holidays would be difficult. Flights to New York City were booked solid. Thankfully, a resourceful ticket agent booked him on a fight to Boston, where there would be more flights leaving for New York, including the New York/Boston shuttle that left every hour.

After more than four hours on the ground at Boston's Logan International Airport, he arrived at New York's La Guardia just after seven and headed into Manhattan.

Marc was going to go directly to Lauren's apartment unsure if she would talk to him. He decided to take his chances and not call first.

When he rang Lauren's apartment, Mel answered the intercom. She hesitated for a moment before telling him to come upstairs.

Two minutes later, when Mel opened the door to the apartment, Marc barged inside. "Where's Lauren?" This was a frantic demand as opposed to a question.

If Marc had looked at Mel, he would have seen she was deeply troubled, but he hardly noticed her. The only thing that mattered was seeing Lauren.

Marc was moving toward Lauren's closed bedroom door before Mel stopped him by firmly grabbing his arm.

"Marc, stop-I need to talk to you!"

Marc tried to shake her off. "And I need to talk to Lauren!"

But Mel only tightened her grip and angrily raised her voice. "No, I said stop!"

Mel had never intended to sound so cruel, but at least Marc stopped and looked at her, stunned, as the manic energy that had come over him dissipated.

Mel slowly released the grip on Marc's arm while making every effort to calm herself down. "Look, I don't have a lot of patience right now. I've had a rough day!"

Marc resented her comment. The only thing preventing him from exploding was fatigue. "That's funny, Mel, because I've had a rough day too! Actually I consider today a continuation of yesterday, since I didn't sleep last night knowing that this morning I would be breaking things off with Miriam. That task was successfully accomplished before nine this morning. Needless to say she wasn't too happy about the breakup, and neither were her parents-or my parents! I made my mother cry and my father called me a disgrace to the family."

Mel remained still as Marc recounted the events of his day. Her day had been smooth and easy in comparison. "Marc...I'm so sorry."

He took a deep breath and continued to recount what had to be the longest day of his life. "Since I'd already caused enough pain in Montreal, I decided to head back to New York. Three major airports, a four-hour layover in Boston and one trip through U.S. Immigration later, I'm here."

Mel could see that Marc was under a lot of stress. She took his coat before giving him what she felt was a much needed hug. Her voice took on a soothing quality. "I just wasn't expecting you back until tomorrow."

Marc was hardly in the mood for small talk. "That was the plan but I'm back now-and I need to see Lauren." He broke free of Mel's embrace and quickly moved to Lauren's closed bedroom door. He called to her while opening the door. "Lauren?"

Marc stood frozen in the doorway of Lauren's room, confused. All of her belongings were gone. He turned back to Mel as his voice caught in his throat. "Where's Lauren?"

Mel could see that Marc was worn down, vulnerable and exhausted as she dreaded what was coming next. "Marc…she's gone!"

For the first time since he arrived, he heard the sadness in Mel's voice, a sadness that now filled his own. "God, Mel! Where is she?"

As she spoke, Mel saw tears fill Marc's eyes. "I don't know!"

With that Marc brushed past Mel as he headed to the front door. But instead of opening the door, he struck it hard with his fist, and then struck it even harder a second time.

Mel was frightened by Marc's unexpected and violent display of emotion. "Marc stop. Please calm down. You're scaring me!"

Her emotional outburst stopped him. When he turned to face her, he was barely audible. "Mel, I'm sorry. I'm so sorry."

Mel watched Marc shakily sink down against her front door before she heard uncontrolled sobs. At first, all she could do was stand and watch helplessly before her instincts kicked in. She sat on the floor next to him while doing her best to console him.

All this time she had only been worried about Marc hurting Lauren, never imagining that Lauren would hurt Marc. But as Marc put his head into her lap, she sadly realized that Marc and Lauren had hurt each other.

Marc slowly drifted toward consciousness, forcing his eyes open but quickly closing them as the bright morning light shot a sharp intense pain through his skull. His surroundings were unfamiliar, and for a moment he had no idea where he was, which confused him.

It could have been a minute or even an hour later when he opened his eyes a second time and realized that he was on the couch in Lauren and Mel's apartment. On the coffee table in front of him was a bottle of Jack Daniel's. He didn't even like Jack Daniel's, but that would certainly explain his throbbing head. He tried to stand, but immediately lost his balance and fell back onto the couch.

Maybe it was his movements that jump-started his brain as the memories of the day before flooded back to him. The day had begun in Montreal, where he ended things with Miriam and infuriated both families. His sister rushed him to the airport, where he boarded a flight back to the States. He had been in Boston for several hours before arriving in New York and making his way to Lauren's place. But Lauren hadn't been here because... he couldn't possibly be remembering correctly. He found himself praying that the day before had been a nightmare.

With great effort he pulled himself off the couch and made his way over to the closed door of Lauren's room, and very quietly, as if not wanting to wake her, slowly opened the door a few inches. Seeing that the room was empty, he opened the door wide and stood staring inside.

As he stood there, Marc remembered how Lauren felt in his arms. He remembered her kisses, her scent, and how smooth, warm and right her naked body felt against his. He remembered the intense few moments of passion that ended abruptly before anything had begun. And now she had literally run away from him.

An unexpected wave of nausea rolled over him, physically knocking him back and away from Lauren's room as he quickly found the bathroom.

A few minutes later, Mel was unlocking her front door as Marc was coming out of the bathroom. She was relieved. "Good, you're finally awake. I was starting to worry."

Marc was too tired to react, but found his way back to the couch as Mel went to the kitchen. Moments later she returned with a glass of water and two white tablets.

"Tylenol. Please take them, since I made a special trip out to get them. You look pretty hung over." She looked at him more closely, studying him. "You look… terrible."

That got his attention. "And good morning to you, too." Marc's head throbbed with every word he spoke. He popped the two pills in his mouth and gulped down the entire glass of water before leaning back on the couch and closing his eyes.

Mel spoke nonchalantly as she took off her coat and draped it over a chair. "Afternoon actually, since it's just after one."

His eyes opened as she slowly and carefully sat down beside him. "Marc, other than being hung over, are you all right? Can you even remember what happened last night?"

Unfortunately, he remembered everything. "I remember spending some quality time on your floor. And Lauren's gone."

Mel was thankful that she wouldn't have to tell him about Lauren's departure again. "That's right. And you were so upset I convinced you to stay here last night. I went to get you a blanket and by the time I got back you'd found that bottle of Jack I didn't even know I had. I didn't have the heart to take it away from you. I hope it helped."

He looked at her, still trying to put the pieces of the night before together. "Mel, why did she leave?"

She wasn't going to get off the hook completely. "This is what I've learned about Lauren. When it comes to anything business-related, she's the ultimate professional. She likes being in control. She can walk into an audition and take over the room. She can manage her finances, her time, and can talk to just about anyone. At *Crossing* everyone loves her. She's great! You couldn't ask for a better friend."

Marc was listening intently.

"But then when it comes to personal matters, she's not as confident. She's very sensitive and can be very shy, especially in uncomfortable situations."

Marc could never imagine Lauren shy.

Mel continued. "Lauren is very emotional. She felt this was one of her strengths as an actor. But in real life, she saw this same characteristic as a weakness. She told me herself that her emotions often controlled her actions, and that sometimes the only way for her to regain control of herself was to shut herself down emotionally."

Mel saw that Marc was looking despondent and considered ending the conversation, but he needed to hear what she had to say. While this conversation was also becoming more difficult for her, she continued.

"I saw this first-hand when she came back from your place the other night. When Lauren got home she was very upset. And then a few minutes later she was uncontrollably upset. Marc, it was bad. But the next morning she was devoid of any emotion whatsoever, and remained that way until the last time I saw her."

There was confusion in Marc's voice. "But why didn't you stop her… from leaving?"

Mel exhaled deeply and told him about the last time she saw Lauren. "A couple of days ago I decided to take the train out to Long Island to visit my family. I begged Lauren to come with me, but she was still feeling awful and didn't feel like being around people she didn't know. I told her that I didn't need to go, either, and we'd do something together in the city, but she insisted I go spend the day with my family." Mel paused for a moment, remembering her last conversation with Lauren. "She *thanked* me for everything I'd done for her, and gave me a hug that was…different. I realize now that it wasn't a 'see you later' hug-she was saying goodbye. " Mel wiped her eyes. "I should have stayed with her."

Marc urged her to continue. "So what happened after you got home?"

Mel continued slowly as she tried to remember details. "I got home just after ten and assumed Lauren had gone to bed since I didn't see a light under her door. I'm positive she was home. But then next morning when I got up, there was a check for her share of January's rent. She didn't want me out financially. Then I found her note saying she'd left. I'm positive the note hadn't been there the night before. That's when I opened the door to her room and saw it was empty. She must have packed up everything when I was out of the city. The furniture is all mine and she really didn't have a lot of stuff, so I guess she was able to move quickly." She got up and grabbed a piece of Kleenex, making no effort to conceal her tears.

Marc could now see the events of the last few days had also effected Mel. He had forgotten that she and Lauren had become close friends. He felt horrible, but urged her to continue. "What did you do?"

"What could I do? She'd pulled a late night vanishing act! In her note she said she'd contact me, but who knows when that'll be. I was worried, to say the least. I called her friend Will, who had spoken to her the night before. She told him she was leaving town, but he never imagined she meant immediately. He wanted her to come spend a few days with him to cool off. He was shocked when I told him she was gone, and has no idea where she is, either.

Marc froze as his spirits sank lower.

"Then late yesterday afternoon I ran into my neighbor from across the hall who works nights. He asked me if Lauren made it home all right. I looked at him blankly, so he explains he just assumed Lauren was going home for New Year's. He told me when he came home at four this morning, he found Lauren struggling out the door with two huge suitcases. He helped her to the curb and hailed her a cab. He heard her tell the driver to take her to JFK. I spoke to my neighbor just after seven last night, a little more than an hour before you got here."

The color drained from Marc's face. "Do you think she went home to Ohio?"

Mel had already considered this possibility. "Sure it's possible-but we both know Lauren. I think Ohio is the last place she'd go now. It's just a feeling."

Mel was still trying to understand what had happened between Marc and Lauren the night Lauren had come home so upset. Lauren wouldn't talk. But she and Marc had always had a special bond. She hoped Marc would give her some insight on why Lauren left him that night, though she had her suspicions. "What happened between you and Lauren that last night?"

Marc didn't know where to begin, and the last thing he wanted to do was to betray any confidences.

"Marc, you've known me forever and you know you can talk to me-and trust me."

Marc replied reluctantly. "The night before I left, she came over to bring me a Christmas present." He was quiet again.

Mel encouraged him to continue. "The Rockem Sockem Robots. She was so excited about giving them to you, and a few times I had to beg her to wait until Christmas." She could see that remembering the events of the week before was painful, but encouraged him to continue.

"Well, I was genuinely touched that someone-that *Lauren*-had gone to the trouble of finding the one toy I'd never gotten as a child, something she knew I'd wanted. She gave me something I've never had."

He stopped talking for a moment, lost in his own thoughts. "I hugged her like I have a hundred times before, and I kissed her. And I kissed her again, and the next thing I knew she was kissing me back… and I didn't want to stop! I've kissed a lot of women. I've been with several but this was different!"

Lauren hadn't told Mel any specifics of that night. Mel tried to keep her expression neutral as Marc struggled to continue the story.

"We kissed… but it was more than physical. I mean it was physical, but there was so much more going on. It's hard to explain. She kissed me with every fiber of her being. It was like she touched my soul."

Marc's last statement replayed in his head. It sounded overly dramatic while bordering on melodramatic. But he had spoken from his heart. "Hell! I don't know much of anything right now."

This brutally honest admission was something Mel never expected. Watching Marc struggling with his emotions was difficult. After a short time she felt she had to say something.

"So, the two of you finally admitted you had feelings for each other. That you're in love."

None of this was making sense to Marc. "You knew?"

Mel shook her head in disbelief. "Apparently you and Lauren were the last to know. The rest of us-Gary and Natalie, Crimson, me, even Wes-saw this coming for months." She thought back to a specific night. "Do you remember the night you got us all together at The Corner Bar to meet Miriam?"

Marc thought for a few moments before weakly nodding yes.

"So, I'm sure you also remember Lauren's date that night, David, the camera operator from my show? Tall. Dark hair. Movie-star-good-looks…"

Marc remembered that he couldn't stand seeing this guy with Lauren and cut her off mid-sentence. "Yeah, I remember. What about him?" The sound of his own bitter voice surprised him.

Mel was also aware of Marc's acidic tone. "Despite the fact that both of you were with other people, the sexual energy between you and Lauren could have lit Rhode Island. And then the next morning you put Miriam on a plane and immediately came here looking for Lauren-and you were clueless as to why!"

Mel watched as Marc suddenly realized he had been in love with Lauren back then. He turned introspective, exhaled and lowered his eyes to the ground.

Mel let him have a few moments before she once again became his confidant "Marc, what happened?"

Marc painfully recalled his memories of that night. "Things got *intense*."

There was an uncomfortable silence as Mel questioned the picture that was starting to take form. "I thought you told me you didn't have sex."

Marc was hesitant to continue this conversation. "No. We didn't! The phone rang. It was Miriam! She was talking all this nonsense about our wedding."

Mel stopped him as a hint of anger seeped into her voice. "What? *Your wedding?* Marc, are you and Miriam engaged?"

The thought of being engaged to Miriam only upset him more. "No! We are not engaged. She's crazy. When we were younger, we had a pregnancy scare. That's all it was-a scare. But afterwards, for whatever reason, I told her we'd get married when we were both out of school. I was eighteen and thought I was in love with my sixteen year old girlfriend… who wasn't pregnant. At the time I think I meant what I said. But that was a long time ago. We're different people and I don't know her anymore. She convinced herself, and *both* families we're getting married this spring. She's been making arrangements and plans and has led everyone to believe I'm onboard with everything. I think both families always wanted this marriage, like it would be good for the business or some other antiquated idea. Both families are pissed that I'm backing out of a commitment I don't think ever really existed."

Now Marc sounded angry, but Mel already knew that. "Marc, don't you get it? Lauren bared her soul to you. Hearing Miriam talking about your wedding plans must have destroyed her, because she thought you were committed to someone else. From what you've told me, you'd already kissed her when Miriam called."

Marc couldn't look at Mel but found himself confessing to where he and Lauren had been when Miriam interrupted them. "We were in bed… when the phone rang."

Mel's mouth dropped open. Though she was angry, she managed to keep her voice calm. "Don't you see? She felt used and who knows what else!" She crossed her arms in front of herself and turned away from Marc. "I warned her she was going to get hurt!"

They both sat silently, neither knowing what to say.

Marc finally spoke. "I never meant to hurt her."

Mel shrugged. "I know."

"I *love* her." This was an honest admission.

Mel nodded affirmatively. "I know that too."

Marc stood to leave. "I should go now."

Mel, while still somewhat upset at Marc for driving Lauren away, was genuinely worried about him.

"No, Marc. You don't have to leave. Stay as long as you like, or as long as you need to. I could make you something to eat."

The thought of food, especially anything prepared by Mel, started to make him feel ill again. "Thanks, but I'd rather be alone now if it's just the same with you." He began looking around the room. "Did I have a coat?"

Mel crossed to the small coat closet, removed his navy blue pea coat and helped him put it on. She handed him the duffle bag he arrived with the night before.

"I'll be calling you later tonight, so please pick up the phone or you can expect a visit from me. And please try to eat something, okay? Trust me, you'll feel better."

He let her hug him at the door, and to his surprise found himself holding her tightly as she tried to console him as he began to miss Lauren all over again.

Finally, he pulled himself away from Mel and began the walk back to his apartment.

On the last day of 1989, Marc awoke to the sound of someone loudly knocking on his front door and a woman's voice calling for him to open the door. While he hadn't had anything to drink since the Jack Daniel's binge at Mel's place, he still felt tired and hung over.

As he dragged himself to the door he realized he was completely dressed. Before he had time to fully comprehend this, he opened the door to find Mel holding two cups of coffee and a white deli bag.

Mel immediately understood that he had spent the rest of the previous day in bed and, hopefully, sleeping. She made an attempt to be civil. "Good morning Marc."

He stepped aside to let her come in.

"You didn't pick up the phone when I called last night, so I'm here to check on you just like I said I would. I'm guessing you came home yesterday and crawled into bed and haven't moved since." She was right.

Mel pushed one of the coffee cups into his hands before quickly moving away from him. "Take the coffee and please, go take a shower! You've been in those clothes since you left Montreal two days ago. I brought you one of those breakfast sandwiches you like, but you have to shower first. I'll be here when you get out."

He saw her go into his small kitchen as he made his way to shower.

Twenty minutes later he returned to Mel, who nodded her approval. "So you look a lot better than you did a few minutes ago." In her eyes this was an important first step forward.

"I feel a hell of a lot better, too. I needed the coffee, and I hadn't even thought about showering or changing clothes. I haven't gotten out of bed since I got home… yesterday?"

Mel nodded and offered him the bacon, egg and cheese sandwich she had brought him. "Why don't you eat your sandwich? I bet you don't even remember the last time you ate."

She watched Marc devour the breakfast sandwich and saw life slowly coming back into him.

"Thanks, Mel. I do feel better, physically anyway."

She reached out and took his hand. "I hope you're ready to start taking care of yourself again because I can't be here every day."

He squeezed her hand. "I guess I don't have a choice." He attempted a smile, which prompted Mel to reveal the other reason for her visit.

"Marc, I have some news. I know where Lauren is. She's fine, and she's safe."

Marc was fully conscious for the first time in two days. "You spoke with her? Where is she?"

She didn't want him to get too excited since she didn't have much to tell him beyond what she just had.

"Marc, calm down. I haven't spoken to her-not yet anyway."

He seemed confused. "Then how do you know?"

She explained. "The friend that she's staying with called me. She had a feeling Lauren hadn't told anybody where she was. Did you ever meet her friend Hannah?"

Marc remembered the night he went to the comedy club with Lauren to see Hannah perform. Then he remembered that Hannah moved to LA earlier in the year. "She's in Los Angeles!" He paused, losing his train of thought for a moment. "Hannah….Hannah Moore moved to LA last spring. She's the one Laurie helped get ready for her move." He sighed with relief. "She's in Los Angeles, with Hannah…and she's safe."

Mel watched him closely.

"Yes. But Marc that's *all* I know. Hannah didn't want to divulge any more than she had to, but she didn't want us thinking Lauren had fallen off the face of the Earth. I didn't push the issue because I imagine Lauren is feeling very much like you are right now: hurt, angry and probably very fragile."

Marc knew where Mel was heading. "So, you're suggesting we let her come around in her own time. Let her sort things out for herself?"

Mel was glad he was beginning to understand. "And maybe you can do some soul searching yourself."

"I know Lauren's safe and she's not alone. If she can't be with me, I'm just going to have to accept that-for now." His eyes wandered to the floor.

Mel took that as her cue to leave. "I have to get going, but call if you need anything-or if you want to talk. If I learn anything more, I'll let you know."

As she headed toward the door she looked at him one last time. He looked exhausted and depressed, just as Lauren had looked the last time she saw her. Marc and Lauren would need time: a lot of time.

Chapter Two
New York City, Winter 1990

For Marc, 1990 began without fanfare as he was still numb from 1989, a year that he would very much like to put behind him, save for a few bright spots that involved Lauren and a successful run in an off Broadway play. He tried to return to his life as a New York actor by beginning to audition again.

He taught a class in stage combat at the American Children's Theater. ACT had hired him as part of a team to develop a curriculum for theater workshops for school children that he and a few others would present around the New York City area. If all went well, the program would be taken on the road with the performance company during the next season. ACT provided a paycheck that allowed him to continue to audition On Saturday nights he tended bar at a small neighborhood place for tips.

Marc was going through the motions during those first few weeks of the year, struggling to get out of bed every morning and pushing himself to get through each day.

Mel became his main support during this time. She took on a role that at times was more maternal than that of a friend. They spoke a few times a week and tried to get together for a meal at least once a week. She even delivered food to him a couple of times out of fear that he might starve otherwise.

As long as Marc kept himself busy, he could get through his days with minimal effort. But stopping for any period of time caused his thoughts to return to the last night he saw Lauren. Maybe he should have run after her. Maybe he shouldn't have left town. Maybe he should have tried to talk to her, no matter how hard she would have tried to push him away. That night played on an endless loop that was difficult to ignore.

One day he was searching for his keys, something that was becoming a frustrating and common occurrence. While moving a pile of papers on his desk, he came across a program from the choreographer's workshop where Lauren had performed in November. He had never really looked at it, but on this day he opened the program and began reading. He was looking for something-anything.

He saw the name of the dance, *And So It Goes,* followed by the names of the dancers, Josh Durning and Lauren Phillips. It was strange to see her listed that way, because now he only thought of her as *Laurie.*

And then, of course, there was the name of the choreographer, Lauren's good friend Will Somers. Marc read Will's biography. That's where he found what he was looking for: the name of the dance studio where Lauren took class. Will's studio.

Then from across the room Marc spied his keys on top of the television. He took this as a sign to leave, but not before making a phone call.

According to the Tempest Dance Studio receptionist, Will would be teaching a class that would be finishing at six o'clock. Marc was going to make sure he arrived at the Tempest studio just beforehand. Marc needed to talk to Lauren's good friend, Will Somers.

The studio smelled of wood and sweat. From the closed door of the dance studio he heard what he assumed was either a jazz or modern dance class in progress. Practically drowning out the music was a loud voice shouting out instruction and encouragement. Marc couldn't help but think that the instructor sounded like a real slave-driver. Then he and remembered that Lauren said Will was tough, which brought out the best in his students.

At six o'clock sharp he heard applause signaling the end of class. The door opened and several dancers emerged from the studio. He heard more than one comment that Will had been especially tough during this particular class, but then that's why they always returned.

Marc watched the receptionist leave her desk, enter the studio and cross to Will on the other side of the dance space. Marc observed Will through his reflection in one of the studio's large mirrors. Will appeared to be helping the last dancer from class with her hip placement. The loud drill sergeant that had been barking orders a few minutes before was now very gentle as he squared his pupil's hips toward the mirror.

Marc gathered that the receptionist told Will that he was in the lobby and wanting to talk to him. He saw Will's expression change slightly as the receptionist returned to the lobby.

"He'll be out in a few minutes and is asking you to wait in his office. It's at the end of the hall."

He thanked her and headed down the narrow hallway.

The small office's walls were covered with photographs of dancers. On the wall behind the desk was a larger photograph of Will and a man he recognized from pictures in Lauren's apartment: Robert, Lauren's cousin. To the right of that picture was a newer photograph that had to have been taken on the night of the choreographer's showcase where Will stood between his two dancers. Marc's eyes were drawn to Lauren, who was still in her dance dress and looking very happy.

Marc heard footsteps coming down the hallway. A moment later Will entered, a water bottle in his hand and a towel draped around his neck. Marc spoke first.

"Will, thanks for seeing me. I'm Marc…"

Will interrupted him as he moved behind his desk and sat down. "I know who you are. And I can probably guess why you're here…but that would be rude. So why don't you explain why you're here."

Will was calm; too calm which made Marc uneasy. "I'm here because of Lauren."

Will showed no emotion. "Lauren. You mean your *friend*, Lauren?

Marc detected a hint of sarcasm in Will's voice. "I miss her."

Will was unimpressed, but Marc continued.

"I realize I'm the reason she left town…and I'm sorry I hurt her. That was the last thing I ever wanted to do. I really miss her, and I want her to come home. I love her."

Will sat back in his chair staring at Marc, silent and making him feel even more uncomfortable. He sat for at least a full minute before finally breaking the silence.

"How is it possible that you can sit here and tell me, a virtual stranger, that you love Lauren while you could never tell her yourself? If the two of you had admitted how you felt about each other months ago, you could have saved yourselves a lot of trouble."

Now it was Marc who was momentarily quiet as he considered what Will had said. "Lauren was in love with me months ago?"

Will's composure started to break. "Do you really have to ask that question?"

His response made Marc sit back.

"Yes, Marc. Lauren has been in love with you for months! She probably still loves you. The rest of us could see what's been developing between you for the longest time. You couldn't be honest with her and you couldn't be honest with yourself. The night of my showcase I watched you and saw the way you looked at her. This was the first time I met you and I could see it."

Marc remembered that it was during that night that he had finally admitted to himself that he loved Lauren, but Will brought him back to the present.

"Does this mean you were the last to know? Not that the information will do you any good now."

Marc now saw that Will was trying to conceal anger. "I didn't know how she felt about me!"

Will practically laughed in his face. "How could you not have noticed? Are you blind, or just stupid?"

Marc didn't react, which Will took as his cue to continue.

"She knew you had a girlfriend but she tried to be your *friend* anyway. The more time she spent with you the more difficult it became for her to control her feelings.

Lauren's an emotional person, especially when she cares about someone. You could have been honest with her. Now she's thousands of miles away, feeling used and humiliated!"

Marc was at a total loss of words.

"And you sit here and tell me that you love her?"

Now Marc was angry. "I do love her, and I'm sorry I hurt her! I know I'm the reason she ran away from home and I'd give anything if I could change things, but I can't!"

Will detected honesty-he hadn't expected that. He wanted to hate this man for driving Lauren away.

Maybe Marc had reached him in some way. "I want her back."

Will looked puzzled. "Did you ever *have* Lauren to begin with? Until very recently, she was just your good friend. She claimed she was glad you were in her life, and that she *respected* your other relationship. You need to decide what you're going to do about your girlfriend, fiancé or whatever she is to you."

As far as Marc was concerned, Miriam was none of Will's business. He returned the conversation back to Lauren. "Have you spoken to her?"

Will shook his head. "Not since she left...and I begged her to stay. She said she'd call me when she was ready. All I know is that she's safe-and looking to start over. And I know Lauren well enough to know that she's determined, and probably won't be coming back to New York any time soon."

Marc's eyes drifted to the floor.

"I'm sorry to be the bearer of bad news."

Will looked at Marc for a few seconds before taking a small framed photograph off the wall from behind him. "Here, I want you to look at something."

Marc took the photograph and recognized Will, but not the person next to him. Then he realized who it was.

"That's Lauren! But she looks so... different."

Will thought back to the first time he saw her. "That's because that Lauren doesn't exist anymore. That's the Lauren that came to New York City when she was eighteen years old and scared to death. She wanted to be in New York, partly because she wanted to be here for Robert, who in a perfect world would have been here to help her adjust to life in the big city. I don't think Lauren had ever experienced a close death and she was still grieving over Robert when she arrived. She wasn't fitting in at NYU or life in the city, and was very close to going back to Middletown, Ohio, which in my opinion would have killed her."

Marc continued to study the photograph of the very young Lauren.

"That's what she told me on the first day she came here. She had been very depressed when, by chance, she found one of our class punch cards that belonged to Robert. Call it fate or divine intervention, but she made it up here and took a class. The receptionist at the time saw her looking at a picture of Robert near the front desk, realized that she had the same last name, put two and two together and got me. Here was this skinny little girl that I'd seen in a ton of Robert's family photographs. That photograph was taken about a week after I met her."

As Marc looked at the photograph, he wondered if this was the girl he'd taken a dance class with at NYU, because this girl looked shy, introverted and could have easily blended into the woodwork.

Will continued his story of his early days with Lauren. "I was pretty sure that she never knew about Robert and me. He had planned to introduce us when she got to New York, but he died months before she arrived. I didn't know if she had the stereotypical Midwestern values, but I told her about us the day I met her, and she let me know that she accepted and respected what Robert and I had. I didn't get to be with Robert at the end of his life, which was very painful; and still is. When Lauren showed up, we were both still mourning Robert's death. We helped each other get through the grief. I stepped in for Robert helping her adjust to life in the city and teaching her about the industry and life as a performer, and she's helped out here at the studio for years. I consider her more than a friend- she's family. I'm still very protective of her, even if this Lauren doesn't exist anymore."

He took the photograph out of Marc's hands and replaced it with the one of her that was taken with Will and Josh at the showcase. "This is the woman that little girl became: confident, talented, beautiful, and a fiercely loyal friend. But I'm sure you know that already."

Marc was almost smiling as he looked at the recent picture. "She's an amazing woman."

He handed the picture back to Will, who carefully put it back on the wall. "Why couldn't she tell me?"

Will was starting to feel sympathy for Marc. "Fear is a horrible thing isn't it? Part of the reason she left New York was that she was afraid of her feelings, not to mention that she didn't want to come between you and any *commitments* you've made. She was afraid, Marc."

There was a knock at the door.

"Will, are you still here?" It was Josh.

"Josh, come in and say hi to Lauren's friend Marc."

Josh came into the small office.

"Marc was at the showcase in November."

Josh extended his hand and said hello.

"Josh, give us a few more minutes, and then I'll be ready to leave."

Josh left, closing the door behind him.

Will still had a few things to say to Marc. "Lauren created a foundation for a good solid career here in New York, but you broke her heart and now she's left town. You've hurt her personally and professionally. Have you thought about that?"

Marc had really not looked beyond his own feelings.

Will continued. "Marc, let me tell you one last thing. I lost someone that I loved very much several years ago, and it still hurts. But Robert died and is never coming back. Lauren is very much alive. I don't know how to get in touch with her, but if I did I'd tell you how to reach her, no matter how upset she'd be with me, because I think you really care about her. But, then again, maybe it's a good thing I don't know where she is. You've got some housecleaning of your own to tend to before you could ever pursue anything real with Lauren." He had nothing more to say. "I hope I helped."

Marc stood to leave. "You have, and thanks." He turned to leave, but turned back to Will. "Please don't tell Lauren about my visit today. I wouldn't want her to think that you've betrayed her by talking to me. I think my betrayal is enough."

Will nodded. "Then as far as she knows, you were never here. And Marc, life is short, so please make some decisions."

Marc sighed, and made his way back down the narrow hallway, past Josh and out into the cold January night.

He had come to see Will for answers to questions he didn't know he wanted to ask. He had been enlightened, and yet he was numb. Marc felt guilt, remorse, and not much of anything else.

The freezer in Marc's apartment severely needed defrosting, with only about a third of the space usable. Days before he had managed to shove a few frozen pizzas into the opening, and now struggled to pull the last pizza from the ice logged freezer. When he succeeded, he also managed to dislodge a small baggie containing some unknown substance. For all he knew whatever it was had been there for years, possibly before he moved into the apartment. He didn't give it any thought and tossed the bag aside as he put the pepperoni pizza into the small oven.

An hour or so later he was throwing out garbage and reached for the baggie which by now had thawed enough to reveal its contents. The bag contained some sort of coarse powdery substance. Curious he opened the bag to take a closer look. Whatever it was, it was tannish in color and smelled earthy. He then came to the assumption that the baggie had probably belonged to Crimson, the Bohemian girlfriend of his former roommate, and was pretty sure that the contents were powdered psilocybin mushrooms, aka *magic* mushrooms.

Crimson had experimented with a variety of organic substances during the time he knew her. Her specialty was *magic* brownies, but she had also brewed *magic* mushroom tea and had offered some to Marc on occasion though he'd never accepted. Not that he disapproved. He just never had the time to devote to a magic mushroom trip that could last up to several hours.

Crimson had started experimenting with mushrooms to expand her artistic realm, as she put it. Some of the paintings that she did while tripping were thrown away immediately, but even Marc had to admit that sometimes she produced some interesting pieces while under the influence.

He had been curious at one point and asked her to describe her feelings during a trip. Crimson's experiences had been mostly positive as she described feelings of joy, relief and euphoria. But she also told him that occasionally she experienced extreme fear and paranoia. He remembered one particular conversation with Crimson. She told him if he ever wanted to try magic mushrooms, to make sure he was with people he knew and trusted.

"While I've never had a really bad experience with mushrooms, I know people who have. You really want to have someone with you who can talk you through and try to talk you down from a bad trip if necessary. If you ever want to try some, let Wes and me know. You'll probably enjoy the feeling. We always have."

Marc looked at the mushroom powder and began to wonder how much powder and water to use to make a tea. It couldn't be that difficult, especially if he used the powder sparingly. He knew that he probably shouldn't experiment alone, but he hadn't felt anything for so long that he found the prospect of feeling anything desirable.

On this night Marc would learn a difficult lesson. Marc would also be reminded that timing is everything.

He mixed the mushroom powder with boiling water and was about to drink when the phone rang. It was Mel wanting to know if he wanted to meet for breakfast the next morning. They agreed on a coffee shop closer to Marc's place. She'd pick him up at ten.

He then returned his attention to the mushroom tea in front of him. The taste wasn't horrible, though he remembered that Crimson said that she often mixed the mushroom mixture with some sort of herbal tea, like peppermint or licorice, to make it more pleasant-tasting. If there was ever a next time, he would remember this detail and continued to drink the mushroom tea straight. He dimmed the lights, then sat back, waiting for something to happen.

Fifteen minutes later, he was still waiting to feel the effects of the mushrooms, when he finally decided that the contents of the baggy had lost their potency due to age and freezing. He turned on the TV instead.

It was almost 9:00, time for *Miami Vice,* one of the few network television shows that cast its actors in New York. *Miami Vice* was a show that he could realistically work on. His agent was constantly on the watch for roles that would fit him on this popular show, though he had yet to audition. But that didn't mean he wasn't preparing for a future audition. He was working on Cuban and Columbian accents to add to his dialect arsenal. That would make him a more viable candidate for *Miami Vice*.

He enjoyed everything about the show, from the actors to the writing and directing. Many times the show took on the look of a music video, due to innovative music composed by Jan Hammer. He'd happily become part of the Miami underworld, especially if it meant several days on location in Miami during the harsh New York winter.

Sometime during the first act of the episode, a painting on the opposite side of the room pulled Marc's attention away from the television. This had been one of Crimson's abstracts which she had given to him for his birthday the year before. He had always loved the mix of swirling blues, greens and purples that he found soothing. But before this moment he never realized that the painting was multi-dimensional. Some of the images appeared to be closer than others.

He walked over to the painting and found that he could actually look *into* the canvas. How had he never noticed that some of the images were outside of the painting's frame? How was Crimson *not* considered an artistic genius? Then the swirls of the painting began to swirl around him, making him feel warm, relaxed, and happy in the fact that he had somehow discovered the secrets that were unlocked deep inside of this artistic masterpiece.

This was only the beginning of Marc's magic mushroom-induced trip.

Finally moving away from the painting, he began to examine his small apartment, appreciating the colors and shapes of the objects around him. The striped print on the loveseat began to extend up the walls, bending and curving throughout the apartment. He followed the lines to the window and looked outside on to the street. From the window the normally dimly lit street seemed to be alive with brightly colored neon lights. He noticed that street lamps and even the lights of the cars on the street trailed streams of bright colors that left him feeling euphoric. Marc felt that the world's secrets had suddenly been revealed to him as he suddenly came to an understanding of everything around him.

He thought about Lauren and now understood what he had to do. He'd have to go to Los Angeles and bring her back home. It was really just that simple and could not understand why he hadn't thought to go get her before. All he had to do was to find her and tell her that he was sorry, and she'd understand. He could leave right now, or at least after breakfast with Mel in the morning.

Lauren was the key to everything. Once she was back in New York, everything would return to normal, and both of them could return to their lives.

By this point in his trip, all he could think of was Lauren and how much he missed her, while the pain he felt over losing her intensified. Suddenly his pleasant trip had taken a sharp and negative turn.

Now his environment became harsh as the colors and lights that had been peacefully surrounding him became severe and unforgiving, causing him to feel as if he were being attacked. He sought refuge in the only safe place he could find: the corner of his front room underneath the window where he laid on the shag carpeting, which was now turning into blades of tall thick grass. At first he felt safe in the grass, but his trip was about to take another bizarre turn.

He started hearing music-distinctive keyboards and synthesizers that created tension throughout Marc's body. He found himself thinking, "That's Jan Hammer." And then he heard voices coming from him across the room. He was terrified, thinking at first that the voices had no bodies at all, until he found the courage to lift his head to look through the grass that had once been his shag carpeting. There he saw *Miami Vice* detectives Crockett and Tubbs on television, creeping through an abandoned building, guns drawn. Sonny Crockett quietly spoke to his partner.

"Our informant swore that our guy was hiding out here." Crockett sounded pretty sure of himself.

"And he's by himself, so we should be able to take him easily. Let's head out this way and split up." Tubbs pointed his gun outward as both men moved forward, stepping out of Marc's television and into his apartment.

Marc crouched down further into the grass. Both detectives were wearing pastel-colored Italian suits over tee shirts. He could see the wrinkles in Tubb's linen pants and the five o'clock shadow on Sonny Crockett's unshaven face. Crockett moved along the left side of the apartment as Tubbs moved along the right.

Crockett called to Marc.

"Marc, this is Miami Vice! We know you're in here. We're not after you! We just need to know what you know. Tell us who's the head of the Mushroom Mafia, and we're gone. Make it easy on yourself and nobody gets hurt!"

This was serious. He had found the mushrooms in his freezer and assumed that they had belonged to Crimson, but then they could have belonged to the previous tenant. He didn't want to rat out Crimson and Wes, but he didn't have a choice. And then he remembered that his ex-roommate and Bohemian girlfriend had moved to California, and for the life of him he couldn't remember where. Both men were moving through the tall grass directly toward him, their guns still drawn.

Marc called to the detectives.

"I'll come out and tell you everything I know...and that's not much! But don't shoot me!"

Then an odd thought occurred to Marc. Maybe he didn't have anything to fear, since he was obviously filming an episode of *Miami Vice*, though he could not remember auditioning. He had to be in Miami because he was hot and sweating. If he was still in New York in January, he would be freezing.

He saw the detectives turn to the other side of the room, giving him the opportunity to look out the window to see where he was, but he couldn't tell because of the bright neon lights. He could be in Miami, or maybe he was still in New York. Then again, he could have been on the moon.

Tubbs was getting impatient. "Marc, come out now! We're tired of wasting time!"

Marc was clutching the grass, trying to remain out of sight. He pleaded with the detectives. "Okay! Just put the guns down!"

Both vice cops laughed.

"You know we can't do that, Marc! What if you're armed? Just come on out with your hands over your head and we'll talk."

Marc was about to surrender to Crockett and Tubbs when a harsh and constant sound reverberated through his body. The sound certainly got the attention of Crockett and Tubbs as they assumed it was coming from outside the window. They ran through the glass, guns still drawn, and disappeared. At least, they were gone for now.

But as Marc lay crouched in the corner of his apartment, the sound still continued. No matter how hard he wished it to stop, it continued at regular intervals, until Marc realized that the sound was the ringing of the front door. He carefully crawled through the grass to the buzzer.

The female voice asked to be let in. Marc remembered that Mel was going to pick him up for breakfast. Was it ten o'clock already? Marc had no idea what time it was since his perception of time had disappeared much earlier into his trip. He didn't even factor in that it was still pitch black outside and never realized it was only eleven- thirty at night.

He unlocked his door for his visitor, who he heard coming up the stairs. Marc crawled back through the grass to his safe place under the window and tightly clutched his knees to his chest as he waited for Mel so he wouldn't have to be alone and afraid. He seemed to wait forever.

Finally there was a knock on Marc's door that seemed to echo through the small apartment.

"Mel, the door's unlocked." Then he found himself pleading with the person on the other side of the door. "Please come in! I'm over here... by the window!"

Slowly he saw the door open. The grass that had grown on his floor became shag carpeting again and the room became eerily quiet.

Looking across the dimly lit room, he saw her standing in the doorway. She was home. She had come back to him. Everything was going to be alright.

Suddenly his fear was gone as he stood and quickly moved across the room, gathering her into his arms and holding her tightly so she could never go away again. He buried his head into her neck desperately trying to smell her perfume, but could not.

Maybe his passionate display of emotion frightened her, causing her to move from his embrace and back toward the door. He did his best to try to regain his composure so she wouldn't be frightened. Not wanting her to run away again, he quickly closed the door.

After a minute or two (or ten), he gently took her hand and hungrily kissed it before leading her to the loveseat. He sat her down, knelt in front of her and collapsed into sobs.

She carefully took his head in her hands and placed it in her lap as she stroked his head neck and shoulders in an attempt to calm him. After several minutes she felt his sobs subside, and his hold on her relax.

There was so much that Marc wanted to say, but he was such having difficulty breathing, he could not speak. Finally, and with great effort he managed a few short sentences.

"I'm so glad you're here! I'm so sorry…I hurt you! I'll do anything. I can to make it up to you. Please believe me! I need you. I want you in my life. You are my life!" He dropped his head back into her lap and caressed her thighs." I swear, I was going to come and get you. But you came back to me…and you've made me so happy! I love you! I love you so much! Please… tell me you're here to stay."

He didn't wait for her to answer, but took his head from her lap and pressed himself into her, kissing her deeply and feeling as if he was disappearing into her and as she kissed him back.

He found himself begging. "Please let me love you!"

She willingly went with him as he led her into his bedroom, where he immediately began undressing her. He helped her under the covers before quickly undressing himself and sliding into the bed beside her.

As he entered her Marc felt alive again for the first time in weeks.

***

The woman who calmly laid beside Marc was oddly satisfied. Their reunion had been emotional, intense and unexpected.

To her surprise she had accomplished what she came to do in a short period of time and with very little effort. She had begrudgingly come to New York not sure of what to expect other than a great deal of resistance. She had been prepared to scream, cry, reason, and beg, or to do whatever she had to do to get Marc to come around and see things her way for both of their sakes. After all, they belonged together.

He had promised her they would be together, and this was a promise that he was going to keep. She had been ready for the fight of her life, but instead he had greeted her with open arms. He had said all of the right things: telling her that he loved her, needed and wanted her. He told her that he had been wrong and would spend the rest of his life making her happy, and then made love to her with an intensity she'd never experienced with any man.

She lay on her back smiling as he slept hard, having collapsed around her. The lovemaking, while intense had been brief, over before it had begun really, yet extremely passionate. She had assumed that this was probably because of the sudden intensity of their union and wasn't going to worry about future encounters.

For now, she was prepared to move forward, even if she had to move slowly. She was going to stay as close to him as she possibly could, being not only his lover, but his best friend- and, if all went as planned, his sole support until she became his wife.

On the night of her return, Marc had only said one thing that confused her. As he had removed the last of her clothing and laid her onto the bed, Marc made her promise that she would never run away again. This was odd, because it was *Marc* who had clearly run away from her. She rationalized that he said this in confusion during the passion and heat of the moment. But still, it bothered her that he would confuse the issue. But as he shifted in his sleep, pulling her closer, she decided she could forget what he said, at least for now.

Miriam's day had been long and full of uncertainties, but somehow many of her problems had resolved themselves. She knew there was still a lot of work and careful planning to do in the days to come.

As she closed her eyes, she turned into his arms allowing him to hold her even tighter. Contented, she allowed herself to fall asleep.

Chapter Three

The morning after Marc awoke from his mushroom trip, daylight presented him with a cruel new reality.

Crimson had always said she never felt any negative effects after tripping on mushrooms. In fact she claimed that she always felt energized and clear-headed afterwards. On the morning after Marc's mushroom trip he felt physically fine and all too alert.

As he slowly awoke, he remembered swirling paintings, trailing lights that had been beautiful, and a bizarre encounter in which Crockett and Tubbs of *Miami Vice* somehow appeared in his apartment.

He sadly remembered that Lauren returned to him. He had begged her forgiveness, then made love to her all night long in a hallucination that was all too real.

That's when he stretched and became startled when he discovered that he wasn't alone in his bed.

With his eyes wide open he looked at the sleeping nude female form beside him. He stared at her in disbelief. His movements caused her to readjust. As she turned over his worst fear was confirmed. It was Miriam.

Marc sat looking at her for several minutes trying to make sense of what was happening and how she came to be in his apartment, let alone in his bed. He tried to reconstruct the events of the night before.

He had buzzed who he thought was Mel into the building. But in his altered state, he saw Lauren…because he wanted to see Lauren while it had been Miriam all along. That meant he had poured his heart out and confessed his love to Miriam.

That's when he realized he was naked, and that he and Miriam had had sex. He fell back against his pillows, eyes closed as he wondered what else may have happened the night before. Part of him prayed that he was still tripping, but when Miriam began stirring a few minutes later, he knew he was dead sober.

She reached out toward him. When her hand found his, she opened her eyes and smiled a smile he hadn't seen in a very long time.

Miriam was beautiful; there was no question about that. But over the years he had begun to see things in her character that diminished her physical beauty. But this morning, barely awake and barely covered by bedding, she had a vulnerable quality that Marc found attractive despite himself. He didn't move as she pulled herself up beside him and kissed him softly and slowly as the blanket fell away from her body.

At her touch he slowly pulled away from her, feeling that everything that had happened, and was currently happening between them, was wrong. He was unsure of what to do next.

Miriam, on the other hand, knew exactly what she was doing and took complete control of the situation.

"Good morning." She slid her arms around his neck. "You've made me so happy! After everything we've been through, to learn that you still love me is more than I ever could have asked."

She pulled herself closer to Marc to sit on top of him while she pressed her breasts into his chest. She cradled his head in her hands and placed her forehead on his and spoke quietly. "I'm sorry, too. I hope you can find it in your heart to forgive me for everything I've done. I'm sorry."

Marc thought he saw tears in her eyes as she suddenly turned away from him in a calculated move. Feeling uncomfortable for her, he reached out and touched her shoulder, making her turn back towards him.

"Miriam, why are you here? I thought I'd ended things between us weeks ago."

He sincerely believed that their relationship was over, especially since he had realized he had fallen in love with Lauren.

"I didn't believe you! There's too much history between us. We hit a rough patch like most couples do during a relationship. And we had a lot working against us, especially with us being apart for so long, and I admit that was my fault. I should have come to you right after I finished school. But I'm here now-and after last night… and everything you told me, I know that we're going to be okay." She took his head in her hands and kissed him.

He moved her off his lap to his side and sat back on the bed. "So you're going to stay here with me, in New York?"

She looked at him surprised. "Of course, I'm going to stay with you, for a little while anyway. One night won't fix everything… no matter how wonderful it was."

Marc did not know how to tell her she was the last person he was thinking about last night, or that in his mind he had been professing and making love to another woman. That would be cruel.

She sensed he wanted to tell her something and somehow knew it was something she wouldn't want to hear, so she played one of the many cards she was concealing. She turned on her happy smile. "I hope you don't mind, but I was so excited about our reconciliation that I got up early this morning and called home. I told our families that there will be a wedding in May after all! Marc, they're all so happy for us!" She threw her arms around him and firmly pressed her naked body into his once more.

Marc felt ill and looked for an excuse to leave the room. That's when he noticed the time. Mel would be here soon. He pulled himself away from Miriam.

"Okay, Mir. Look, I made plans for breakfast with Mel. I obviously didn't know you were coming, but if you'd like to join us… that would be fine. Let me get in the shower."

He rolled away from her leaving her in bed as he made his way to the bathroom. Miriam sat back on the bed feeling confident and relaxed. As long as she remained calm and in control, everything was going to go her way.

Marc had been in the shower for just a few minutes when Miriam heard what she believed to be the front door buzzer. She ignored it, hoping that whoever it was would go away. The buzzer stopped, but a few minutes later there was a loud knocking on the front door and a voice that sounded vaguely familiar.

"Marc, it's just after ten. Don't tell me you overslept because I'm starving."

Miriam had never cared for any of Marc's friends, and she found Mel especially annoying, though she could never put her finger on why. She knew that Mel was one of Marc's closest friends who had known him since he arrived in New York as a college freshman, and that he talked about her often. She didn't fear any sort of romantic involvement between the two of them, but feared Mel knew Marc better than she did. The Marc that Miriam knew as a teenager no longer existed, having been replaced by this adult New York version of Marc that puzzled Miriam- a Marc that Mel knew very well.

Mel continued to rap on the door. Miriam got out of bed and considered answering the door naked. That would certainly send a message. Instead she grabbed the shirt that Marc had been wearing last night when she arrived. It was on the floor along with other items of clothing both of them had been wearing the night before. She had barely buttoned the shirt as she opened the door.

Mel stepped back, stunned. Between the undone shirt and Miriam's disheveled appearance, it was clear what she had done the night before.

Miriam was cool as ice. "Mel! What a surprise. It's so nice to see you again." It was too late for Mel to pretend not to be thrown by Miriam's presence and unkempt appearance.

"Miriam! I'm sorry… I didn't know you were in New York. When did you arrive?"

Miriam lied. "I arrived a few days ago. Marc and I have a lot of plans and decisions to make. And we've decided that it might be easier for me to be here in New York for a while."

"Marc didn't mention that you were coming to town."

Miriam shrugged. "Does Marc tell you everything?"

Mel felt the negativity coming from Miriam and didn't trust her. "Is he here?"

Miriam leaned closer to Mel, letting Marc's shirt fall away from her body. "He's in the shower. We had…well let's just say a very late night and we were late getting out of bed this morning. I'm sure you understand. We've been apart for a very long time and we're…well, getting to know each other again."

Mel felt the anger rising within her. Marc had led her to believe that Miriam was part of his past and that he honestly wanted Lauren back in his life. He had been a shell of himself since she left, and Mel had felt sorry for him…until now.

"Miriam, would you please tell Marc that something came up and I can't join him for breakfast this morning."

Miriam maintained her frozen smile. "Sure, I'll do that for you."

She lowered her voice. "Mel, I wouldn't expect to see much of Marc over the next few months. And I would appreciate it if you could give us time…and space. We've got a lot of work to do. I hope you understand."

Mel understood that Miriam wanted her nowhere around Marc. She was happy to oblige and decided to leave before she strangled her.

"Oh, I think I understand *everything* perfectly, so I'll just leave you two alone. Great to see you, Miriam."

She turned and left.

Miriam, happy with the small victory of getting rid of Mel, returned to bed, never mentioning Mel's visit to Marc.

Marc couldn't understand why Mel had stood him up for breakfast, and was upset when he never got so much as a phone call to explain why. He needed to talk to her about several things, including Miriam.

If Marc had his way he would put Miriam on a plane and send her home, but in light of the events surrounding her arrival, he knew he couldn't do that. She was insistent on staying, and to avoid conflict he allowed her to stay, thinking that she would leave on her own after a few days.

Over the next several days Marc tried to reach Mel at home and at work, but she wouldn't return his calls. This perplexed him, to the point where he waited for almost an hour one evening outside of her building as she returned from work. He called to her as he approached her and immediately noticed her cold glare.

"Mel…what's going on? Why haven't you returned any of my calls? I was really worried about you."

She stepped away from him and chose her words carefully. "I thought Miriam didn't want me calling or seeing you. Does she know you're here talking to me now? I'd hate for you to get into trouble!"

He was surprised to learn that Mel knew that Miriam was in New York. His life was becoming more complicated with each passing day.

He tried to explain but Mel cut him off. "There's no need to explain. It's clear that you and Miriam are back together. I believed you when you said the two of you were over. I believed *everything* you told me! To say I'm disappointed in you would be a gross understatement."

For a moment he thought he was tripping again. He had no clue of what she was talking about.

She continued to seethe at him. "Honestly, I feel like an idiot for thinking you'd changed and had fallen in love with Lauren! I thought *she touched your soul!*"

It stung him to hear his own words spat back in his face. If only she realized how much he truly loved Lauren.

Mel continued. "Marc, how could you have you used Lauren like that? She was your friend, and she fell in love with you…and you knew that! It would have been less cruel for you to let her down easy and tell her that you could never care about her the same way she cared about you! Why did you have to pull her into bed?"

Marc was dumbfounded. "Mel, please listen to me! I do love Lauren! What happened with Miriam was a mistake…and there were other factors…"

Mel snapped back. "I came by to pick you up for breakfast and I'm greeted by Miriam who might as well have been naked! She made sure that I knew that you'd slept together, like she was laying claim to you."

Now Marc was getting angry. "I didn't know you stopped by, Mel. Miriam never mentioned that you stopped by."

This didn't surprise her one bit. "Of course, she didn't mention me! She told me to stay away from you! I'd be careful around her if I were you."

"I'm sorry! I don't know what else to say!"

She could see that Marc was confused and upset. While he had told her that he loved Lauren, she also now knew that Miriam was still very much in Marc's life, and apparently in his bed.

It was time for Marc to know that Lauren had also made some decisions. Mel had dreaded this conversation and had hoped to talk to Marc under more idyllic circumstances- but he was here, and she didn't know when or even if she was ever going to see him again, now that Miriam was still in the picture.

There was a part of her that hated Marc for what he'd done to Lauren. She hated the fact that Miriam was back in his life and seeming to control him. She especially hated that their friendship was in jeopardy. But Marc needed to know what Lauren had decided to do so that maybe he could also make some choices of his own.

She did not want to put this conversation off any longer. Mel worked on a soap opera and was tired of the soap-like drama affecting her friend's lives.

She forced herself to speak calmly. "Marc, I've heard from Lauren."

Marc froze and gave Mel his full attention.

Mel carefully continued. "She called to tell me it was okay to find another roommate, because she's staying in LA... permanently."

Once again he went numb.

"She's found an agent, an apartment and bought a car. Marc, she's moved on. She told me that she has to move forward because looking back is too painful. And in light of current events, maybe her move is for the best."

Marc processed this information. "Did she even mention me?"

Mel remembered Lauren's exact words.

"She asked me to tell you that she's safe and doing okay."

Marc's face dropped. "That's all? Mel, where is she? I want to talk to her."

Mel knew that what she had to say next would be difficult for both of them.

"Marc, she doesn't want to talk to you. She doesn't want you to know where she is, or how to contact her. I need to honor her decision, so please don't ask me for numbers or addresses because I can't give them to you. And, besides, with Miriam still in your life... would that be a good idea anyway?"

Marc had no expression as he turned and walked away. He wanted to be upset with her, but couldn't-she was only delivering a message.

Lauren was gone, and any hope of her returning was also gone. He had held on to hope for weeks. Now that his hope was gone, he had nothing.

Marc made his way home fully expecting to take out his anger on Miriam. But once he arrived home, he found that things were very different. At first he thought he had walked into the wrong apartment, because this space was clean, neat and organized unlike the chaos he had been living in for the last several weeks. Everything smelled fresh and clean.

He was taking all of this in when Miriam came out of the kitchen, smiling as she crossed to kiss him. "Your timing is perfect! Dinner will be ready in just a few minutes. Take your coat off and relax for a few minutes."

He now became aware of a wonderful aroma coming from his tiny kitchen. This was no frozen pizza. Miriam had prepared a home- cooked meal-certainly the first real meal prepared in this kitchen since he had lived here.

Marc had expected to be screaming at her by now, but this new sweet attentive Miriam had thrown him off guard. He didn't know this woman who seemed to be catering to his needs like it was a regular and normal occurrence.

By the time he had taken off his coat she had returned with a bottle of his favorite European beer.

"I hope this is the one you like. I couldn't remember the name, but the colors on the bottle looked familiar, so I took my chances. For dinner I made meatloaf, roasted potatoes and a green salad. I hope that's all right"

By this time Marc's anger had totally diminished. "That sounds good. And you were right; this is the beer I like. I haven't had any in a long time. Thanks… but you really didn't have to do all of this."

Miriam turned around and looked to Marc. "Yes I did. I owe you so much more than a dinner and picking up a couple of things. Marc I haven't treated you very well in a very long time. I guess it took you leaving me a few weeks ago to fully understand that I've been acting selfish and childish and hardly a woman who you would want to spend the rest of your life with. I am so sorry, but I want to start making things up to you, starting now."

For a moment she seemed like the girl he had fallen in love with many years ago. But that was ancient history. Things between them would never be right.

"Miriam, thank you for all of this, but…"

She was becoming aware of irritation that he was trying to conceal.

"Marc…is something wrong?"

He had come back to his apartment wanting to throw her out, but now he wasn't so sure. Maybe he was wrong and needed to reexamine his feelings toward her.

Miriam pulled Marc down on the loveseat beside her. "Marc, I'm here. I will *always* be here. I'll never run away from you."

These words brought his eyes to hers. Miriam was here and wanted to be here, while Lauren had run away from him and did not want to be found. This thought angered and hurt him deeply.

Miriam saw the tension on his face and brought her hand to his cheek. "Love, I can see that you're upset about something, but you're home now. Please, let me take care of you."

Now she moved both of her arms around his neck and held him until she began to feel him relax. Then she kissed him. When she felt him kissing her back, she slowly took one of his hands and moved it to her breast. When he began to move his hands to the buttons of her blouse she took both of his hands in hers as she took her mouth from his.

"We've got plenty of time, so why don't we have dinner first? I'm not going anywhere and we have the rest of the night ahead of us."

She took him to the table where she pulled out his chair. "I promise I'll take very good care of you, and I'll do my best to make you forget about whatever it is that's bothering you. Enjoy your beer while I put the food on the table."

Marc was exhausted physically and emotionally. He was incapable of thinking rationally and fell victim to Miriam's less than subtle manipulation.

The Connellys had left in May, with Wes and Crimson leaving shortly afterwards. For all he knew his friendship with Mel was over. Lauren was gone and wanted no contact with him. In Marc's mind the only person left in his world was Miriam. And it was under Miriam's direction that Marc's life started to move forward again-but in a path he never imagined.

Years later, when Marc looked back at this period of his life, he would ask himself many questions. Why hadn't he sent Miriam home as soon as she arrived instead of trying not to hurt her feelings? Why had he not gone after Lauren, even if that meant going to Los Angeles and looking for her? Why was he so easily persuaded by Miriam to go ahead with a marriage that he knew was wrong from the very beginning? Why had he not fought for his own life?

He always came to the same conclusion: During this part of his life, he had given up on his own happiness and became overly concerned with pleasing Miriam and going through with the wedding that their families had been looking forward to for years. As a result, Marc lost his sense of self.

In May of 1990, and just as Miriam had planned, Marc and Miriam married in a lavish, over the top ceremony that rivaled weddings of members of the British Royal Family. He had no say in the planning, as Miriam saw to every detail with her mother. Apparently this extravaganza had been planned over a number of years. During the last few months a well-known wedding planner was brought in to organize the many details that were escalating in cost.

FALL AGAIN: LOST BOY

Miriam told Marc that everything had been taken care of, and all he had to do was to show up on time. Marc took Miriam at her word, his only pre-wedding activities involving tuxedo fittings (her family gave him a custom-made tuxedo as a wedding gift) and posing for a few photographs. He was able to stay in New York until the Friday before his Saturday nuptials, arriving in Montreal just before noon.

He had expected Miriam to meet him at the airport, but was surprised and relieved to see his sister Marie-Christine waiting for him at the gate. The upcoming wedding had caused Miriam to spin out of control. He would see her later.

Marc embraced his sister and kissed her forehead. "Chrissie, I'm so glad you're here! I didn't expect to see you until later tonight at the rehearsal dinner."

Marie-Christine was happy to see her brother, but hated the circumstances. She had many reservations about this wedding. She hugged him back before stepping back to really look at him. "Welcome home! Miriam was so overwhelmed with everything that I told her I'd pick you up. I've been hoping to talk to you alone anyway."

Her tone made Marc nervous as he followed her first to baggage claim and then to her car.

Once in the privacy of her car she wasted no time. "Marc, you know I love you and only want what's best for you. Do you remember the last time we were at this airport? It was only a few months ago."

Marc was intentionally not looking at his sister and pretended to fidget with his seatbelt that thoroughly annoyed her. She was not going to let him shut her out.

"As I remember you had broken things off with Miriam, which was something that personally made me very

59

happy. You had to get back to New York because you were in love with someone else. I've never seen you so fixated on anything like you were that day I drove you to the airport. And it wasn't that you wanted to get back-you *needed* to get back! When I got back home I thought our parents were going to disown both of us-you for breaking your engagement and fleeing the scene like a criminal, and me for driving the getaway car."

Marc never thought about what Marie-Christine must have gone through once she returned home that day and suddenly felt guilty. "Thanks for being there for me, and I apologize for any grief you had to endure because of me. I never wanted to put you into the situation of having to answer for my actions."

He sat back against the seat and really looked at his sister for the first time in a long while. Somewhere along the way she had become an adult. Marc felt that Marie-Christine was one of the only people that genuinely cared about him and his well-being.

She reached over and took her brother's hand.

"Look, it's just the two of us. Tell me what happened back in December."

Marc didn't want to talk about December- or anything else before today. He wanted to look forward. He removed his hand from his sister's. "Chrissie, I'm getting married tomorrow. Don't you think this conversation is inappropriate?"

Marie-Christine refused to be shut out. "Marc...tell me her name?"

It was obvious that Marie-Christine found nothing inappropriate about this conversation and wouldn't leave the airport parking lot until they had spoken.

Marc was hesitant to say her name aloud. "Lauren." He relaxed. "Her name is… *was* Lauren."

Marie-Christine smiled as she considered the name before repeating it. "Lauren…that's a beautiful name."

She was right, Lauren was a beautiful name. He smiled at the thought of her. "A beautiful name for a beautiful woman. Chrissie, she was beautiful inside and out."

She saw her him physically relax as he thought about her. She encouraged him to continue. "Tell me about her? I'd really like to know."

Marc breathed heavily as he tried to describe Lauren to his sister. He realized for the first time that he'd never described her to anyone. "The first time I saw her…" He remembered her sprinting up the steps toward him the night he met her. "I thought she was a little perfect princess, which is funny to me now because I learned that she was very nice…pretty, personable. As I got to know her better, I saw that she was a beautiful woman. She was smart and sensitive-and totally unselfish. She was passionate and driven. I've never met anyone like her, Chrissie. She frightened me."

Marie could see that this woman had affected him on a deep emotional level. "She frightened you? I don't understand."

He smiled slightly and shook his head. "Lauren was a force of nature I didn't understand. She was an optimist, always seeing the glass half full-unlike me who always saw the glass half empty. She was full of possibilities." The smile left his face. "But Miriam was in the picture and I tried not to look at her as anything but a friend. That's what I kept telling everyone around me. And that's what I told Lauren-and that's what I kept telling

Lauren. And the worst part was, that's what I kept telling myself!"

Marie-Christine had seldom seen her brother show emotion. If he couldn't say it, then she would. "You fell in love with her!"

He didn't say anything.

"And she was in love with you, too!"

His silence said everything.

"Marc, what happened?"

He looked off into nowhere. "I was never able to make a complete break with Miriam. I finally told Lauren I loved her, but it was too late. I ended up hurting her, and she felt she couldn't even stay in the same city with me."

Marie-Christine stopped her brother. "But you *did* break it off with Miriam just after Christmas! You upset a lot of people when you left, but you didn't care about anything other than getting back to New York." Marie-Christine watched as her brother started to shut down emotionally.

"Chrissie, by the time I got back to New York Lauren was already gone. I'd missed her by less than twenty-four hours. Miriam had come between us too many times and she couldn't stand it, or me, anymore. She picked up her life and left New York without telling anyone where she was going. I know she's in Los Angeles, and seems to be doing well… but she doesn't want to have any contact with me." Marc looked totally defeated.

This time Marie-Christine sighed heavily. "Marc, I'm sorry. But you're here to marry Miriam. Do you love her?"

He looked straight ahead. "Years ago I thought I was in love with Miriam. But we grew up and apart and became different people, but that doesn't mean we don't have a history. We have a lot in common: the same type of upbringing, the same religion. Our families have known each other for years. They've looked forward to this marriage ever since Miriam and I told the families we'd planned to marry when we got out of school. I haven't been the best person during the last few years. I've lied to many people, including myself. In January, Miriam came to New York to see me. She seemed to care about me despite the way I'd treated her. We've gotten to know each other again. I can see a part of her that she doesn't like to show many people, and I like what I see. She's agreed to move to New York, which had always been a problem. You know she hates New York, but she's willing to be there with me, as my wife. So I'm here to make amends and to make good on a promise I made years ago. I think we could be good for each other."

Marie-Christine didn't like what she was hearing. She clutched the steering wheel of the car to steady herself. "Marc, after you get married I promise that I'll never intentionally say anything bad about your wife. But right now Miriam is *not* your wife, so I'm going to speak my mind."

She waited until Marc gave her a sign to continue. If he didn't want to hear what she had to say she'd respect his wishes. But eventually, he turned to face her.

"Marc, Miriam is a spoiled little brat who is used to always getting what she wants, and right now she wants the big wedding she and her mother have been planning for years! She has a sense of entitlement, like this wedding is her God- given right. I don't believe either of you are going into this marriage for the right reasons. I see her as someone who wants to be at the center of attention. And then I look at you and I see you not marrying for love, but out of some twisted sense of loyalty-or guilt. I saw the way you looked when you talked about Lauren. You looked happy and calm. I'm sorry I never got to meet her. I've never seen you look like that when you've talked about Miriam. When you talk about her all I see is stress. Are you sure you know what you're doing?"

Marie-Christine knew her brother well. Everything she said was absolutely true. But Marc had come home for a reason, having come to terms with his decision to get married weeks ago. Now Marie-Christine would also have to accept his decision.

"Chrissie, I wish you could have met Lauren, too! Both of you have the same fire, sense of determination and a sparkle that comes from deep within you. You would have loved her- but she's part of my past. I loved her, and I suppose a part of me always will. But I've decided to move on with my life, like she has with hers. I know you're only looking out for me, but I hope you can understand that I'm doing what I feel I need to do. It will be all right."

Marie had finally released her grip on the steering wheel and asked her brother again.

"Marc…do you love Miriam?"

Marc remembered the all-consuming love he felt for Lauren. He had never felt that type of love for Miriam or anyone else. A heavy silence hung between them before Marc reached over and hugged her.

"I'm going to do my best to be a good husband to Miriam." He knew this wasn't the correct answer, but felt better when Chrissie returned his hug.

Marc eased out of his sister's embrace, unable to look at her as he once again began to pull on his seatbelt. "Chrissie, why don't we head home? There're probably a lot of people waiting for us, so we might as well get going."

During the drive to the Guiro family home Marc and Marie-Christine said nothing, their silence speaking volumes.

The next day, after Marie-Christine was dressed in her blue satin bridesmaid dress, she went to check on her brother. Marc was sitting in a chair in the second floor sitting room. She had never seen her brother in a tuxedo and thought he might look handsome if he didn't look so sad. He had a drink in his hand that looked like scotch. She correctly assumed this was not his first drink of the day. He looked serious and lost in deep thought. Maybe she shouldn't have interrupted him, but she felt she had no choice.

"Marc, are you sure you really want to go through with this?"

If he had given her the word, she would have rushed him back to the airport and gotten him on the first plane back to New York...or Los Angeles. But Marc had no intention of leaving. He managed to produce something resembling a smile for his little sister.

"Sure, why not? I'm already dressed."

Marie-Christine knew there was nothing more she could do.

Less than two hours later, for better, for worse, Marc and Miriam were married.

Chapter Four

New York City, 1991-1992

Marc and Miriam's extravagant wedding was followed by an Italian honeymoon, a gift from Marc's parents. The couple was able to relax after the stress of the wedding, though the couple was stressed for entirely different reasons. Miriam was trying to decompress due to the intense wedding preparations. Marc struggled with the lifelong commitment to a woman he no longer knew.

Together they enjoyed Italy's art, history, architecture, food and wine. They explored Florence and its museums. They spent four days on the Amalfi Coast in an opulent hotel suite overlooking the Mediterranean Sea.

For Marc the three weeks in Italy created a strong hope that his marriage had been the right decision, because feelings for Miriam that he had not felt in years began to resurface.

But when the couple returned to New York, the realities of life and the complexities of a marriage emerged.

Marc and Miriam had considered several neighborhoods before deciding on the East Village. The apartment they selected was only slightly larger than the apartment Marc had shared with Wes, though it was in a nicer building. He hoped Miriam would feel comfortable.

Their first several weeks in New York as a married couple were spent making a home together and unpacking wedding gifts, of which there were many. Miriam happily wrote thank you notes over a period of several weeks.

Meanwhile, Marc began auditioning often and even returned to working special events. He took his role as a husband and provider seriously and fully supported his wife during her first few months in the city.

During this time Marc patiently helped his new bride become a New Yorker. She learned how to navigate the city on foot and via subway, though, of course, she preferred taxis. She learned where to eat, where to shop and where to find the best bargains. She learned the best places for carry out and where she should take her dry cleaning. In Marc's eyes she seemed to be adjusting well.

At first their marriage was polite and civil. This changed once Miriam finally understood what her husband did for a living. She was the wife of a working New York actor. Marc's schedule was unpredictable with auditions sometimes starting early in the morning, with others running late into the night. Plans that were made sometimes weeks in advance were often cancelled due to last minute calls. Miriam found this frustrating and unacceptable.

During the first six months of their marriage Marc booked several jobs which meant he was in rehearsal for several hours during the week, or when at home was preoccupied with memorization or research. In addition to any acting work Marc was also working day jobs. He was teaching stage combat at ACT and tending bar whenever possible.

Miriam often felt neglected due to Marc's sometimes erratic schedule. Marc reminded her that she had married a New York actor, and being uncertain of one's schedule was a normal part of the profession. Miriam said she understood, but she was experiencing more and more bouts of boredom and irritability due to Marc's absences.

When Marc realized that she seemed comfortable in her new surroundings, he suggested that maybe now was a good time for her to begin her own career. He offered his support in any way he could, first by bringing her trade papers for the fashion industry and even getting the names of employment agencies that catered to the fashion industry.

At first, Miriam appeared grateful and began to peruse the trade journals. She even went to one of the employment agencies where she submitted an application and resume. But Marc soon realized that she was merely going through the motions of looking for a job with no intention of finding employment. Her *idea* of marriage meant a husband who would support her.

By the time Marc and Miriam returned to Montreal for the Christmas holiday, their marriage was beginning to crumble. The trip was brief due to one of Marc's work commitments. The holiday season meant Marc could earn good money working holiday parties. While he looked forward to spending Christmas Eve and Christmas Day with their families, he and Miriam would be returning to New York the day after Christmas.

Marc ended up returning to New York alone with Miriam choosing to stay at home for just a few days more. Those few days turned into a few weeks, until Miriam's mother told her to get back to New York and be a wife.

Meanwhile, Marc realized he had not missed his wife at all. In fact, he had enjoyed the peace and tranquility he had at home for the first time in months. Nevertheless, Marc was determined to make his marriage work when his wife returned home.

On her first day back from Montreal, Miriam had to make her own way back to the East Village since Marc was working. She entered her small apartment that she had spent months arranging and decorating. The apartment was comfortable and cozy, but compared to her spacious bedroom back in her family home in Montreal, it felt like a prison cell. As she unpacked her two large suitcases she felt claustrophobic as if the walls were closing in around her.

Marc arrived home shortly after she did and was genuinely happy to see his wife, especially since he had some very good news to share.

"Miriam, welcome home!" He gave her a big hug which she half-heartedly returned. "I want us to go out and celebrate! I booked a role in a film that works next month. It's a substantial supporting role in an indie film that's shooting in Boston!"

All Miriam seemed to hear was Boston. She pushed herself away from him and exploded. "You're leaving me to go to Boston? Marc, my God! How much longer do you expect me to put up with this?"

This outburst was unexpected. Marc was genuinely hurt that his wife could not be happy for him and this major career accomplishment. "Miriam, I auditioned for this film early in December, don't you remember? It was the espionage project where I read for the role of a scientist? I was excited because this role would be something different for me. I went through two different auditions, hoping that they'd make a decision before the holiday, but as usual they took their time. I got the news that I booked the role today. I really hoped you'd be happy for me."

She looked at him as if she hadn't heard a word he said. "How long do you intend to do this?"

Marc had heard this exact same phrase from his own family for years and had learned to ignore them. But hearing it from his wife felt like a knife through the gut.

She continued her tirade. "Didn't you enjoy being back home? We could have a real life there right now with a house, and you could have a *real* job-and friends and a social life."

It was all Marc could do to restrain himself. "Miriam, please stop." He said quietly.

At that moment he realized for the first time that she had no idea what he did for a living.

"I have been working, somewhat successfully, as an actor here in New York for the last few years," he continued. "You would have been aware of this if you had come to see me from time to time, but you were always busy, or ignored my invitations. Since we were teenagers you knew that this is exactly what I wanted to do, and so far I'm very happy in my career. As for being home, New York *is* my home-it's *our* home. I come home today, happy to see you, and to let you know that I'd made a significant step forward in my career. I wanted nothing more than to share this news with you and you can't even say congratulations! You stand here and yell at me like a two–year- old because you're going to be home alone for a few days next month. May I remind you that I've been here alone for almost three weeks." In reality, he hadn't missed her at all.

She looked ashamed as he continued, his voiced tinged with sadness. "Miriam, why is everything always about you? Let me tell you what this role means to me. I've been cast in a film that stars some major players and is being directed by an established director. The script is good...no, it's very good. This is a film that very well might get some attention, which means I'll get some attention, and hopefully more doors will open for me."

Miriam wasn't even looking at Marc. "I'm sorry, but I don't understand any of this. I'm not sure what you expect of me."

Marc believed her. "I want your love, respect and support. Is that too much to ask from my wife?"

He could have sworn he saw her cringe.

"Ever since you came to New York I have been nothing but supportive toward you. I want you to be happy here, but you've done nothing to support me, or yourself for that matter. I've invited you to join me for events and performances when I can, but you never want to join me. You might actually enjoy yourself. I don't know what you have against the artistic community, but it's really bothering me because it seems you want to have nothing to do with my professional life."

He thought back to the challenging year before. "Last year several of my closest friends left town. For a while my life was very difficult because my world had changed so drastically. When you came, I thought things would get better because you were with me. I'll admit it to you now, but I wanted to send you back home to Montreal right after you arrived."

This came as a major revelation to Miriam.

"You *wanted* to get rid of me? It certainly didn't appear that way when I got to your door that first night! As I remember, once you got your hands on me I didn't think you were ever going to let me go."

Marc also remembered that night, but his recollections of that night were very different from Miriam's. In Marc's memory Miriam was not even present.

For a moment he considered telling her everything. But then he remembered his marriage vows-specifically, for better or worse.

"I remember seeing a part of you that I hadn't seen in a very long time. It was a part of you that I'd forgotten and wanted to get to know again. I chose you over several things-and people-in my life at the time."

Miriam was incredulous. "You gave up people for me?" She didn't believe him, so Marc revealed something else that he had kept to himself.

"I know that Mel came to see me the morning after you arrived. I know that you were not very nice to her, lying to her and making it appear that I didn't want to see or talk to her."

Miriam's face turned red.

"I was very upset when she didn't return my calls so I went to see her. It was all she could do to talk to me because she was so angry. That's when I realized that while she had kept her breakfast date with me, you sent her away. How could you do that to me, and to one of my best friends?"

He watched Miriam slink to the couch in shame as he continued to speak. "I don't even know why you did what you did. I was thinking it was jealousy which would be ridiculous! The fact is that Mel was one of my closest friends who I'd known for ten years. She was responsible for helping me get through some pretty tough times here, and I miss her! But in the end I chose you, and as a result I haven't spoken to her for almost a year."

She looked like a child who been caught doing something very bad and awaited punishment.

She fumbled for a response. "I thought it was important that you and I get to know each other again. I wanted to spend time alone with you. That's why I sent her away. Are you still mad at me?" Mac didn't know what to say, but at least she had admitted to her wrong doings.

"It took me awhile to get over what you did, but I chose to look forward and tried to make things work. I married you, and made a vow to share my life with you. I wish I felt that you were doing the same with me."

At that moment it became clear to Marc that she had no understanding of what a marriage really was.

"Marc tell me what I can do... to make us better." Maybe she had begun to hear him.

"Support me unconditionally. Be there for me emotionally, and professionally. While I'm always here for you, please don't depend on me for everything. You might want to make more of an effort to find a job...or maybe I should say start your career. Maybe you'll be happier if you created a life of your own in New York that you could share with me. Miriam, you're very talented and there's no reason you can't pursue your own goals."

Marc watched her as she sat lost in thought.

Miriam had achieved her only goal of marrying Marc. She had not thought of life beyond her wedding.

After a long silence she stood up, crossed to Marc and looked into his eyes before giving him a tentative hug.

While it was difficult, she said what she thought Marc wanted to hear. "I'm sorry for being selfish, and I promise to try to be more supportive of your career." She took a step back and tried to smile. "I'm happy you got the part, Marc."

Marc thought that just maybe, just maybe, this was a start.

A few days later, as Marc was preparing to leave for his bartending gig, Miriam asked if she could go with him.

He hadn't expected this at all, but seemed happy that she wanted to spend time with him.

Once the couple arrived at the bar, Miriam took a seat at the end of the long bar, slowly nursing a couple of glasses of wine through the evening. She was pleasant, engaging and seemed to be having a good time as she interacted with several of Marc's regular customers.

One of Marc's regulars, George, was a man in his seventies who came in alone and usually stayed through two shots of Canadian Club whiskey before leaving. George was totally captivated with Miriam who gave him her undivided attention. She even flirted with him, which amused and touched Marc.

George loved Miriam's accent, and when he learned she was French Canadian, tried to speak with her in French that amused her, though Miriam, treated the effort with respect, speaking slowly and trying her best to understand what George thought he was saying or asking her. She never laughed, though several times Marc had to cross to the other side of the bar to laugh himself.

When George left at the end of the night, he gave Marc a generous gratuity. "You have a beautiful and fascinating wife. Treat her nice or I may have to steal her away from you."

On their way home Marc thanked Miriam for the extra attention she had paid to his customer. She was slow to take the compliment.

"He's a lovely man, but very lonely, Marc."

He could never remember her doing something so unselfish. But this was only the beginning of Miriam's surprises.

A few nights later Marc was memorizing lines for his upcoming film role. The dialogue was heavy in scientific terms and jargon, not to mention that many of his character's speeches actually advanced the plot of the film. Before the dialogue could make sense to an audience, it had to make sense to him. Marc wanted to be completely comfortable with the dialogue and was devoting at least a few hours a night to memorization and research. As he was working, Miriam quietly came into the room, placed a cup of tea on the table in front of him, and then left just as quietly. Marc was surprised and appreciated her kindness.

But one of the biggest gestures came a week later as Marc was working on a series of particularly difficult speeches. Miriam had been bringing tea to Marc as he worked regularly, but on this night she didn't leave immediately. She stood quietly on the other side of the room until Marc noticed her.

She sounded nervous. "If you would ever like me to help you study-I mean-learn your lines-just ask." She exhaled, smiled and started to leave the room.

Marc was floored. "You'll run lines with me?"

She brightened as he reminded her of the correct terminology. "Yes, running lines! I'll run your lines with you whenever you'd like."

Marc touched by her offer, moved to one side of the couch and motioned for her to sit beside him. "If you have time, I could really use your help right now."

She joined him on the couch as he handed her the script. For the next forty-five minutes, Marc ran lines for his upcoming film role with his wife. Maybe this was the way it was supposed to be.

On this night Marc sincerely believed that maybe he and Miriam had a chance of making their marriage work.

They had a nice Valentine's Day. He brought her roses and took her out for a romantic dinner. They enjoyed a pleasant evening-in fact the past few weeks had been pleasant as he saw Miriam trying to be supportive and was grateful for her change in attitude.

But Marc was feeling horrible, because now, he was starting to feel that he was only going through the motions of being a good and attentive husband. He wanted to feel an emotional connection to Miriam but could not-especially in bed, where their sexual encounters were becoming less frequent. He knew the precise moment when he realized this unfortunate reality.

He had come home one night and turned on the television when he heard a familiar voice call to him from the screen.

"Pizza's here!"

The scene on the television screen was a girl's college dorm room. Three attractive coeds were starting to devour a large pizza, enjoying each bite more than the last.

But Marc only noticed one coed. It had been over a year since he had last seen her. He had made a conscious effort not to think about her anymore, considering the changes in his life. But for the next thirty seconds he noticed everything about her. Her hair was pulled back with a headband which framed her face and allowed him to clearly see her beautiful eyes. Her skin looked bright and velvety smooth. She was dressed in shorts and a generic college T shirt, which showed off her slim figure and long beautiful legs. Her cheerful smile lit up his dreary apartment like a thousand-watt bulb.

Marc thought she looked absolutely beautiful. Her presence somehow went through the screen and momentarily wrapped him in a comforting warmness, before the commercial ended. He then found himself in a dimly lit room, feeling cold and empty.

When Miriam came through the door a few minutes later, he pretended he was happy to see her. And yet he felt guilty.

It was ridiculous, but by watching Lauren on television for a few seconds, he felt he had just cheated on his wife. How could he ever love Miriam when his heart still belonged to someone else?

During the last weeks of February, Marc travelled to Boston, where he spent two weeks working on the espionage thriller. Most of his scenes were filmed on the MIT campus in Cambridge. He enjoyed the trailer and attention from the students who had their peaceful campus invaded by the motion picture industry. But mostly, Marc enjoyed the work and left Boston, secure in the knowledge that the job had gone very well.

Marc returned home to find that Miriam had gotten a job as an assistant to a designer known for her Modern American Classic aesthetic. Miriam's duties would not include actual designing, but the opportunity would allow her to get to know the business, and move up within the company.

When Marc walked through the door he could tell that she was genuinely happy, something he had not seen in months. That night proved to be the happiest of their marriage. They were both able to celebrate professional achievements as they celebrated over dinner and champagne.

Marc honestly thought that Miriam's new job would give her a sense of purpose, not to mention a boost of self-confidence. And at first, that happened.

Miriam was energized with her first project at her new job which involved scouring Manhattan for ethnic influences for an upcoming line. She had an excellent eye and purchased items from many New York neighborhoods, coming back every day with a variety of items ranging from textiles to pottery to food items-anything that might inspire the design team. Once she had the items back at the studio she would photograph and catalogue them. While she enjoyed this part of the job, she was also asked to answer phones and perform other minimal office duties, including making coffee and getting lunch for more senior employees. Those menial task, to no surprise, she hated with a passion.

It wasn't long before Miriam felt that her entire job was beneath her.

When Marc got back from Boston he immediately began working on not one, but two roles in a play reading series to be done at the main branch of the New York City Public Library. The plays were new unproduced works by newer authors. The readings didn't involve a lot of time for any of the participants. The actors would meet with the writer and a director the Tuesday and Thursday before the reading to rehearse. On Sunday afternoon the staged reading would be performed in front of an audience, and afterwards the audience could ask questions to any of the participants regarding their preparation, choices and processes. The pay was very good for three days of work, in addition to the work that the participants did outside of their two days of rehearsal.

Marc's first staged reading was in late March. *Gate 13* was a four-person comedy about three strangers trapped at New York's JFK Airport during a blizzard. Marc played a European tourist who was sick of the States and fed up with Americans, only to find himself trapped in an American airport. He found a way to make his annoying and frustrated character likable and endearing.

Miriam attended the Sunday reading and seemed to enjoy herself and her husband's performance. Marc thought this was good, since lately she didn't seem to be enjoying much of anything.

A few weeks later, Marc was in rehearsal for the second staged reading. Little did he know that this job would have a catastrophic effect on his marriage.

The one act play, *Vows,* was a two- character drama involving a parish priest and a married parishioner who fall in love. The conflict arises when these two people must decide whether to honor their vow or surrender and fight for their love and pursue a relationship that would be condemned by God and man.

The one-hour play was intense, emotional, and extremely well received by the library audience. The question and answer period went for a full hour after the reading was completed. Most of the questions were for the play's author, though the actors also received several questions.

Marc was genuinely excited about this reading. The play was well written, and the complex role allowed him to work on a deeper emotional level. He also enjoyed being the romantic lead, which up to this point in his career had been a rarity.

Of course, he asked Miriam to attend. She had watched him working on his script all week, but was completely unaware of the play's subject matter before the Sunday performance.

During the question and answer period Marc answered an audience question about how he approached the role of a celibate priest in preparation for the reading. He answered the question with a touch of humor, saying first that since he was a married man he decided not to take a method approach to the role. The audience laughed.

Then he turned serious as he explained to the audience that the character of the priest is simply a man-a man with needs, desires, emotions, a heart and very strong ideas of right and wrong. While he loves and has committed to God, he has also fallen in love with a woman and is severely conflicted. Marc took a long thoughtful pause. "The Catholic Church, has always regarded the love between a man and a woman as one of the most precious gifts that God has given mankind. When I began thinking about this role, I first saw his love for this woman as a test. Then I started to think about his love for this woman… as a gift."

Marc's answer had been brutally honest, but he was no longer talking about the play. His wife noticed this as well.

He noticed her sitting several rows back in the audience looking angry. At this point he had no idea why. She continued to scowl for the rest of the question and answer period.

There was very little conversation on the train ride back to the East Village.

Once they arrived home Marc casually began discussing the reading. "The audience seemed to enjoy the program. The role was different from what I usually play, but I feel I turned in a good strong performance. What did you think?"

She could hardly look at him as she tried to suppress her anger. "The play's words and story were beautiful. You and the woman…" She didn't know his partner's name.

"Erica. She's a wonderful actor! She was very generous and very easy to work with. She made my performance better."

She looked at him as if he had just slapped her. "Performance? How can you call what the two of you did on that stage a performance? The emotion and feelings between the two of you...were *real!*"

Miriam's words confused Marc. He had not done a full production, which would have involved physical interaction and a fully developed performance. For this reading he and his acting partner were seated at a table with scripts in front of them, and a narrator reading stage direction seated at a small table a few feet to the audience's left to avoid distracting the audience from the actors. The only physicality between Marc and Erica was when Marc reached out once and grasped her hand, an action that had been purely spontaneous.

"Miriam, we were *acting*. Recreating the human experience. I know I've explained this concept to you many times."

But Miriam was so angry she was having difficulty expressing her thoughts. "Yes, you've explained it to me! And yes, Marc. I understand. You are an *incredible* actor because I saw things...emotions in you that I've never seen you express toward me!"

Marc crossed to her and put his hands on her shoulders. But she angrily pushed him away.

"Don't treat me like a child!"

Marc did not understand. "Are you jealous of Erica? Because there's no reason. I met her for the first time on Tuesday at the first rehearsal. " To his frustration, that seemed to anger her more.

"I don't have any opinion about the woman you were reading with. Just with the way you *acted* towards her!"

"Miriam…what are you saying?"

"You had more intimacy with her than you've *ever* had with me. You were tender and loving toward her in a way that you've never been with me. I could see it! And worse… I could feel the connection between you."

Marc was still looking at her in a state of confusion as she began to cry.

"What I witnessed on that stage today was *real.* Real feelings-honesty, and very real emotions. But here at home… with me, I feel you're only going through the motions. I can only pray you-or any man for that matter-will look at me the way you looked at your partner onstage today!"

She was right. The emotions seen that afternoon were very real. He may have told his audience earlier that he had not used a methodic approach to his role, but in reality he had used a method approach called *substitution.* This is when an actor substitutes genuine feelings and emotions they have experienced in their own lives for the feelings of the character in a script. This method, when practiced correctly, can be quite effective and very powerful.

In *Vows,* Marc remembered the only time he had truly been in love, and brought up his feelings for Lauren. Ironically, he had never allowed himself to feel or express these feelings for her when she had been with him in New York.

Allowing himself to experience these feelings was something he was hesitant to do, because his feelings for Lauren had been so intense that at times they frightened him. But he *wanted* to think about Lauren and express his feelings for her. He wanted to *talk* to Lauren, even if it was within the context of a play where no one could possibly get hurt. Instead of talking to his acting partner's character, he was talking to Lauren-and his performance became very real, raw and extremely emotional.

In Miriam's mind, her husband had cheated on her not physically, but emotionally. The sad thing was that Miriam was absolutely right.

"I'm sorry, Miriam." Now Marc was experiencing very real guilt.

Now, Miriam became brutally honest. "The last time I felt anything even close to what I saw onstage today, was when I came to New York last January when you didn't know I was coming. You were so *happy* to see me... and I felt you really *loved* me... and *wanted* me. The experience was powerful. I believed you when you said you loved me, and I thought we really had a chance at a marriage and a real life together. But now... I don't know!"

By marrying Miriam, Marc had dismissed his own feelings in an attempt to fulfill a promise made years before under stress. But now he could see that he had deeply hurt Miriam. He was at a loss.

"Please, tell me what I can do? I don't like seeing you like this."

Her answer shocked him. "You don't have to do anything... because I don't feel anything for you, either."

He looked at her stunned.

"I tried to like it here in New York because I was with you. I thought being married would be different. I was looking for magic, but I guess magic really doesn't exist. Marc, I like you, but is that really enough? I hate New York! I hate this apartment! I hate not knowing if you'll be here or not when I make plans for the both of us! I hate that I'm not the center of your life."

Miriam's honesty hurt him to the core, but he deserved everything she could throw at him.

"Miriam, are you enjoying any part of your life in New York? What about your job?"

She started to shake her head no as she fought to maintain her composure as she spoke about her embarrassing career in the New York fashion industry. "I *hated* that job. Another position opened up in the company, so I applied and interviewed. The job would have involved some actual designing. I thought this position would solve many of my issues because they'd get to see my talent. It came down to me and another guy who'd been with the company for about a year…and they gave the position to him…so I quit! That was two weeks ago."

Marc had assumed that Miriam had been going to work every day for the last few weeks and wondered what she had been doing with her days, but he didn't need to know this instant. Miriam was distraught and he wanted to be supportive.

He hugged her with compassion. "Mir, I think I understand. It's hard when your talents aren't realized. But you'll find another job, one that's better suited to your talents. I'll do whatever I can to help you, just like you've helped me over the past few months. It's going to be okay."

Her reaction surprised him. "Is it *really* going to be okay, Marc?"

Before he could answer she stood and walked to the door of their bedroom. She paused, contemplating what she would say next. When she spoke, her words were ice cold. "Do you remember the accident that happened not too far away from here?"

A few weeks before there had been a horrible accident just two blocks away from Marc and Miriam's apartment. A driver had lost control of his car after taking a right turn too fast. The car jumped the curb, hitting a pedestrian who was killed instantly.

Marc nodded. "Of course, I remember. You saw the report on the news, but remember, I saw the accident site first hand on my way home that night. I remember thinking that it could have easily been me, since that's a route I normally walk."

Miriam spoke with no emotion. "I know. That's what I was thinking, too. When I heard the report on the news it occurred to me that you were late getting home. The victim's name had not been released to the public, pending notification of the family. I began to wonder if it *had* been you. I imagined what I would say to the police officers who would show up at the door to deliver the horrible news and wait for me to dress so they could take me to identify your body... which would have been difficult. But at least it would be over. After all the unpleasant tasks involved in planning a funeral, I'd finally get to pack up and go home to Montreal. And no one could ever blame me for anything. I'd be free."

Marc sat stunned and motionless as he continued to listen.

"But then you walked through the door which put an end to my little fantasy." She thought for a moment. "Part of me was disappointed that you'd come home."

Marc, who had been intently staring at Miriam could no longer look at her as she continued.

"That's who I've become. I don't love you. Sometimes I don't even know if I like you. I do know that I don't like myself. This marriage was a huge mistake. I hate my life...and I want to go home!"

Miriam calmly stepped into their bedroom and closed the door behind her.

At the moment, he felt his entire life slowly come apart.

The next morning, Marc took his wife to JFK and put her on a flight to Montreal, uncertain of the state of his marriage.

Ironically, the best thing about their marriage was ending their union. For the first time they worked as a team to achieve a common goal, and both felt relief as they moved toward correcting a terrible mistake.

Two weeks after Miriam returned to Montreal she called Marc. "We both know that our marriage is over, but our families are devastated. They want me to come back to New York and for us to start marital counseling."

Marc was uneasy about this prospect. "Marriage counseling? Is that really going to achieve anything, Miriam?"

Miriam had obviously thought this through. "No, we both know that counseling will change nothing. But if we go through the motions of seeking help, maybe it will be easier when we tell our families we never should have married in the first place. This might make it easier for them to come to terms with the divorce."

The word *divorce* suddenly made their situation very real.

"I have the name of a therapist who's rather progressive. She'd like to meet with us one on one before she sees us together. Why don't you make an appointment for yourself, and I'll do the same."

Marc agreed.

A week later Marc met with the marriage counselor and tried to explain his reasons for getting married, and revealing from his perspective, why they had no foundation for a marriage; he was never in love with Miriam.

In Miriam's own session, she told the doctor that her perception of marriage was based in fantasy, and the realities of her actual marriage were overwhelming.

In their only session together the counselor asked if either of them could think of any reason to fight for their marriage, or if there was even a marriage worth saving. Marc and Miriam agreed there was not.

The rest of the session was spent with the counselor giving them advice on finding closure, and even peace with each other. The session turned out to be productive and would help them through the next several days.

Marc had offered to stay someplace else while Miriam was in town, but Miriam saw no need for Marc to leave what was also his home. They were cordial and supportive toward each other as they divided their belongings, deciding who got what, and together packed what would be shipped back to Montreal. With the pressure of being married off their shoulders, they were able to communicate openly for the first time in years while truly enjoying each other's company.

Finally the last of the boxes had been shipped to Canada. All that Miriam had to do was to pack her last suitcase and get to the airport.

Both of them were surprised that they were experiencing sadness. They were coming to the end of a relationship that had been going on since they were teenagers. They had history.

When Marc took Miriam to the airport for the final time he told her a few last things. "I'm sorry that I couldn't be the man you wanted me to be, Miriam. I never wanted or meant to hurt you. I sincerely hope that one day you'll find what you're looking for in life, and in a husband."

She suddenly looked like the sixteen –year-old-girl he had fallen in love with several years before.

She nodded sadly. "I'm sorry I couldn't be the woman you wanted me to be, either. I just thought… it would be different. At least we had a nice wedding and honeymoon before everything fell apart." She was trying to keep the mood light, but the knowledge that this was really the end brought tears to her eyes.

He put his arm around her and pulled her close. The last thing he wanted was for her to fall apart. "Miriam, it's all going to be okay."

She pulled a tissue from her purse and dabbed at her eyes.

"I know." She calmed herself down with a few deep breaths and told Marc something that she felt was important. "You're going to be getting some very scary looking official papers in the mail- but, remember, we agreed to make this as quick and as painless as possible. My father says there shouldn't be a problem with the annulment, either, probably due to a large donation he recently made to the Church."

As Catholics, their marriage had to be officially dissolved by the church, especially if either of them ever wanted to marry in the Church again.

"We're not blaming one another for anything. We're just ending something that never should have happened in the first place."

He could see that she was trying very hard to keep herself together. He spoke with an unexpected tenderness.

"Miriam, I've never blamed you for anything. I think there were too many circumstances beyond our control."

She nodded affirmatively, though Marc knew she really didn't know what he was talking about.

She had never known about her ill-timed phone call that ended with the woman he had fallen in love with literally running out of his life. She never knew that her unannounced visit came in the middle of his experimentation with a mind altering-substance that allowed Marc to see what he wanted to see-Lauren, the woman he loved returning to him.

Miriam never needed to know about these things. The only thing that mattered now was getting her home safely, so they could both begin the healing process and move forward with their lives.

The first boarding announcement came over the PA system. "Good afternoon ladies and gentlemen. We are happy to announce that Air Canada's flight 733, nonstop service to Montreal is ready to begin boarding through gate 37. Please have your boarding cards ready, and welcome."

As the gate attendant repeated the same announcement in French, Marc and Miriam stood together for the last time, neither knowing what to do or say.

Miriam spoke first. "Thank you for everything."

Her sincere words touched him. He took her in his arms one last time, holding her close. "Thank you, Miriam. I want you to be happy." He suddenly found himself struggling to maintain his own composure.

On seeing Marc's emotion, she touched his cheek, and kissed him lightly on the mouth.

Marc hadn't expected this but found himself returning her kiss because he knew this was goodbye. This was the least he owed her. The kiss ended and she stepped out of his embrace.

"Goodbye Marc." She began to move toward the gate.

Marc wanted to say something that would make her feel better whenever she remembered this moment. He wanted it to come from the heart.

"Miriam…"

She turned to him one last time.

"You were… the most beautiful bride."

Miriam smiled for the first and only time that day before turning to board the plane.

Marc didn't leave the gate immediately but instead took a seat where he could watch the plane from the window.

His last unofficial act as Miriam's husband was to watch her plane push back from the gate and taxi toward the runway. When he could no longer see the plane, he left the gate.

His sense of relief equaled his sense of guilt. Surprising were the feelings of sadness and loss. He had been married for three hundred and fifty nine days, not even making it to one year.

While Marc felt numb, he concentrated his efforts on getting back into the city. He had an audition.

Chapter Five

New York City

1996-2001

Marc was in a cab heading toward a theater near Times Square for the premiere of an independent film. The producer John Paris, a friend from NYU, had invited him to the premiere because first, they were friends. And secondly, because Marc was currently in an Off-Broadway play for which he'd received excellent reviews, he was known in the theater community.

Since most theater venues were dark on Monday nights, many New York filmmakers held their premieres on Monday evenings which would allow the members of the theatrical community to attend. The filmmaking and theater communities in New York mixed freely at events such as these because everybody loves a good party, especially a party where there were good networking opportunities and press exposure.

The Empire Theatre, where the premiere was taking place had once been a lesser movie palace that had fallen onto rough times. After they stopped showing movies back in the sixties the theater had been a strip club and later an adult movie theater. It had been abandoned in the seventies and was brought back to life during the revitalization of Times Square in the early 1990's. Dry wall had been removed revealing the original art deco motif. The theater was a favorite place for indie filmmakers to premiere and screen their films since it had a decent sized auditorium and a good space for after-parties.

Marc gave his name to the event hostess positioned at the door.

Instead of consulting her list she looked directly at him, smiling and struggling to maintain some degree of professionalism. "I saw *Tales of the Dark City* a few weeks ago. You were amazing!" She was actually blushing.

This part of the job did not come easily for him. He was an actor whose priority was the work, not any celebrity that might come along no matter how minor. But as usual, Marc was cordial. "Thank you, that's very kind."

She smiled and blushed even more before looking down at her list of invitees. "Oh, I see you're doing the red carpet."

Marc hoped he'd just be attending the event, but he wasn't surprised that he was expected to do some press, helping the producer, (and hopefully himself in the long run).

Twenty-two minutes later, the carpet was over. It had not been horrible. It was a smaller carpet and he spoke primarily to local press. He gave his friend John high praise, and even told a college anecdote involving John to one of the film magazines that had sent a reporter. As he neared the end of the carpet his producer friend joined him for a few photographs before he headed into the lobby of the theater.

The artistic community in reality is very small, and the chances of running into people you know at these events are good. Marc realized that he knew at least two of the actors in the film and found several other people that he knew or had worked with in the past. He joined a director that he had worked with the year before for the actual screening. Thankfully, the audience enjoyed the film, meaning it would be easier to talk to people afterwards.

The party that followed the film's screening was lively and Marc found himself running into even more people he knew. Marc was actually having a good time and returned to the bar for another drink.

As he turned to leave the bar he found himself face to face with an attractive young woman with dark hair and smoldering dark brown eyes. She was wearing a clingy blue satin cocktail dress with a plunging neckline that showed off an incredible body. Under any other circumstance, she was the type of woman Marc would be attracted to physically. But he was working. Marc had a hard rule never to mix business with pleasure. He smiled and then tried to step past her, but she stepped back into his path.

Now that he got a good look at her, she was a lot younger than he realized. She tossed her long dark hair over one shoulder and flashed a bright coquettish smile. "So what did you think of the film?"

Marc politely answered her. "I enjoyed the film very much. Did you?"

This seemed to encourage her. "I thought it was wonderful! I loved the lead actor and the story wasn't predictable. I hate plays or movies where you can see the end coming in the first ten minutes. Are you involved in the production?"

As Marc listened to her he thought that she couldn't be older than nineteen or twenty. "No, I'm a guest of the producer. We were in school together."

She liked this tidbit, and continued to talk to Marc about the film, the venue and whatever else popped into her head.

She had seen him on the carpet earlier in the evening and wanted to know why he was doing the *press thing*. Only then did he tell her that he was an actor currently appearing in a show. She excitedly told Marc that she was also an actor and moved in closer to him. That only made him feel uneasy. Marc hated this sort of attention. If this girl wanted help with her career she was certainly flirting with the wrong man.

He even tried to make a graceful exit, telling her it was nice talking to her and wishing her luck with her career. She didn't take the hint. Instead she playfully batted her eyelashes at him while touching his chest with her perfectly manicured hands.

"Oh please... don't go yet."

Marc reached out, and with one hand took her by the shoulder and quickly pulled her close in an action that could only be perceived as forward and aggressive. His mouth was almost touching hers and his voice took on a cautious tone. "Don't start what you can't finish, little girl!"

This bold action took her by surprise and for a moment Marc saw a hint of fear in her eyes, which told him that she was in over her head. But she tried to regain her composure by appearing to be offended. "I'm...I'm not a little girl..."

Marc cut her off and relaxed his grip on her shoulder while stepping a full arms-length away from her. "Yes, you are. You're very young and very pretty. If you're not careful some horrible man is going to take advantage of you. You seem like a nice girl, but this isn't high school. Do you understand?"

She hesitated before nodding yes.

Marc removed his hand from her shoulder. "Have a nice night."

She quickly moved away from him and disappeared into the crowd.

His pulse was still racing from this incident when he heard a familiar female voice behind him.

"Well, maybe you have some sort of moral compass after all."

Marc spun around and found himself face to face with Mel Holden. She had upgraded her wardrobe and haircut and looked great. He hadn't seen her in five years.

"Mel!" He had missed her and warmly embraced her as she hugged him back.

"John told me he had invited you and I was hoping I'd run into you." She took his hands in hers, immediately noticing that he was not wearing a wedding band.

"I've missed you." he said.

"Me too."

She asked about Miriam.

"We're divorced. We didn't even make it to our first anniversary."

She couldn't read his expression but that was just as well.

"Marc, I was getting ready to leave. Would you walk me out so we can talk for a minute?"

He escorted her to the street where it was cooler and quieter.

"I owe you an apology." she said. "I never should have let Miriam come between us and our friendship. But please understand that I was very angry with you and Miriam when she came back to you. Maybe I should have put my own feelings aside, but instead I held a grudge-that was wrong! Friends are too valuable to kick to the curb. I'm sorry."

Marc had never held any ill feelings toward Mel, having always blamed himself for excluding her from his life.

That means a lot to me," he said. "Thank you. And you had every right to be mad at me. I'm still mad at myself for a lot of the things I did back then."

Mel had an idea. "Are you free for breakfast on Saturday morning?"

Marc was. They exchanged information and agreed to set a time and a place over the next few days. Then Marc hailed Mel a cab and sent her home.

He had planned to return to the party, but he had done enough networking for the night. He hailed a cab for himself and went home.

***

Mel sat across from Marc in the Greek coffee shop that they used to frequent with Wes, Crimson and Lauren years ago.

She was amazed at how different he looked in the daytime. When Mel had seen him the other night, with his long hair, mustache, and goatee and black leather jacket, he looked menacing. For his show, he had allowed his hair to grow well beyond his shoulders, longer than he had ever worn it. Onstage he wore it loose. But this morning, Marc seemed different. His long hair was pulled back into a respectable ponytail. Seeing him dressed in jeans, T shirt and denim jacket made her remember the old Marc.

"The other night you really had the bad boy thing going on, but today you look like the Marc I knew back at NYU; approachable, and a little goofy."

The word goofy made him laugh. "Well, the bad boy thing, as you call it, is a persona that helps me keep my privacy when I feel I need to."

Mel remembered the attractive coed from the other night. "That didn't seem to keep that nubile young thing away from you."

This embarrassed him. "I didn't say it worked all the time. Anyway isn't it true that girls crave bad boys?" He was enjoying taunting Mel.

"Keep my personal life out of this, okay?" She could feel herself blushing.

"Deal." He sat back and smiled. He'd almost forgotten how good it felt to relax in her company. "I've really missed you. There have been several times I would have loved to have used you as a sounding board. You were always a good listener and easy to talk to about anything. Communicating on a personal level has never been one of my strong points."

She wanted to remind him how he and Lauren never communicated properly, which eventually led to irreversible problems. But she thought better of it.

"Blame it on youth. You seem to be doing well. *Tales of the Dark City* has been running for months now. Your reviews were great. My favorite was the one that mentioned your 'dark brooding intensity.' I wasn't sure if the reviewer was describing you or your character." Mel had missed teasing her friend like this and was now enjoying watching Marc blush. Marc may have been slightly embarrassed but couldn't help smiling.

"Landing that role was a fluke! When I auditioned for the role initially I thought I'd done horribly-you know the typical actor's story. And I was especially upset because I thought the role was amazing. I tried to forget about the audition, but I couldn't. That audition haunted me for days, and I kept thinking if I only would have done this or that, then maybe they would have brought me back. And then two weeks later, my agent calls and tells me they want to see me again-that afternoon. And the next day the role was mine. This has been an unbelievable experience!"

Yeah, this was the Marc she knew.

"You've had a few really good years, though. I know you've done a few other plays that have been well received."

Marc seemed surprised. "You've kept up with my career?"

"Of course, I've kept up with your career. Why wouldn't I? Just because we weren't talking didn't mean I didn't think about you. By the way, I loved the credit card commercial-you as the kind and caring French concierge? I admit, at first I thought it was kind of a stretch for you, but then I decided I believed you. Really, it was a nice spot."

He missed her taunting. "You noticed that they hired me instead of a Frenchman… or should I say they hired the accent. My folks were offended that I put on the Parisian accent until I told them how much money I was making, and suddenly they were all *Viva la France*! And they're holding the spot, which means they could run it again, and in the meantime I'm still making money from a job I did almost two years ago. No wonder Lauren loved commercials so much."

Mel froze momentarily at the mention of Lauren's name. If he wanted to talk about her she would, but she wasn't going to press the issue. An uncomfortable silence hung between them for a few moments before he finally changed the subject.

"Mel, how about you? How are things over on *The Crossing?*"

"Things are going very well. We're getting close to forty years now, and I feel like I've been working there for at least fifty. Soaps are losing their popularity in general, but our ratings are still good. The executive producer is open to any ideas that will keep the show current. Some of the older shows that have been cancelled over the past ten or fifteen years never progressed with the times, and their core audiences literally started dying off. My bosses, thank God, have always supported my choices of direction and storylines. I just wish I could find the secret to finding younger viewers."

Marc flashed her a wicked grin. "Maybe *Miss Pretty Young Thing* from the other night should have been coming on to you!" She playfully threw a packet of sugar at him and then they shared a laugh.

"You're the bratty little bother I never had…and that's a good thing because I would have killed you."

Her laughter subsided as an idea came to her. "Marc, would ever consider doing my show?"

Marc also stopped laughing. "Sure, I guess…but I'm not exactly a Southerner."

"No, but not everybody on the show is from the South. We've introduced characters from other places, and of course our characters travel to places outside of the American South."

"What are you thinking? Do you see me as a sympathetic Frenchmen?"

"Maybe. Actually there are several types of characters you could play on the show. We hire good actors, so you already fit the criteria."

"Thank you Mel. That means a lot coming from you. Gary worked your show several times while he was in New York and said *The Crossing* was one of the friendliest sets in town. He loved working on your show."

Mel noticed he didn't mention Lauren, especially since she had worked the show often and could have possibly become a regular had she stayed in New York.

"Speaking of Gary, you know he and Natalie are on baby watch? She's due late next month."

Marc had spoken to Gary earlier in the week. "I know. He's terrified! Thankfully Natalie has enrolled them in every parenting class to keep him focused and to make him feel like he's doing something. You know they're having a girl. Gary's never been happier."

She shook her head in disbelief. "We actually have friends who are leading somewhat normal lives."

"That all depends on your definition of normal. Frankly the idea of a wife and child is completely foreign to me. The life that I'm living seems perfectly normal-at this point in my life, anyway. Seriously, can you imagine me living any other life right now?" He gave her a knowing smile. "You didn't seem at all surprised when you didn't find a wedding ring on my finger the other night."

Marc watched Mel turned red. "You were hardly subtle." He smiled knowing that he had embarrassed her.

"Oh, guilty... I guess," she said nonchalantly. "But I didn't want to assume anything. I mean, I was halfway looking for Miriam in case..."

Marc finished her thought. "In case she was there and ready to chase you away? It's alright Mel. I get that she didn't treat you or any of my other friends very well, and that was just one of many problems. We did the right thing by ending the marriage."

She liked that he was opening up. "It still couldn't have been easy for you."

Marc thought for a moment. "It wasn't easy for either of us...the marriage, I mean. We both married for the wrong reasons. She was in search of a fantasy and someone to take care of her, not realizing that a marriage was a lot of work. I married her out of guilt. I learned the hard way that two wrongs don't make a right. And then we were hardly in love with each other."

Mel's mouth dropped wide open. "What do you mean she didn't *love* you?"

Marc thought it sounded odd hearing this out loud. "No. She didn't love me. Not the way you're supposed to love a spouse. We both cared for each other, but that's as far as it went. There was some drama during the last few months, but we were able to create a united front and end it.

It was the best part of the marriage and we actually got along during those last few weeks. It's kind of strange when I think about it."

Mel was having a hard time believing that Marc had changed the course of his life for his now ex-wife. "What about your family? They must have been upset, from everything that you've told me about their relationship with Miriam."

He spoke with reflection. "That was another strange thing. When I told my father he hardly said anything other than saying that he would talk to my mother, and to please not mention anything about the divorce to her. He'd take care of it when the time was right. It was all pretty weird. My father took the divorce pretty hard. I think he mistook the marriage as a business merger of sorts and we haven't really spoken since. He paused for a moment. "I may have been glad the marriage was over, but I didn't expect to go through a depression after Miriam left. It took months for me to feel like myself again."

Mel understood perfectly. "You had just ended a relationship that had lasted for years, and like it or not, she *was* a part of your life!"

"I know that now. I've also learned that I always cared about her, and maybe felt responsible for her in some weird, twisted way. Maybe that's why I couldn't completely let go of her when I should have. My life could have been so different."

"How did you get through those first few months?

Marc shrugged. "I was very depressed and was carrying around a lot of guilt and anger. Strangely enough, none of these feelings were toward Miriam. I felt guilty for marrying her in the first place, and I was very angry at myself, at the past, and at situations that were beyond my control. Instead of wallowing in self-pity I decided the best way to deal with everything was by throwing myself into my work, and the efforts have paid off. I've done three major shows, several workshop productions, the commercial, and a couple of films. I'm doing what I always wanted to do: earning my living as a working New York actor. I've also taken some directing workshops. I have a good eye and I enjoy the process. I'm directing one of the shows at ACT next season. They've always been good to me, and they're giving me a chance with one of the elementary school productions. I'm excited about this, and rehearsals don't even start until summer. So you see things are good. Professionally I'm doing well."

"And I'm happy for you." She smiled. "And how are you doing personally?"

"I don't have a personal life. I've spent the last few years building a career and anything outside of that would just take away time and energy that I'd rather channel into my career. And if you're talking about women and relationships, I'm not looking for anything serious."

Mel gave him a knowing glance. "Well, I can't imagine you…"

He finished her thought. "I'm hardly a choirboy if that's what you're insinuating."

"Yeah! That's exactly what I was insinuating. I was surprised you came to the premiere by yourself the other night."

"You know as well as I do that those events are work and hardly an ideal date situation. I usually go to these things alone so I can get in and out at my leisure."

They talked over another couple of cups of coffee before leaving the coffee shop. As they hugged goodbye, she took a chance and answered the one question he had not asked. "Marc, I talk to Lauren once or twice a month, and she's doing well."

On hearing this he hugged her even tighter. The gesture spoke volumes. She hadn't realized it, but she'd make his day a little bit better.

***

Several months later, Marc made his first appearance as Detective Julian Dumont on *Clayton's Crossing.* Mel had written the character specifically for him, though he had to go through the formality of the audition process.

Mel had only given him one piece of advice the night before his audition. "Just be yourself, because you're Julian in more ways than you'll ever know. Just be you with a Parisian accent!"

The role worked twenty-five days over the next thirteen weeks as he searched for one of *Clayton's Crossing's* ingénues who had run away to Paris to be with her artist boyfriend. Of course, there were many twists and turns before Detective Dumont was able to close the case and send the love-struck girl back to her family in America.

On the other side of the country, a former cast member of *Clayton's Crossing* tuned in to watch and videotape every single one of Marc's episodes. When his storyline ended, she felt as if she had lost him all over again.

***

A few years after they resumed their friendship over breakfast, Marc received an email from Mel.

You might want to record *On the Couch* this Wednesday. Lauren's in the episode.

Marc knew that Lauren had been working fairly steadily over the past few years. He had seen her in at least two commercials. There was also a soft drink commercial where he saw someone that could have been Lauren but couldn't be sure.

In a strange fluke he saw her as a lab technician on a Los Angeles based soap when he came home one afternoon to change for a last minute audition. He caught less than two minutes of her scene. She didn't appear for the rest of the episode.

Mel left him the date, time and channel.

He programmed his VCR immediately fearing that he might forget to record the episode. He couldn't imagine why, but he was taking no chances.

When Marc returned home from the theater on Wednesday night he followed his normal post performance unwinding routine of a long shower and television. But on this night he found himself having a hard time relaxing. Instead of David Letterman, he would be watching *On the Couch*.

He had seen the show once or twice and admired the show's star Robert Parker and the sharp writing. Robert Parker played a successful and competent psychologist who could easily fix the lives and problems of his patients, but had problems in his own seemingly normal life. The show was smart, witty and innovative. This episode involved rekindling the romance in his own marriage.

Mel had told Marc that Lauren's scene was in the second act, which began with an establishing shot of Rodeo Drive in Beverly Hills, before cutting to Robert Parker entering what appeared to be an upscale lingerie boutique. The doctor is completely out of his element.

Parker, the Tony and Emmy Award-winning actor known for his extended silences on screen, bumbles around the boutique, both embarrassed and fascinated by the store's sensuous inventory. His erratic actions attract the attention of a striking sales associate who begins, discreetly at first, to follow him throughout the store.

The sight of the sales associate drew Marc closer to the screen. The actress playing her was Lauren.

She looked so different, he could not believe his eyes. She was dressed in a form-fitting black dress that showed off an incredible figure. The severe makeup accentuated her eyes and cheekbones, while her hair had been styled into a messy chic up do. When the camera pulled back it revealed that Lauren was wearing sky high stilettos that made her appear taller while accentuating her toned legs. The girl he knew years before in New York had become a woman. He could not take his eyes off her. She was more beautiful than he remembered.

Mesmerized, he carefully watched Lauren keep up with Parker in an understated performance that was smart, precise and very funny.

A few minutes later the scene ended on a huge wave of applause and laughter from the live studio audience.

Marc sat in front of his television, still laughing and mentally cheering Lauren's performance.

He quickly rewound the tape, and watched the scene again, this time studying her every move as she hit every acting beat and nuance in an amazing comedic performance that he felt was no less than brilliant. When had she become a comedienne? He was so proud and happy for her. If only he could tell her somehow.

Marc's mood changed from happy and excited to pensive as he moved to his desk and typed an email to Mel.

Lauren was wonderful! I'd like to tell her myself and hoped you could give me a phone number...

No. He couldn't just call her after all these years. He quickly deleted the last sentence and retyped.

Would you please tell Lauren congratulations? I am so happy and impressed...

This time, he deleted everything before retyping the note to Mel for the third and final time.

Lauren was very funny.

He hit send, just as the credits of the episode began to roll. He watched until he saw her name, "Lauren Dey." Funny, he still thought of her as Laurie Phillips, the eternal teenager.

Later that night as he was trying to fall asleep, he continued to think about her. Tonight was the first time he had seen her in an adult role. She had to be in her early thirties by now. He didn't know why this surprised him.

Lauren Dey-*his* Laurie, had become an incredibly talented actor, and a beautiful woman. She had been his best friend, and regrettably, only his friend. But he loved her; maybe he *still* loved her. He couldn't understand how things had gone so horribly wrong between them so long ago.

Chapter Six

ACT Fall Tour

Fall 2001

The acting profession is cyclical. Mark continued to work steadily as a New York actor. As a direct result of his work in the theater, he landed a role on TV's *Law and Order,* as well as a few substantial film roles. For Marc it was all about the work. He could be working in large or small theaters, or on a film set. He had also enjoyed his brief run on *Clayton's Crossing,* far more than he expected and sought work on the other New York based soaps, or "daytime dramas" as he learned to call them.

Then in the summer of 2000 he booked another national television commercial for a world-wide delivery service, playing the stereotypical brooding Frenchmen. The spot was humorous and ran often.

The commercial's timing was excellent, because a few weeks later the Screen Actors Guild would be on strike against the producers of television commercials. His commercial and earnings were not affected. Marc seldom did commercials because he didn't have a typical "commercial" look and therefore didn't actively pursue them. He was lucky in that the strike didn't have much of an impact on his life, though he saw its effects in the lives of those around him, actors as well as those who supported the commercial industry. By the time an agreement was reached there had been a negative shift in the industry. He could not explain it, but things were never the same.

Marc had also been honing his directorial skills by working with several small theaters. ACT first hired him in 1996 to direct one of their productions for younger students, and had since called him back to work on other company productions. In late August of 2001 he was nearing the end of the rehearsal process for an adaptation of William Shakespeare's *The Taming of the Shrew*, written by his good friend Gary Connelly.

The ACT Company's rehearsal period was unique in that the cast was in rehearsal for two shows at once. Marc had to share his cast and the rehearsal period with the director of the other production, a modern adaptation of *Goldilocks and the Three Bears*.

The two directors had their own challenges with each production, but managed to be civil during rehearsals, while making sure that they each got an adequate amount of time with their casts. During the last week of rehearsal the casts would run through both shows in a single day to get the cast used to performing two different shows in one day, as they would on the road.

Marc had just finished the last full day of rehearsal with his cast when the managing director of ACT, Ben Stewart, asked him to stop by his office. Marc assumed it was to find out how the show was coming along, but soon learned the true reason for his visit.

His boss sat him down. "Marc, we are extremely happy with your work and have a proposition for you. We know your commitment with us ends in a few weeks, but maybe you'll stay with us a bit longer. A position has suddenly opened up and we'd like to see if you'd be interested in taking it."

Marc was intrigued, especially since he had not lined up a gig after this one finished.

"You were on the team that developed our program that does acting workshops with students after our performances," his boss continued. "They get the regular performance or performances, and then we'll present an acting workshop with some of the school's acting students. We've offered this program to our clients for the past couple of years, and more and more schools are taking advantage of the program. Your cast will be presenting several workshops as part of their tour this year. How would you like to join them?"

This wasn't what Marc had expected.

"Ben, I haven't been on the road in years! I'm afraid I may be too old for another tour."

Ben had expected this response. Marc now had major credits under his belt and leaving New York for any period of time could be detrimental to his career path.

"Marc, hear me out, please. We want to offer you a position as a company manager, whose duties are slightly more detailed than they were when you toured with us in the nineties. You'd be looking after the company in the day to day operation, but you would also be the liaison between the company and the educational community. You would be very hands-on in the execution of the classes- in fact you'd be running the classes."

Marc was interested, but leery. His boss picked up on both.

"Marc, we're not asking you to do the entire season-just the first couple of months, or six weeks even. To be totally honest, we had someone lined up, but he's received an offer to stage manage an off-Broadway play. They pay more, and since he hadn't signed a contract with us, he's taking that position, which has left us in a bind. We have someone who we think can handle the position, but he's never worked with us, and I don't believe he's ever taught high school kids. We'd basically like you to go out and train him in our procedures and get him up to speed while you're on the road. You would be the manager, and he would be working under you until you both feel that he's ready to take over. Then we'll bring you back to New York. You'd really be helping us out."

Marc thought about it, but the possibility of leaving town and travelling around the country in a van for an unspecified period of time did not appeal to him. "Ben, I'm just not sure. It would be a major change for me."

Despite his reservations, the boss made him a generous offer. He had a lot to think about.

By this time, Marc had moved from the East Village to a loft downtown near Wall Street in Lower Manhattan. Mel had described the area as funky, with its array of colorful characters and businesses. At first she would only visit him during the daytime because that's the only time she felt safe. She quickly got over her fear. Marc assured her that the area was changing. More artists and professionals were moving into the area which was a stone's throw away from the Wall Street, The New York Stock Exchange and The World Trade Center.

Marc's rent was dirt cheap and his loft was spacious. In the future he saw using his living space as a studio for readings and rehearsals for a variety of projects he was developing.

He picked up a gyros for dinner and weighed the pros and cons of accepting Ben's offer.

The big con was that he would be out of New York. Then again, he had nothing lined up workwise.

He hated the idea of being on the road again, this time being in charge of the company. But then the experience would be good as he was branching out beyond acting. He saw himself producing in the future. This position would look great on his resume.

Ben said that he wouldn't be gone for the entire nine month season, but only for six to eight weeks before returning to Manhattan. He wanted to be back in time to audition for the Public Library's play reading series which now took place in November. He had done the series for the first time the year he was married and, since then, had been a part of the talent pool, doing anywhere from one to three readings a year.

He then thought about what ACT had done for him over the years. They had always found a way to employ him, whether it was teaching, or developing a new program. ACT had given him his first professional directing job. Now he was directing his third ACT production, to be performed in schools all over the country.

And then, of course, there was the money. It appeared that the powers at ACT wanted him to take this position badly.

Marc couldn't sleep for most of the night because he was still thinking about the offer from the American Children's Theater. Each time he found a reason not to accept the offer, he found two or even three reasons to accept. At one point the voice inside his head screamed, "ACCEPT THE OFFER!"

Finally, at about four o'clock in the morning, he made up his mind. He would accept the position and tell Ben that he was willing to leave town for a few months. But he wanted a few things in addition to the salary.

He called Ben at ten the next morning.

"Ben, I'd like to say yes to your very generous offer, but I'd like a few more things on top of the salary that I feel are reasonable. First off, I'd like to produce the New York showcase for the company in March."

Ben seemed surprised but said yes. "I don't think that will be a problem. What else?"

Marc's next request was fairly big. "You've talked about doing a full length production in New York over the summer. I'd like to be involved in some real capacity."

Ben also agreed to this request. "Okay, if our summer production becomes a reality, you're involved. We'll see how at a later date, but I could always see you performing, and depending on the show, producing or even directing. What else?"

Marc's confidence was increasing. "I want to be back in New York no later than November 1."

Again Ben saw no problem. "Dan Steele, the guy you'll be training is sharp, so I don't think that will be an issue. Is that all?

Marc had one last request. "Can ACT assist me in subletting my loft? I have less than ten days and really won't be able to do it myself since I'll be in rehearsals with the company?"

Marc heard relief in Ben's voice. "Of course we'll help you sublet your place. Does this mean you'll accept the offer?

Marc felt himself relax. "Yes, Ben. I accept, and thank you for the vote of confidence. It's strange, but for some odd reason I'm suddenly looking forward to doing this tour. It'll be nice to get out of the city for a while. I'll make sure that Dan will be a competent company manager by the time I head back to New York."

Ben was genuinely relieved by Marc's acceptance. "Thank you for doing this for us."

Marc felt he was coming out ahead on this deal. "I'm glad I'm available, and can do it for you. I'll let you get back to your family, so I'll see you Tuesday."

Ben was happily relieved. "And hopefully I'll have something for you to look at contract-wise by Tuesday afternoon."

Marc heard shuffling papers.

"Okay, I'm looking at your current contract which ends on the ninth. I'll date the new contract September tenth, which is the day the tour starts, with the first performance being the next morning in Philadelphia."

Marc was honestly pleased with his decision. "That sounds good, Ben. And thanks."

As Marc hung up the phone he made a mental note of ACT's first performance date: Tuesday, September 11 2001.

***

The ACT Company left Manhattan at 9:00 AM on Monday September 10, 2001 with its two vans for the company and truck for the sets, lights and other items required for the productions. They had a fairly easy time getting out of the city. Once they reached the Jersey Turnpike, it was smooth sailing into Pennsylvania. Not long afterwards they reached the Philadelphia city limits. The trip had taken only two-and-a-half hours.

Since the Philly shows would be presented in a downtown theater, there would only be one load in, which was done after the company grabbed lunch at a nearby sub shop shortly after their arrival. In companies such as this, all cast members had responsibilities during the show's load in. Thankfully the two sets for both productions were minimal and the company was able to unload the truck and vans fairly quickly.

Once the set was in place the cast did a quick walk-through of both productions onstage for lighting purposes. While both shows used general lighting, the lighting director needed to set a handful of special lights for a few key moments. With both walk-throughs complete, the company settled into the theater's house for a brief meeting.

The cast met the staff of their host theater, and then Marc reviewed the show schedule for the next three days with everyone.

"Tomorrow we have a morning performance of *Goldie.*"

Goldie was the show for the elementary school students.

"The show starts at 9:30, we'll break for lunch here at the theater, and then *Shrew* will be presented at 12:30, with a workshop to follow here in the theater at 1:45, where we're expecting about forty participants. Wednesday starts the same, but there's no workshop, so you'll have some free time in the afternoon. Thursday is the big day, with *Shrew* at 9:30 with a workshop following, and a second performance of *Shrew* at 1:30, also with a workshop to follow. I'll get counts on the number of students for the workshops closer to the time. Friday there will be a morning performance of *Goldie* at 9:45, followed by lunch and the load out. We'll leave Philadelphia the next morning. As for tomorrow, the vans will leave the Holiday Inn at 7:45 sharp, so I suggest everyone leave a wakeup call for themselves. Any questions?"

There were none, but that was no surprise. It had been a very long day, and Marc knew the company just wanted to get to the motel and relax.

"Alright then, in ten minutes we'll meet at the vans, get checked into the motel, and you're free for the rest of the evening. Good work everybody!"

Less than an hour later the company was checked into a nearby Holiday Inn Express.

Marc shared a room with Dan on this leg of the trip. He collapsed onto one of the double beds as soon as he got into the room. "I forgot how much work these tours could be. I'm beat! "

They were too tired to go out to dinner, so they ordered Chinese takeout. They got to know each other over chicken lo mien, beef and broccoli and eggrolls.

By the time Marc showed Dan how to fill out the daily company log, he was exhausted and went to bed, thinking he was too old for this demanding schedule.

How had Ben talked him into going on tour again? But then he remembered he had found himself really wanting to do the tour for some obscure reason that hadn't yet revealed itself.

The next morning began at 6:15. When Marc was just a performer he rolled out of bed throwing on whatever was close by, but as company manager he spent a few more minutes dressing. He even remembered to bring a jacket to the theater, since he was the direct liaison between the company and the educational community.

The company arrived at the theater shortly before 8:15 and began preparing for the morning's performance before an audience of four hundred grade school students.

All seemed to be going well. The stage manager wanted a few of the actors on stage to check spacing for a dance number in *Goldie*. Dan was also on the stage placing glow tape in key areas to assist the actors as they maneuvered onstage during blackouts.

Marc was in the booth reminding himself of the schools attending this morning's performance, since a huge part of his job was public relations. Everything was going according to plan.

He was still in the booth chatting with the theater's resident stage manager, Doug, who would be basically babysitting the ACT Company while they were at his theater for the Philadelphia shows, when the phone rang.

He went back to his binder of information while Doug took the call. He wasn't listening to the conversation at first, but the odd tone of Doug's voice got his attention.

It was shortly after 9:00AM Eastern Time.

"Doug, is everything alright?" Marc asked concerned.

Doug was crossing the room to turn on the television that was on the other side of the booth. He looked uncertain. "Marc…something's going on in New York."

By now the television was on CNN, and revealing an unbelievable image of the World Trade Center's Twin Towers. The South Tower had black smoke billowing from a huge gash in the upper portion of the building.

Marc could not believe what he was seeing. "What the hell…"

Doug stepped back to let Marc get a closer look. "That was my wife on the phone. Details are still coming in but it looks like a commercial airliner hit one of the Towers."

And then as Marc and Doug watched the screen, something flew behind the North Tower and almost immediately, a huge fireball erupted and travelled several floors up on the second Tower. Both men looked to one another. It was 9:03.

The phone rang again, and as Doug answered, Marc called Dan, who was still on the stage, to the booth.

"Dan, they're saying an airliner hit one of the Towers of The World Trade Center. We just found out about a minute ago, but I'm pretty sure that we just saw something hit the other tower."

Doug was now on the phone with someone else. "Yeah, I saw that, too! My God, are we being attacked?"

There seemed to be nothing but confusion coming from the television anchors and reporters. Marc changed the station and this channel showed a closer view of the burning Towers. He changed channels again to see yet another horrifying angle.

"Dan, would you please go backstage and see if the company has heard anything about this yet."

Dan quickly headed backstage as Marc dialed the ACT offices in New York from his cell phone. All of the circuits were jammed. It was impossible for anyone calling New York to get through.

Doug hung up his phone again. "Okay, that was my boss who heard from somewhere that there have been reports of several hijacked planes across the country. There could be more planes in the air right now…"

"We don't really know anything yet, so let's try to keep calm," said Marc. He was thinking about his twenty-member company of New Yorkers that was preparing for a retelling of *Goldilocks and the Three Bears*. He took a few deep breaths before the in-house phone rang. It was Dan from backstage.

"Marc, they're not aware of anything yet. What do you want to do?"

Marc didn't know. "Is there a television anywhere backstage?"

Dan looked around. "Not that I can see."

This was a good thing. "Then get back up here because we're going to have to start making some decisions."

Marc started to look through his school information binder and began highlighting phone numbers as he spoke to Doug.

"We don't know what's going on, but can you get a few numbers for me to have on hand, like the school board, and the area police station. And if your boss calls back, let me talk to him."

Now Marc spoke to Dan who'd returned to the booth. "Dan, I've made no decisions, but we might want to cancel today's performances simply because we don't know the extent of this thing. I have eight phone numbers that we can split if we have to start calling schools."

Doug looked at his watch. "You may want to start calling sooner than later since they'll be loading the busses soon-that is if they haven't started already. And I can make calls, too."

The phone in the booth rang and Doug answered.

"Yes. Yes we are very aware of what's going on. No, we understand completely, and thanks for calling."

Doug hung up. "Okay, one of the school's is on lockdown and not letting any of their kids off campus until there are more details." He shook his head. "If I were a parent anywhere right now, I'd be doing anything to get back to my kids."

That was all Marc needed to hear. "Doug thanks for being the voice of reason. Guys, let's start making phone calls. We're cancelling today's performances!"

It was the first major decision Marc made as the ACT company manager. This turned out to be the right decision, as most schools across the country closed for the day. Schools in other time zones never opened.

The next order of business was to inform the cast. Marc asked Dan to call the entire company to the backstage green room immediately.

Marc and Dan met the company, their energy noticeably different from their own.

Marc began slowly. "Guys, I need your attention please." The cast was slow to settle.

At about this time Doug came into the green room and passed a note to Marc with information he'd just received from a news report. Then he headed back to the booth to be close to the phone.

Marc looked at the note, exhaled deeply and then passed the note to Dan. "People, please…"

Dan momentarily took over. "People, WE NEED YOU TO SETLE DOWN NOW!"

The room went silent as all eyes turned to Marc and Dan.

"Thanks, Dan. Ladies and gentlemen, we've decided to cancel both of today's performances."

A rush of whispers went through the company along with a smattering of laughter. Some thought that Marc was joking.

"Unfortunately, I'm very serious." He had a difficult time believing his words as he spoke. "A short time ago, two planes-we believe two commercial airliners-crashed into both Towers of the World Trade Center."

The room fell into complete silence as Marc continued to convey what little information he had.

"The thing is that there are so many reports coming in that nobody knows exactly what's going on. I felt it best to go ahead and cancel, or at least postpone our performances until we see how this plays out."

The company looked stunned, until one of them spoke up.

"Is this some sort of weird coincidence or is there something more to all this?"

Marc thought about a few of the television reports he had just seen. "In one of the reports something was said about *possible* foul play."

Everybody started to talk again, before Dan again demanded quiet. Marc continued.

"I think we should prepare to leave the theater, following the end of the day procedures so we can all get back to the motel and watch the reports as they come in… together."

By now a few people had pulled out their cell phones, only to find they couldn't get through to New York. A wave of anxiousness to came over the company.

One of the actors suggested that they all head back to the city."

"You don't understand," said Marc. "WE CAN'T GET TO NEW YORK!" Marc's uncharacteristic outburst quickly silenced the room. "Nobody can get into or out of Manhattan! All of the bridges and tunnels going into the city, as well as all of the New York City airports have been closed. This is serious!"

Doug was at the door of the green room again.

He looked to Marc, unsure whether or not to talk.

"Doug, it's alright. Do you have any new information?"

The adrenaline rush was making it very difficult for Doug to speak. "There's another plane down, this time near Washington DC…at the Pentagon!"

Marc didn't wait and took control of the company. "LISTEN, EVERYONE! In fifteen minutes we all meet back here, and we'll leave for the motel together. Fifteen minutes. GO!"

Fifteen minutes later, the entire company was once again assembled in the green room. To make sure, Dan did a quick roll call and, once finished, nodded to Marc.

But before any of them could move Doug was back at the door red faced and out of breath. "The South Tower... it just collapsed!"

There was an audible gasp. Marc spoke slowly and deliberately.

"All right everybody, let's go!"

The company went out the back door of the theater with Marc being the last to leave. He extended his hand to Doug. "Thanks for your help today. Please tell me you're locking up and heading home yourself!"

Doug nodded. "Good idea. Thanks. Will I see you tomorrow?"

Marc hadn't thought that far ahead. "Yes, Doug. We'll be back first thing in the morning." At least, that was what he hoped.

The company made it back to the Holiday Inn Express in less than twenty minutes and headed to their rooms to turn on their televisions. Unfortunately they were just in time to see the collapse of the North Tower.

Marc and Dan went to their own room and watched the same disturbing pictures while listening to the same tragic stories.

Marc had the binder of the company's personal information in front of him.

"Dan, I don't see anyone who lives anywhere near the Towers from the addresses here. We do have a few people who are married, and I'd like to talk to them now." He handed Dan a piece of paper. "Would you start with the first name on the list? He has a couple of kids."

After Dan left the room, Marc took a few minutes for himself. He now knew why there had been an inner voice insisting he take this job. Had he been at home, he would have been just a few blocks away from The Towers. But instead he was on the road far away from the disaster, and safe. After pondering this reality, he turned his attention back to the company.

An hour later Marc had spoken with all of the company members who had spouses and children in the city. None were concerned that their loved ones were in harm's way, though they were eager to contact their families. All were willing to wait until communications were restored to see if there was any need to return to the city.

One report said that mail service would continue in New York, so Marc asked Dan to get to a Post Office and purchase sixty prepaid post cards for the company.

Now he had to make some serious decisions. There was still no way to contact the ACT office in New York City, so his decisions would have to be made independently of ACT's management. He had to look out for the welfare of the company, its members and the tour. He had already decided to stay in Philly through Saturday morning as planned. He was hoping that the performances would go on as scheduled the next day, even if they were only playing to partial houses. Beyond that, he was uncertain.

He made a few calls to his schools in the Philadelphia area. A couple of principals had no problem with their kids attending the performances the next day, as long as school was in session and the situation had calmed down. Marc felt slightly better.

By now there was a fourth plane down in rural Pennsylvania. All US air traffic had been grounded. The footage of New York- home-was heartbreaking.

Marc was angry. How could anyone dare to do this to his city and worse yet, to his neighborhood? Eventually he had to turn off the television so he could concentrate.

Dan returned from the Post Office with the postcards.

"Dan, I pray to God all you have to do as company manager will be to manage the day-to-day activities of the company. This is insane. We still don't know what's going on!"

His thoughts turned to the company members. "How are they doing?"

Dan nodded. "They seem to be doing okay. They're between three rooms watching television."

Marc tried to smile. "That's good. They need to support one another now."

By now it was 12:30. It seemed they had just returned from the theater.

Marc placed a pizza order for the company, while he asked Dan to head to a nearby market for snacks.

Dan had started to leave the room, but stopped. "Marc... you're doing an incredible job. All of this is unreal." He felt that Marc needed to hear a vote of confidence.

"Thanks Dan. And I'll try to make this your last errand. We need to discuss a few different scenarios of how we're going to continue this week."

Dan headed out.

Less than five minutes later there was a very soft knock at the door. Marc wasn't sure if he had heard anything at all, but a second soft knock sent him to the door.

Waiting at the door was April, his primary Goldilocks in *Goldie,* and his secondary Bianca in *Taming of the Shrew*. She was a wonderful and engaging actress, but right now she was clearly upset.

"April, come in. Are you alright?"

She shook her head and began to cry. Instinctively, he put his arms around her. This young woman reminded him of his younger sister, Marie-Christine…and maybe someone else. April was one of the youngest members of the company, having just turned twenty-three, but she was a very young twenty-three, unlike other twenty-three-year olds in his past who had confidence and self-esteem to spare.

He felt April calming down. He stepped away from her to grab a box of Kleenex, and then walked her to a chair on the other side of the room. He took a seat in another chair that he pulled in front of her.

Marc was uncomfortable. Dealing with personal issues was not one of his strengths, but he tried his best to look confident in front of his company member. "April, please tell me what's going on." He saw tears come to her eyes again.

"I'm so frightened right now. I hate feeling this way, but there's nothing I can do about it. I feel so helpless!"

But he already knew this. On this day of unspeakable horrific acts she was frightened, just like everybody else.

"April, I know. I'm scared, too! This is horrible being so far away from home and not being able to do anything. But…you're safe, that's the important thing right now."

She reached for a piece of Kleenex. "Maybe I feel guilty because I'm not *there*, and maybe I should be…I don't know." She continued to wipe her eyes.

"April, where do you live?" She looked at Marc as if he had asked her the strangest question in the world.

"Harlem. Why?"

That was far away from The Towers.

"I just wanted to make sure that you lived away from The Towers, that's all. Do you have any friends or family that would have any reason to be in Lower Manhattan this morning?"

She shook her head no.

"Then that's good. Hopefully everyone you know is alright. Please hang onto that thought until you're able to make contact, which I pray will be very soon."

She seemed quieter now.

"April, where is your family?"

She blew her nose. "Indiana."

Marc took his own cell phone from his pocket. "Here, why don't you try to give your family a call?

Sometimes talking to the people you care about, or talking to the people who care about you can totally change your perspective."

He extended the phone to her, but she was hesitant to take it from him.

"April, this will be our secret. This is my personal phone so no record of the call will show up in New York if that's what you're worried about. Please, try to get through to your family, and take as long as you need."

Slowly she took the phone from Marc and began to dial. He crossed to the other side of the room to give her a bit of privacy. He was relieved when he could hear that someone in Indiana had answered. He busied himself with the daily log, which was going to take considerably longer today.

A few minutes later, she was coming across the room to return his phone. "Thank you for that. You were right and I do feel better, and not so scared anymore. I'm sorry I acted like such a baby."

Marc took her hand. "Never apologize for being human, April."

She tried to smile. "Okay, I'll try to remember. Thanks again." She gave him a quick hug before Marc walked her back to the door and sent her back to the rest of the company.

He knew that eventually he'd have to deal with the personal issues of company members-he just never expected it to be on day two of the tour. He hoped he had done and said the right things.

That's when something occurred to him. April had dialed her family in Indiana with no problem whatsoever. She had spoken to someone she cared about, and someone who cared about her and came away with a whole new perspective. Maybe it was time he followed some of his own advice.

He took his phone back out, scrolled down his list of contacts and pressed send. Moments later, and thousands of miles away, a phone in Culver City, California began ringing.

"Hello?" Gary Connelly answered on the first ring.

"Gary, its Marc Guiro."

There was relief in Gary's voice. "Thank God! Marc, where are you?"

It was good to hear Gary's voice. Marc was already feeling better. "Philadelphia. It's a long story, but I accepted a short-term company manager position with ACT, and we left town yesterday if you can believe that!"

Gary asked him to hold on for a moment as he heard Gary excitedly relating his story to others in the room. He was back fairly quickly.

"Marc, I'm here with Natalie and Lauren."

Hearing Lauren's name, and realizing she was just on the other side of the line, took him away from the thoughts of The Towers and the company and everything else going on around him. On this, one of the most difficult days of his life, he would have one pleasant thought-if only for a few moments.

"Lauren?" He relaxed. "Gary, how is she?"

Gary was surprised to see that the mention of her name still affected him. "She's good, but worried sick like the rest of us."

While Marc was glad to hear Lauren was well, he knew he had to put any personal feelings aside and be the ACT company manager. He needed to talk to someone who knew what was involved in this specific position, and at this moment that person was Gary Connelly.

"Gary, first of all part of me is relieved to be out of the city. That may sound selfish, but I'm glad I'm in Philly!"

Gary could only imagine. "Marc, you shouldn't feel bad about being out of harm's way. I know that your friends and family must be relieved. I know we are here."

Marc hadn't thought about his own family. "Great! I guess I need to call Montreal and let them know I'm okay. I let my sister know I was leaving town, but for the life of me I don't know if I told her when. I didn't know anything about this job until ten days ago when Ben asked me to take the position as a favor

Gary voiced something that Marc had only been thinking. "Marc... you weren't supposed to be in New York this morning. You know the Universe works in mysterious ways and we've all experienced things like this from time to time-though most of the time it isn't this obvious. Not to get all mystical on you, but I think you're right where you're supposed to be: taking care of the company. How are they doing?"

Marc exhaled deeply. "They're scared... and angry. There's a sense of helplessness. All we can do is sit back and watch the television and get even more angry and upset. I mean our hometown has been bombed...literally."

Gary could hear the helplessness in Marc's voice. "Marc, how are *you* doing?"

Marc didn't know how to answer this question and struggled to articulate an answer. "I'm having the same feelings as the company. I'm upset-that's a given, and I'm pissed that I can't do anything. I'm hurting inside and can't do anything about it. Gary... I'm so angry!"

Gary thought that was more than understandable. "We're all angry at whoever did this!"

This wasn't what Marc meant at all. "No, Gary! I'm angry because it's just not me! If I had to look out for only myself I'd be in a much better place, but I am responsible for the well-being of the entire company! That's twenty New Yorkers when I include myself. I'm in charge of twenty people on a day where everything as we've known it has changed! We don't know the whole story, or if there'll be more attacks. Gary, I was the one who told the company about the attack this morning. They're getting ready to go onstage, and they're up and excited, and then I tell them I've cancelled today's shows and why. Some of them thought that I was joking."

Gary wanted clarification. "*You* cancelled the shows? I mean it was your decision?"

"Yeah, I didn't feel I had a choice in the matter. I couldn't reach the office in New York so I had to make the call on my own. The best place for the kids was in their own schools or at home with their families. I think most schools across the country closed or never opened today."

Gary agreed. "That's right. Sabrina wouldn't have gone to school today even if classes were in session. That was a good call on your part. What happened next?"

Marc tried to remember the events of just a few hours before that seemed to blur all together.

"Marc, it sounds like you're doing everything right!"

Marc was still unsure. "I hope so. Just a few minutes ago there was a girl…a company member in here crying because she was frightened. It was heartbreaking, but I think she'll be okay. I gave her my phone and let her call her family in Indiana."

Gary approved. "As the father of a daughter, thank you! Marc, that action showed some real sensitivity on your part. Part of your job is being able to listen and to look out for people emotionally as well as professionally."

Marc shot back. "But I didn't sign up for that part of the job, Gary!"

Gary shot right back. "Too bad! It's easy to handle the day-to-day operation of the company and give out call times and mount the shows and move them from point A to point B. But your company just isn't actors and stage managers and technicians. Your company is made up of people, and people are complicated, especially when they're in crisis!"

Marc was quiet for a few moments. "I know you're right. But…well, I haven't handled my own personal relationships very well, and now being expected to help others handle…what could be tough personal decisions…I don't know."

But Gary knew. "Marc, are you scared?"

There was no hesitation. "Hell yes, I'm scared!"

This was the answer Gary had hoped to hear. "Good! You *should* be scared along with the rest of us. But in this case, fear becomes the great equalizer. You know where your people are coming from because you're feeling the same things. From what you're telling me, you're doing a good job, and that's why Ben wanted you out there with his company. You're the type of person I'd want working with me. Aside from your talent and professionalism, I could trust you to make tough decisions… and Ben trusts you! So I think you need to start trusting yourself."

Marc thought about what he'd done today and wouldn't have done anything differently. "Gary, thank you. Thanks for the vote of confidence."

Gary knew that Marc was going to be okay. "So Marc, what do you need from me now?"

Marc's tone shifted from personal to professional. "Gary, I need to talk to someone who knows the position I'm in, and you're the only person I can think of right now."

They spent the next forty minutes discussing decisions that Marc would have to make. By the time they finished their conversation, Marc's perspective had changed completely because now, he had a plan.

He ran his ideas past Dan who agreed that his plan was the best course of action. He then presented his strategy to the company later that night at a restaurant near the hotel.

"First of all, I'd like to thank all of you for your professionalism and understanding during a situation that has been strange and bizarre, to say the least. Like many of you, part of me wants to be at home doing something…anything to help our city, and our friends and loved ones. Part of me feels guilty for being only two hours away from home, and safe. But we're here for a reason, even if that reason is performing for school kids during a difficult time. It may sound cliché, but the show must go on."

A small buzz went around the table. He allowed it to subside before he continued.

"I think it's in the best interest of the company to go ahead with the tour beginning tomorrow morning. There's a strong possibility that we may be playing to half empty houses, but that's okay, because we'll be giving our best. We may actually help some of these kids forget about this tragedy for a little bit. We may be able to forget too, if only for the duration of the performances. I've made this decision independently without ACT management because, as you know, it's impossible to reach the city right now. I hope to have contact with the office by Saturday before we leave for Pittsburg, but we'll just have to wait and see."

He had the table's undivided attention.

"Earlier today I spoke to a few of you who I thought may have reason to get back into the city, but my door is open to all of you. If any of you would like to leave the company and try to get back into the city, I understand. I'll even try to help you get back. But please think about a few things. First of all, you're currently employed and earning a salary. Who knows what will be happening in the industry in the weeks and months to come. We are all safe and healthy, and like it or not, our lives have order and purpose. We see the pictures coming from home and they're upsetting, but I feel that we need to look ahead."

The company members were listening intently as Marc saw a few people nodding affirmatively.

"Dan and I are here to help with any concerns. We don't know what's ahead of us now, but we're here to help make sense of all of it. The US mail will be delivered into the city and Dan has picked up some prepaid postcards if you'd like to drop a line to anyone in the city. I wish we could do more for you, but I promise we'll get through this... together."

Marc sat down. Before long the entire table broke into applause. He finally started to relax.

Later that night one of the company members ran into Dan by the vending machines.

"I guess continuing the tour is the right thing to do. Who knows what we'll be coming back to in November?"

Dan agreed. "I just can't imagine what's happening there right now. Television is making New York look like a war zone, and while part of me wants to be there, I'm glad I'm here."

The company member shook her head in agreement. "I guess we're pretty lucky as a company. It seems, for now anyway, that nobody can think of any reason why any friends or family members would be in or around The Towers. And I don't think any of us lived anywhere near The Towers."

Dan stopped and looked at her. He had something to say to her, but wasn't sure that he should.

She noticed and became curious. "Dan, what is it?"

"That's not true. Marc lives near the financial district and very close to where The Towers stood. He doesn't know the status of his home."

Dan got his soda and said goodnight as the stunned company member stood speechless.

The following day, September 12, The American Children's Theater officially began its 2001-2002 season. The theater may not have been full, but the audiences were enthusiastic.

Before both performances Marc greeted the audience who thanked them for coming and allowing them to forget about events in New York for a few minutes, and in return hoped they could do the same for them.

His decision to greet the audience was spur of the moment, but it set the tone of the performances for the audiences and his cast. The thing that Marc remembered most from these performances was the laughter of his young audiences.

Ben Stewart was finally able to contact Marc and Dan on Thursday, thrilled that with the exception of Tuesday, the performances continued and gave the company the go-ahead to continue the tour as scheduled. On Saturday morning the company found themselves heading to Pittsburgh.

When recalling the events of September 11, 2001, Marc would remember the fear and uncertainty surrounding that day. He would also remember that probably for the first time in his life, he put the needs of others before his own. In Marc's mind, September 11 was the day he finally became an adult.

***

The fall portion of the 2001-2002 ACT Season was the best tour that Marc had ever done. After the events of 9/11 the company united in a strong front against the tragedy as they brought live theater to the country's school children. In the big picture what they were doing may have seemed trivial, but for the company it was the most important thing they could be doing. The company thought it was a very strange set of circumstances, but all made the best of the strangeness by doing some of their best work.

The company of New York actors was overwhelmed by the outpouring of support they received from their young audiences. Many rose to their feet at the end of performances and sustained their applause much longer than normal.

The first time this happened was after the last performance of *Shrew* in Philadelphia where the high school audience cheered the actors, refusing to let them leave the stage. The actors began to applaud their audience as the curtain was finally lowered.

Nobody in the company had ever experienced this type of ovation and questioned the action.

Marc saw what was happening. "They're not just applauding you for your work on stage, but they are also applauding you as New Yorkers. I guess we've all become ambassadors from a place that has become a symbol lately."

Marc was unprepared when several of his company members, men and women, burst into tears.

In the first several days after 9/11 emotions were erratic and unstable, but the company pulled together for support. That took on extreme importance when news from home started to trickle in. A few company members learned that they had known someone who had died in The Towers. Many company members began to hear the harrowing stories from friends and relatives about where they were, what they did, and for a few, how they escaped and cheated death.

Within a few weeks of the attacks, two company members decided to return to New York. One member wanted to get back to his family, while the other felt he needed to be at home to help in any way he could.

Marc and Dan were able to fill the roles with other company members. The tour continued as normally as possible.

By the second week of October, Marc gradually took a back seat as Dan assumed management of the company. He was impressed when he saw Dan having a very serious discussion with a company member that appeared to be of a personal nature, another part of the job that he accepted freely.

At this point there were only a few weeks left on this leg of the tour before the company returned home to New York for the November/December break. Due to the extreme circumstances, the New York office told Marc that if he wanted to complete this leg of the tour with the company, he was to feel free to do so, and that his contract would be extended into November.

Marc seriously considered staying since he had grown close to many of these people-that was not always easy for him. But he also felt that Dan needed to fly solo as company manager, even if it was only for a few weeks. Then when the company resumed the tour in January, Dan would feel completely comfortable in the position.

The company arrived in Minneapolis late in the afternoon on Tuesday, October 30. Dan held a brief company meeting, giving the company the schedule for the Minneapolis/St. Paul area, and assigning them a 7:00 o'clock call time for the next morning, before releasing them.

Dan and Marc went to their shared motel room. Dan collapsed onto one of the beds, exhausted.

Marc laughed to himself. "Dan, you seem to be very comfortable as company manager. You're organized, a good problem solver, and you're easily handling the logistics of the company. I'm impressed."

Dan was pleased by Marc's compliments. "Thanks. Coming from you that means a lot. You've put me in a good place to take over the reins of the company. I've learned things that I never imagined were a part of the job, like being able to handle the personal stuff…which was kind of strange at first, but you gave me the best advice, which was to listen. I know I'll be ready come January."

Dan was expecting him to finish this leg of the tour with him, and for a moment, he considered doing just that, but his common sense cancelled any such thoughts.

"Dan, do you need to ask me any questions about anything as far as the company's management is concerned?"

"Nope, I'm feeling pretty good about everything." Dan replied.

That's all that Marc needed to hear. "That's great, because as of right now, you're officially assuming all duties as ACT's company manager. I'll leave for New York in the morning."

Dan seemed stunned. "Marc, are you sure? I mean there are only a few more weeks to go and-"

"Dan, you were ready a few weeks ago. In fact you've been handling everything while I've just been taking up space in the van. You need to be out here by yourself."

Dan was suddenly looking unsure of himself.

Marc reassured him. "Don't worry, you have the respect of the company. Just keep doing what you've been doing. And most importantly, trust yourself."

Marc knew he had made the right decision. That night Dan insisted on treating him to dinner at a nearby steak house as a gesture of thanks.

The next morning Marc was at the vans at 7:00 with the company as they groggily climbed on board to begin their day. None seemed to notice that Marc was carrying his packed duffle bag.

Dan was the last to board the van but stopped to say a few final words to Marc. "You didn't say goodbye to the company."

Marc nodded. "I hate goodbyes, but I'll forget that for a moment and say goodbye to you. It's been great working with you, despite the circumstances. The company is very lucky to have you. And look, if you ever have any questions, or just want to run something past me, feel free to give me a call. And I mean that."

They shook hands.

"Thanks for everything, Marc."

The horn of one of the vans sounded.

Marc looked toward the waiting van. "You better get going."

Dan was still unsure. "Marc, are you going to be okay?"

At that moment, a cab pulled up right behind the vans. "Dan, the cab is for me. I'll be fine. Now get going."

Dan hesitated one last time. "What do you want me to tell the company?"

Marc was opening the cab's door. "Tell them it's been great working with them, and I'll see them all for the company showcase in New York this spring."

Dan gave Marc one last nod, climbed into the van and shut the door.

Marc got into the cab. "I'm going to Minneapolis International, Northwest Terminal, please."

The taxi followed the two company vans to the exit of the Holiday Inn Express. The ACT vans turned left to head to their day's performances, while the taxi turned right, as Marc began his journey back home to New York.

Chapter Seven

New York City,

October 31, 2001

The New York that Marc left six short weeks before no longer existed. There was a new normal that he witnessed first-hand at the Minneapolis International Airport where he saw the strong National Guard presence patrolling the airport with assault weapons, not to mention the increased scrutiny during the check in process.

His flight was non-eventful, though the tone on the flight seemed strange as passengers were overly polite, patient, quiet and very attentive to the flight crew. Even stranger was that, as the plane touched down at New York's LaGuardia Airport, the passengers applauded.

But this was only the beginning. Marc was about to enter a surreal *Twilight Zone* version of New York City.

Marc decided the best way to get into Manhattan was via one of the Port Authority buses that would take him to Penn Station. From there he could either take a cab or the subway to Lower Manhattan.

October 31, Halloween, was chilly, overcast and very dark to Marc. This was despite the fact he had arrived in Manhattan in the middle of the afternoon.

Once he reached Manhattan, he realized that things were very different. There was a strong military presence that reached beyond the airport and into the city itself. Armed soldiers patrolled the streets with weapons at the ready.

American flags were everywhere-on cars, in windows and storefronts, in graffiti, on clothing, on buildings and fire trucks and police officers. He observed many makeshift memorials.

Most disturbing to Marc were the missing posters. It had been several weeks since the attacks, but the posters seemed to be everywhere. He had seen these mostly handmade posters in television news reports. But on his first day back in New York he came face to face with these posters as he went down into the Penn Station subway station. Posters covered walls, token machines and any other any available space. As he waited for his train he found himself drawn to the posters closest to him. He studied a few photographs, reading names and descriptions, and the one fact that connected them, "Last seen, 9/11/2001." He only read a few of these posters before looking throughout the station and seeing hundreds of these notices. A sickening feeling came over him as he realized each poster represented a person who more than likely had died in the attacks.

His train arrived and he quickly boarded, not quite knowing what to expect next.

He reached his stop and climbed to the top of the stairs. While it was shortly before 3:00, the sky seemed unusually dark as a light cold rain began to fall. While he had expected the familiar sounds of a busy street, he was immediately aware of an eerie quiet. There seemed to be more stillness than motion.

As he began his three-block walk towards his loft, he was aware of dirt, or very fine sand, under his feet. As he walked the vaguely familiar streets, he thought that the entire neighborhood was in need of a good dusting because he seemed to be inhaling dirt.

But the worst part was the smell throughout the city. The acrid scent of metal and wood hung in the air. Weeks later, there was the distinct aroma of rot and decay which caused Marc to feel nauseated.

As he finally entered his building he thought, "My God! I'm in Hell!"

***

Paul Chen was a photographer from Seattle, Washington who had sublet Marc's loft while he was on tour. He was in the loft on the morning of September 11 and heard a large plane flying way too low and the subsequent explosion. He grabbed his camera and headed in the direction of The Towers, not believing what he was seeing.

He saw thick black smoke billowing ominously from one of the Towers, and thousands of pieces of paper, some on fire, floating over Lower Manhattan.

He got as close as he could before he and many others could go no further due to the large number of people who had poured into the street. But when the second plane hit the South Tower, he came to the conclusion that this was no accident but rather some sort of attack and immediately wanted to leave the area. But as strong as his desire was to leave, he felt compelled to capture these frightening images with his Nikon. But then he saw what he thought were objects starting to fall from the upper floors of The Towers. To his horror, he realized these were not objects but people.

That morning images were burned into Paul's mind that he would never forget.

Sometime after The Towers fell, Paul was eventually able to make it back to Marc's loft, intending to get out of New York as soon as possible. And yet he was still there when Marc returned on the last day of October.

Marc unlocked the door of his loft and found Paul sitting on the couch looking at a stack of black and white photographs.

"Marc, welcome home, man."

Marc entered the loft and looked around not knowing what to expect. Thankfully, he found his place just as he had left it, and breathed a heavy sigh of relief.

He shook his hand and thanked him for staying, especially under the circumstances.

Paul clearly saw that Marc was shaken and unsettled. "Well, believe me it's much better than it was. And you're very lucky that your place is outside of the Frozen Zone."

Marc was unfamiliar with the term. "I don't understand."

"Basically, an area has been closed off to all vehicular and non-resident pedestrian traffic. We're just a few blocks outside of the barricades, though this area still looks-and feels-like a war zone."

Paul had seen a lot over the past few weeks and was mentally exhausted. He offered a stack of photographs to

Marc. "These were taken a few days ago just outside of the barricaded area."

While Marc had an idea where some of the photographs were taken, it still didn't look like the New York he left only six short weeks ago.

Paul told him that he had taken hundreds of photographs the morning of the attacks that he'd show Marc, but warned him that many of the photographs were difficult to look at because many photographs froze tragic and horrible images.

"I've sold many of my photos over the past several weeks, but honestly that doesn't seem important now. I came to New York to experience the city but became an unwilling documenter of historic and tragic events."

Over the next several minutes Paul told Marc about the neighborhood and the fact that many people had just picked up and left. He had been keeping an eye on the loft next to Marc's, since the couple who lived there didn't feel that this was a good environment for their newborn though they hoped to return. The man who lived in a corner unit one floor above Marc hadn't been seen since September 11. His family feared the worst.

He showed Marc the dust that had accumulated over the past day throughout the loft and explained that it was always getting in somehow. He advised Marc to always take his shoes off at the door so as not to track dust throughout the loft.

Marc remembered the dust he walked through on his way home. "Is this the same dust that's all over the streets and buildings?"

Paul answered wanting Marc to fully understand. "Yes. Marc it's the dust from the collapse of the Towers. The dust *is* The Towers."

Sadly Marc understood.

An hour later Paul took Marc on a walk of the surrounding area, pointing out which businesses had closed. They saw many police officers and the armed guards with their assault rifles. For the first time Marc really noticed the fire fighters. There were so many weary looking firemen on the street wearing all different types of uniforms.

Paul explained that while most of the restaurants were closed to the public, they were operating for the emergency personnel.

Marc spotted a fire truck with a name of someplace called Bismarck painted on the side.

"The only Bismarck I know is in one of the Dakotas."

Paul nodded. "You're right. That company is from North Dakota. They've come from all over the country."

To Marc none of this seemed real and part of him wished that he'd stayed in Minnesota. There, things were normal.

As Marc continued to look at his neighborhood he was continually distracted by the smell of burning: burning metal, burning wood, and burning buildings. Marc was actually smelling the smoldering remains of the collapsed towers. Paul told him the smell had diminished but even he was still aware of it. It was something that you just never got used to.

"And Marc, you're also smelling the smell of collapsed buildings."

Marc looked at him strangely.

"That was a new one for me too."

They continued to walk in the direction where The Towers once stood until they reached the guarded barricade. A gate opened long enough to allow a few emergency vehicles to exit. Just blocks away he could see the unbelievably huge pile of crumbled concrete and twisted metal that had once been the Twin Towers of The World Trade Center. He'd seen images of this many times on television over the past six weeks, but the *pile* depicted was nothing compared to the reality of seeing it firsthand. Marc quickly inhaled as his stomach tightened. The enormity of the disaster causing an unexpected physical reaction.

The gate slowly closed as Marc looked to Paul, confused. "While the layout of the streets is the same, and I recognize buildings and landmarks… it's just all so different. I don't know this place anymore!"

Marc saw Paul suddenly become aware of something as his body stiffened and his eyes quickly moved skyward. A roaring sound in the sky reverberated off the buildings causing everything shake. Looking up he saw two military fighter jets flying low over the area.

"They make regular patrols, but I can't get used to them." Paul explained. "I'm not sure if I ever will. To me they just sound like planes flying too low. I find myself waiting for the explosion when they make impact…"

He stopped to gather his thoughts. "I saw and heard things that morning that I'll never forget! It's been an experience, to say the least. I know it can't be easy for you looking at the aftermath, but consider yourself lucky that you were far away from here that morning."

They headed back to Marc's loft in silence.

A short time later Paul gathered the last of his belongings and said goodbye. He still had one more month in New York and had found another sublet near Columbia University, far away from the chaos that was Lower Manhattan. A friend picked him up to drive him to the new place. He had come to the city thinking he might want to relocate, but now wasn't so sure if he was cut out to be a New Yorker.

That night, Marc was home in his New York City loft in Lower Manhattan, where nothing was the same.

This was Halloween night. The city should have been alive with the energy and excitement of the holiday. But from his window he only heard the occasional sound of a car-or, more than likely, some sort of emergency vehicle driving past the front of his building.

He had looked forward to coming back home, but the city he remembered no longer existed. He felt alone, out of place…and lost.

Chapter Eight

New York/Cincinnati/

Assorted Regional Theaters

2002-2006

Marc tried to acclimate to this strange new place called New York City. He observed that the further uptown he went, the less he was aware of Lower Manhattan and the chaos that existed in his neighborhood.

People uptown seemed to be leading normal lives: walking about freely, eating in restaurants, shopping, going to the theater, and *enjoying* life.

The only thing that continued to strike him as strange was that everybody was so nice; overly nice, and he found himself wondering how long this would last.

Less than a week after he arrived home, Marc decided he had to leave Lower Manhattan. Finding an apartment was fairly easy, since there were a lot of vacancies. Many people from all over the city had fled following the attacks. Marc found a place near NYU. The unit was much smaller than his loft, but it was clean and comfortable. He was finally able to get a good night's sleep.

Immediately after he settled into his new place he began to audition again, though there was a decline in the volume of auditions. He read for the library reading series, three plays and two films.

ACT asked him to participate on a panel that would update and develop contingency procedures for emergencies and other types of situations on the road, so that no other company would be stranded without a documented plan of action, as Marc's company had been. This was work he hadn't expected, but happily accepted.

ACT's board was very happy with Marc since he may have saved the season by keeping a cool and level head on 9/11 and keeping the company intact. Dan Steele told the board everything that had happened during those first two weeks after the attacks and praised Marc for his actions. The board gave Marc an unexpected bonus at the end of the year.

Marc's business savvy paid off. Part of his deal for going on the road was to produce the ACT actors Showcase before the third leg of the season, as well as participate in the first ACT summer production to be produced in Manhattan. The showcase was successful and he directed ACT's summer production of *You're A Good Man Charlie Brown*, his first full-length musical.

Marc was surprised at the choice of shows, but the ACT board thought an upbeat non-offensive musical would be good for a first summer effort that would appeal to family audiences. The four-week run did well enough to make the board consider making a summer production an annual event.

In August, Marc was working with ACT again, this time directing Gary Connelly's adaption of *The Tempest*. This was the last show he had done with Gary years before.

But by the time the company began their tour, just after Labor Day, Marc was fed up with life in the city. It had been almost a year since 9/11 and life in New York was still challenging for him.

He discussed this with Mel over breakfast one Saturday morning. "I still don't feel completely comfortable here. I feel out of place and out of step, like I don't belong in New York anymore."

Mel sipped her coffee. "Please don't tell me you want to leave New York?"

"Well, no. Not permanently anyway. Leaving New York would be admitting defeat and giving up. I'm an actor and I live in New York, but I don't know this incarnation of New York and it's disconcerting to say the least."

Mel thought that Marc had not looked like himself ever since he returned from his brief tour the year before. She hoped he would settle into the post 9/11 New York, but he had not. She had known him for years and was used to his moodiness from time to time, but he had been depressed for months.

"What are you doing to cope with this problem?"

"I've been thinking about doing regional theater. I could still be based in New York and still do some good theater in places outside of New York."

She had a hard time imagining him anywhere outside of New York for any period of time. "Have you given this any real thought?"

Marc shrugged. "It's an option and I need to do something before I go insane. I've been back for almost year and I've been working pretty steadily, but I've been miserable. Maybe I need a change of pace and location, being somewhere where I don't have to worry about the city and can concentrate on the work."

She agreed that he needed to do something. "Okay, so how do you get into these theaters?"

So this is how he'd break his news to Mel. "Several regional theaters cast in New York. I auditioned for a few of them in July. I leave for Cincinnati next week."

Mel almost choked. "No! You're kidding me!"

Marc expected her reaction. "I've signed the contract Mel…and I'm excited about going. This is what I need to be doing right now. I'm looking at a month of rehearsals and a month of performances. The more I talk about it the better it sounds."

Mel sat back and looked at her friend with concern. "But, Marc… Cincinnati? That's in Ohio!"

There was no further discussion. Marc left for Ohio the next Tuesday.

***

Cincinnati, Ohio was a beautiful city located on the Ohio River. The theater where Marc would be working, Playhouse in the Park, was one of the best regional theaters in the country, and had won several regional Tony awards.

The artistic director was originally from New York and knew his Midwestern audience well. He planned a well-balanced season that featured a variety of productions, from safe family friendly productions like *Oliver,* to classics like *A Streetcar Named Desire.* Every season he would also introduce his audiences to newer edgier productions like *Tangled Web,* which was a post-Cold War spy drama. Marc had a prominent role in *Tangled Web.*

Playhouse in the Park was a favorite regional theater of many New York actors. The theater itself was a beautiful state-of-the-art facility, located in Eden Park, which was located just outside of downtown and bordered an area called Mt. Adams.

Cincinnati, like Rome, Italy, is built on seven hills. Mt. Adams was a hill that overlooked downtown Cincinnati on one side and the Ohio River on the other. The neighborhood was the trendiest in the city, with several unique restaurants, shops and an arthouse-type theater that ran smaller independent and foreign language films. The accommodations for the actors were apartments located in Mt. Adams, so the actors could walk to the theater. Marc's apartment overlooked downtown Cincinnati.

After rehearsal on the first day, the artistic director took the cast to dinner. Marc was surprised to learn that two of the six cast members were professional actors living in Cincinnati, while the other four were from New York.

The artistic director let the visiting New Yorkers know they would be receiving several invitations to parties and receptions throughout the city. He let them know that just before and during the run of the show some of them might be asked to do publicity for the show by appearing on local television and radio shows, as well as being interviewed by the local press. He would try to keep the first few weeks of rehearsal relatively free so the cast could concentrate on getting the play on its feet. All of them could attend a performance of the current production running at the theater, simply by calling the box office. He also asked if any of them would be willing to speak to school groups after the show opened. Marc thought about doing that.

The staff of Playhouse in the Park wanted to make sure the visiting actors enjoyed their time in Cincinnati.

Contrary to what Mel had predicted, Marc would not die from boredom.

The rehearsal schedule was Monday through Friday initially, with adjustments made closer to the play's opening. The performance schedule was Tuesday through Saturday evenings, with matinees on Wednesday, Saturday and Sunday. The schedule was similar to New York City theater schedules.

Once the show opened he found the Cincinnati audiences warm and appreciative. The show received good to excellent reviews. Ticket sales were good.

The cast split the publicity duties, with Marc doing one local morning television show and two radio interviews.

Marc also happily went to the Cincinnati School of the Performing Arts, where he spoke to high school acting students about being a working New York actor. He didn't paint any unrealistic pictures and felt his young audience appreciated his candor.

Marc and the other cast members were also invited to performances at other theater venues, all being surprised that Cincinnati had a thriving theater community.

Every once in a while, he thought about Lauren. She had grown up in Middletown, a small town very close to Cincinnati. After all these years he still remembered it. Lauren had often told him that, to her, Cincinnati *was* the big city. A few times he found himself wondering if she had ever been to Playhouse in the Park, or to Mt. Adams, where he was currently living.

But then he would remember the last time he was with her and berate himself for not running after her that night. After all these years he still had regretted that Laurie, the woman whom he had fallen in love with despite himself, had run away from him, and his life had never been the same.

It had been more than ten years since Marc had last seen Lauren Dey Phillips. He missed her.

Marc called Mel three weeks after his arrival in Cincinnati. He told her things were going well, and could understand why so many actors did regional theater, and that he hoped to do more himself.

"In New York there are so many of us, but here we're a novelty and are treated very well by the locals. So far it's been a good experience."

Mel laughed. "Well it sounds like you're having a better time than I am. *Crossing's* budget has been cut... again."

Marc groaned. "Are you going to be alright?"

Mel tried to remain upbeat. "We're going to be alright only because we have to be alright while turning out an hour of television five days a week. The thing is, I know they're going to make another cut in our budget within the next six months, and I don't know how they can cut it anymore than they have already."

He knew she had been dealing with consistent budget cuts for the past two years. "Well, hang in there. Your fans are loyal and don't seem to be going anywhere."

She groaned. "I just wish we had younger viewers to keep us going. Television has changed drastically, but daytime dramas have pretty much remained the same. I don't think we'll be here in five years. Hey, why don't you watch us in Cincinnati since it sounds like you're going to be free in the afternoons? At this point every viewer counts."

Now he was laughing. "It's not like I'm lying around eating chocolates, you know. But sure, I'll tune in when I can. I'd like to see what you're doing story wise. Your show has some of the best writing on daytime…and I really mean that."

He'd gotten to her. "Thanks. And to think I wasn't sure if I wanted to stay in daytime television for any period of time." She sighed. "I miss not being able to vent to in person. What, you have like five more weeks in the Midwest?"

"Something like that. But I'm having a good time. Believe me!"

There was silence on the other end of the line. "Okay... I get it now." She said. "Of course, you're having a good time on the road. You told me yourself a long time ago that you're no choirboy."

In fact, there was a woman, but it wasn't worth talking about. With Marc, it never was. She was more of a recreational diversion than anything else.

Her name was Victoria Brighton. She was a British actor working in New York. Marc met her in *Tangled Web*. They had several wordy scenes together that were getting the best of both of them. They had apartments in the same building, so running lines in the evenings was something they both agreed would be beneficial for both of them. Their extra work paid off and during the second week of rehearsal they both finally felt comfortable and no longer felt it necessary to work in the evenings.

But Victoria, never Vicky, arrived at Marc's door one night after rehearsal. Instead of her script she carried a bottle of wine and two glasses. He invited her inside and soon learned that the play was the last thing on her mind. After forty minutes of rolling around on his couch, she asked if his apartment had a bedroom.

He pulled away from her. "Victoria, just so you know, I'm not looking for anything right now."

She smiled seductively and stroked his face. "I'm not looking for anything either. But darling, we're in Cincinnati."

Their affair would last through the run of the show, ending right before they returned to New York.

Marc let Mel know she was right. Beyond that, he said nothing.

She noticed the time. "I've got to get back to work. Let me know when you're coming home so we can do breakfast. And call me if you get bored. Keep in touch, okay? I miss you!"

They both hated ending their calls.

"I will. Miss you too Mel." As he hung up, he again wondered if they had been siblings. Their connection was too strong for anything else to make sense.

***

For the next several years this was Marc's pattern. He'd go off to do regional theater, meet a woman who most of the time was another cast member (though there was one stage manager in DC and a wardrobe mistress in Baltimore), and have a short-term affair that always ended before he returned to New York.

Mel was afraid that he had regressed to his college days when his relationships were always casual. But Marc was not nineteen anymore. She started calling him Casanova, which he resented.

As far as Marc was concerned he was doing the best work of his career and reaping the benefits...all the benefits. "I'm enjoying myself!"

But she shot back. "How long do you intend to go on *enjoying* yourself?"

"For as long as I'm feeling good." He hated this conversation.

Marc never thought about living beyond the present. His affairs certainly helped him with the loneliness he often felt, especially when he was on the road. Maybe he was subconsciously trying to recover something he had briefly years ago.

She was worried for Marc, in part because of the current, and probably the final man in her life, Eric Richman.

She had been seeing Eric seriously for more than a few years. Marc had never met him due to the impossibly busy schedules of three busy people, though Mel had casually dropped his name in passing. She knew her good friend Marc still had a problem with the concept of romantic love, for himself anyway.

Eric helped Mel see life in a new light and helped her deal with the challenges that had been thrust in front of her, especially since she had been named head writer on *Clayton's Crossing*. She knew the show was in its final days, and at this point was only waiting for a cancellation notice from the network. But thanks to Eric, the love of her life, she continued to write the best show possible and knew when the final day of *Clayton's Crossing* came, her life would continue.

But when Mel looked at Marc and his string of endless meaningless relationships, she found herself filled with regret. If she could somehow travel back through time, she would have helped Marc find Lauren. They were so perfect for each other and had been in love-the romantic kind of love Marc no longer believed existed.

And things had not exactly gone well for Lauren romantically, either. Lauren had often admitted she was always falling for the wrong men and had more than a few less than perfect relationships, including one that was dangerous and abusive.

Mel was still in contact with Lauren on a regular basis, plus they had a mutual friend, David Diaz, who more than once had been Lauren's guardian angel. He often gave Mel updates on Lauren's life in Los Angeles- not for the sake of gossip, but out of concern.

Mel observed that Lauren, like Marc, was doing well professionally, at least now. But personally she felt Lauren had come to the conclusion she was meant to be alone.

When Mel thought of her two friends lately, she felt sad…until she thought about Eric. And that's when Mel counted her blessings while keeping her friends in her prayers.

Chapter Nine

New York/Montreal

2006

In July of 2006 Marc was at home in New York. On this Saturday morning, he was keeping his regular breakfast date with Mel at their usual coffee shop.

He had made sure to arrive early, so he would be there to greet her. He knew she had to be miserable and going through a rough time, since her show had finally been cancelled the week before. He had spoken to her briefly on Tuesday evening after the cancellation had been made public, but had been unable to see her until now.

Marc had settled into a booth and already had his first cup of coffee in front of him when Mel burst through the door. Something was off. He was expecting her to look serious, subdued, and depressed. But she was radiant!

He could see the brightness of her smile from across the room and there was a spring to her step that he never remembered seeing…*ever.*

Mel practically ran across the restaurant to greet him by throwing her arms tightly around his neck, before kissing one cheek and then the other. Marc was stunned as she settled into the other side of the booth.

Their regular waitress appeared with a coffee pot. "Can I pour you a cup of coffee?"

Marc answered for her. "Yes please. And while you're at it could you please bring my friend a sedative?"

The waitress had known them for years, and simply smiled as she poured Mel's coffee and left menus on the table.

Marc watched her as she sweetened her coffee and observed that she was smiling like a teenaged girl.

"I don't get it. Shouldn't you be…I don't know…sad? Suicidal maybe?"

Mel started to laugh which only confused him more.

Once she realized this, she apologized. "Please forgive me. And, no I shouldn't be sad, and I couldn't be sad or upset because… I am so happy right now!"

She then presented her left hand to Marc. His mouth dropped at the sight of the diamond ring.

"You're engaged?"

Mel started to laugh again. "Well, for a minute. But if you take a closer look, you'll see two rings!"

Marc took her hand in his and clearly saw a slim wedding band below the diamond engagement ring. He could only look at Mel who was uncharacteristically starting to tear up.

"I'm married Marc! Do you believe it?"

Marc could still say nothing, so instead he got out of the booth, went to her side of the table, pulled her out of the booth and kissed her on both cheeks before he found his voice again.

"Congratulations! I had no idea! Who is he?"

That's when she told him about Eric.

Marc had never seen her this happy. "So, when do I get to meet him?"

Mel dried her eyes. "Next Saturday here at breakfast if that's okay? He had to get back to Oregon…where he lives…where we'll be living. I forgot… I'm moving to Portland!"

She continued to rave about her husband, but Marc couldn't hear a word. He was still trying to process, "I'm moving to Portland." He continued to smile and was truly happy for her, but was already starting to miss her. Marc hated goodbyes.

Marc looked forward to meeting Eric the next Saturday. However, the two would not meet for another five years. By the next Saturday, Marc would be in Montreal.

***

Marc sat in the chair next to his sister's hospital bed watching her sleep. He was still upset that she had not called him herself to tell him that she was having surgery, but grateful that her husband, Michael, had the good sense to call him.

Marie-Christine was in recovery and her prognosis was good. But Marc felt that he that should have been with her. Marc had gotten on the first flight to Montreal and had come directly to the hospital from the airport. The important thing was that he was by Marie-Christine's side.

Marc heard the door open and was relieved to see his brother in-law.

Michael was pleasantly surprised. "Marc! Thank you for coming. When did you get in?"

Before Marc could answer, Marie- Christine began to stir and opened her eyes, blinking a few times to make sure she was not hallucinating. "Marc?"

Marc took her hand and kissed her forehead. "Yes, I'm here, Chrissie."

She squeezed his hand while giving an annoyed look to her husband. "I told Michael not to call you. Really, I'm fine. And I would have told you everything myself...later."

She started to sit up but a sharp pain caused by her incision forced her back down into the pillows. This made Marc anxious.

Marie-Christine found the control panel for the bed and easily raised herself to a sitting position.

"See, I'm alright now, and there's no need to worry. What I'm feeling now is just a little residual pain from the incision, and that will heal sooner than later. I expect to be home in the next few days."

Marc still looked to Michael to see if she was telling the truth.

"Chrissie, your brother is here because he was worried about you. He's come all this way, so why don't you tell him what's going on instead of letting him jump to conclusions?"

Marie-Christine nodded and gestured for Marc to sit in the chair beside her. "For now you get the short version. Please, don't be alarmed but I had a breast cancer scare. Some suspicious cells showed up in a recent test and my doctor felt it was best to remove and biopsy them immediately."

Marc listened, but was unsure of what she said. "Are you saying you found a lump?"

She had not used that term. "Not even a lump, but cells that could have possibly become a lump."

A nurse came into the room and asked the men to leave for a few minutes while she changed Marie-Christine's dressing.

Marc was still agitated as he stepped outside of the room with his brother in-law.

"Michael, I can't thank you enough for calling me. I should have been here with her...with both of you. Why didn't she want me to know?"

Michael calmly explained what had happened. "She didn't want to alarm you and wanted to call you herself when everything was over and done with so you wouldn't worry. But as she was being prepped, I remembered how close the two of you are-and if it was my sister I'd want to know. I totally went against her wishes and called you. Marc, your parents don't know she's here, either. She wanted to keep this as quiet as possible. She's probably going to kill me later, but I thought someone else in the family should know about the surgery, and I think she feels the most comfortable with you."

Thank God for his brother in-law.

The two men waited for a few minutes before the nurse told them to come back inside.

Marc was calmer now. "Chrissie, how did you know the cells were there?"

Marie-Christine was still trying to play down the incident. "The doctor's found them during a routine mammogram."

For some reason this surprised Marc. "*You* had a mammogram? But you're so young. I didn't think you started to get those until you were older."

She nodded. "That's true under normal circumstances. Forty is when most women start regular screenings. But in my case, since there's a family history, I've been getting regular mammograms since I was in my twenties."

Again Marc didn't understand. "What are you talking about, Chrissie? What family history?"

Michael got up and left. Marie-Christine needed to discuss this with Marc alone.

"Marc, I'm sorry but I honestly thought you knew by now, but it's obvious you have no idea what I'm talking about. I hate that you're finding out this way, but mother had breast cancer several years ago."

Marc sat straight up not knowing how to react.

"She's cancer free now and has been for years. Her doctors were able to do a lumpectomy, and she did both chemo and radiation which she felt was much worse than the disease, but she's fine now, really. It's because of mother that I began my own screenings so early."

Marc couldn't comprehend why he was just learning about his mother's illness. "Chrissie, when did this happen?"

She relaxed back into the pillows. "She was diagnosed early in 1991 and underwent treatment all that spring, so about sixteen years ago. There's never been a recurrence."

She saw her brother starting to connect the dots.

"Spring 1991. That's when Miriam and I told the families we were separating, and shortly after that we were divorcing. I thought it was strange that Papa didn't want me to mention anything to Mother. He said he'd tell her about the separation himself, and I could never figure out why. I just assumed it was because he hated me! All this time I thought they were furious with me for not making things work with Miriam and causing problems with the business, but their tension had nothing to do with me! My mother was sick and I should have been here at her side instead of feeling sorry for myself in New York."

Marie-Christine hated to see her brother beat himself up like this.

"Marc, it's not your fault. Mother knew you were hurting and didn't want to cause you more stress and pain. She begged me not to tell you, and promised that she'd tell you when she thought the timing was better."

He didn't respond.

She slowly extended her arms toward him being careful of her incision. He hugged her so gently that she reprimanded him.

"I know you're being careful, but you can hold me tighter than that."

He hugged her just a bit tighter.

"That's better. Thank you for coming. I'm glad you're here."

He helped her settle back onto her pillows. "Are you comfortable?"

She was smiling again. "Yes, and I seem to be getting more comfortable by the minute. I don't think we should talk about anything important for a while. That nice nurse gave me some very nice pain killers…and I'm starting to feel loopy. See if Michael's outside. I think the two of you will enjoy making fun of me when I start to talk nonsense."

Marc brought Michael back into the room to be with his wife. Then he went into the hallway and tried to process the information he had just received.

***

He spent the next several hours with Marie-Christine and her husband. They talked about the family and what they were both doing.

Marie-Christine told him about an old flame. "I've run into Miriam more than a few times over the past few years. She seems to be doing well. I think she's happy."

He smiled. "Then I'm happy for her. I know she remarried five or six years after we divorced."

She was glad he already knew. "That's right. She married a doctor. She has a son and a daughter who I met once when they were little kids. Little spoiled kids at that!"

They both shared a good laugh.

"As long as she's happy. I never had any bad feelings toward Miriam, we just never should have gotten married. Once we figured that out, we got along very well and ended everything. I think both sets of parents took it harder than we did."

Marie-Christine nodded in agreement. "But thankfully, everybody got over it and moved on."

Marc was not so sure. "Really? I think Papa still resents me for not making the marriage work. We haven't really spoken in years. I've always felt I've been a disappointment. "

The relationship between her brother and their father had troubled Marie-Christine for years. This was a situation she wanted to remedy sooner than later and had an idea, but for now she changed the subject. "So, Marc, I know you're during well professionally, but what about your personal life? I'm assuming you have one."

He didn't want to discuss this. "Chrissie, I date … but I don't think what you have, or what Miriam has will ever be in the cards for me."

She shook her head. "I don't believe that, but I'm not going to push the issue either." This conversation had been fast and brief.

She gave her brother a long hard look and took a deep breath thinking that there may never be a perfect time for her to broach the next subject. "Marc…would you like to call the folks to let them know you're in town? It's bothered me that you haven't been close to Papa. He may not understand you, or your personal career choices, but you're still his son and he loves you. He's never been a man who's been able to express emotions easily. So maybe you should make the first step. There's no time like the present."

While Marc's relationship with his mother had normalized, he often felt guilty about neglecting the relationship with his father. Their relationship deteriorated even more after his divorce from Miriam years before. Maybe his sister was right and he should try to reestablish a relationship with both of his parents.

Marc sighed, knowing that he would do almost anything for his sister. "Chrissie, I'll make a deal with you. You call the folks and let them know you're here, and I'll be here by your side when they arrive because you know they're going to run right over to be with you."

She reached for the phone, fearing that Marc might change his mind. "This is blackmail, but I'll hold up my end of the bargain if you hold up yours."

He stepped out of the room as his sister spoke to her parents. His brother in-law followed him.

"Marc, I've wanted Chrissie to call her family since we found out about the surgery and she was against it. Thank you. And thank you for agreeing to make peace with your father. That's been on Chrissie's mind, too. I guess this is a lot for you to take in all at once?"

Marc nodded. "Yeah, it is a lot to grasp but maybe it's time I take some responsibility as far as the family is concerned. You weren't around for the explosion over the collapse of my marriage several years ago, but the family dynamic was damaged, and she's right. It's time to try to make things right. I thought I'd disappointed them by divorcing Miriam. But there was so much more going on back then. You're right. It is overwhelming."

Michael tried to lighten the mood. "And you know they were upset with Chrissie for a while? Remember, she married an American."

Both men laughed as they reentered Marie-Christine's room just as she was finishing her call. She looked at her husband and brother, shaking her head.

"They'll be here within the hour. Marc, they still don't know you're here, my thinking being that when they see you that most of the focus will be taken away from me.

She reached out to her husband. "Michael, I'm so sorry you're going to have to see the dysfunctional side of my family, but then I'm remembering that our vows said *for better, for worse*, so I guess this qualifies as worse."

Michael kissed his wife and reassured her. "Don't worry, I'm not going anywhere."

At this moment Marc was grateful that his sister had found a good man who loved her. He wondered if he would ever be that type of man.

Fifty-two minutes later the senior Guiros arrived at their daughter's hospital room. To their surprise, they saw their oldest son, Marc-Adrien, calmly sitting next to her.

Marc heard both his parents gasp as they stopped in the doorway.

Marc stood, and took control of the situation. "Don't worry. Chrissie is going to be fine, especially now that you're both here."

He crossed to his parents, hugging and kissing his mother before turning to his father.

Until this moment Marc never realized that he had missed his father. He took a deep breath, and warmly embraced his father.

Charles Guiro was initially stunned upon seeing his eldest son and hardly returned Marc's embrace. But a moment later he firmly grasped Marc's hand. "Thank you. Thank you for coming to be with Chrissie. Thank you for coming home! I...your mother and I have missed you, too!" This time it was Charles who reached out to embrace his son.

For the Guiro family, the healing process had begun.

***

Marie-Christine was released from the hospital a few days later. The biopsied cells were benign, so no further measures would be taken. However, she would be getting screenings more often.

Marc flew back to New York and got back to his routine of auditions and his regular dealings with ACT.

Since the fall of 2001 Marc had been a valued member of the ACT team as they credited him with saving the 2001-2002 season. He proposed doing a workshop for company managers since ACT now had more than one touring company a year and would need more qualified people ready to step into this specialized position.

Marc still directed productions from time to time, preferring his friend Gary Connelly's Shakespearean adaptations. ACT now had the rights to nine of these adaptations, most of which were comedies. All were well written. Marc had no problem putting money in Gary's pocket every time one of his adaptations was produced. ACT was doing more educational workshops in the Tri-State area, with Marc picking up workshops in Manhattan whenever he could. He was a wonderful teacher who worked very well with young people.

In the fall of 2006 Marc booked a series of industrial training films for an airline, plus he performed in a staged reading of a new play to be presented in October. He landed a role on a soap that worked for a month. Shortly after that role ended, he won a large supporting role in an independent feature- a comedy, playing an arrogant chef in an upscale restaurant. He was happy to be doing a comedic role after doing primarily dramas for the past several years.

In October, the day Marc had been dreading arrived. He had been helping Mel pack up her condo for several days. Now the movers were loading the last of her belongings into the moving van. They would begin their cross-country trip to Portland Oregon within the hour from the looks of things. The couple renting her condo would be moving in the next week.

Mel asked Marc if he would drop in before her tenants arrived to make sure that the unit had been cleaned properly. He was dreading coming into her empty unit, but said yes because he would do anything for Mel. For more than twenty years he had been the constant man in her life, and now he was relinquishing this duty to a man he had never met. All he knew was that Mel was happier than he'd ever seen her.

Clayton's Crossing shot its final episode in September, which aired three weeks later. Closing the *Clayton's Crossing* production office took a couple of weeks. Once her duties at the soap opera ended, Mel was able to focus all of her energy on getting to Portland to be with her husband and begin her new life.

Mel said goodbye to her own family the night before she left for Oregon in her family home on Long Island. She preferred to have the goodbye meltdowns in a private place as opposed to a busy airport before dawn, where they would only be able to see her as far as the first TSA checkpoint.

So it was Marc who escorted Mel to LaGuardia early the next morning. Both were used to travelling with only a carry-on these days to avoid inflated luggage fees, but this was a special circumstance. Mel gladly paid Northwest Airlines the $100.00 in fees to make the start of her new life in Portland a little easier.

With her baggage taken care of and her boarding time approaching, Mel and Marc walked to the TSA check-in area. That was as far as he could take her.

They stood together saying nothing at first. Marc wasn't the only one who hated goodbyes.

Marc spoke first. "You know it's going to be horrible here with you gone."

Mel promised herself she wouldn't cry today, but that was a promise she couldn't keep. "Please don't say that. It's not like I won't be back from time to time. Once a New Yorker, always a New Yorker." She blinked her eyes as they began to sting with tears.

She took an envelope from her purse and put it into Marc's jacket pocket. "Don't look at that until you get back home, okay?"

Marc nodded as he felt his own eyes start to moisten.

Mel wiped her own eyes. "It's getting late and I should…"

He didn't let her finish but instead hugged her tightly and kissing her forehead one last time. When they finally let each other go, Mel could hardly speak.

"I'll let you know I got there…and I'll be talking to you over the next few days. I should really go now."

There was so much that Marc wanted to say to this incredible woman, his friend who had supported him through some of the best and worst times of his life.

"Mel..."

She stopped him from speaking by quickly shaking her head no and putting her fingers to her lips, and then to her heart.

"I know." She dropped her eyes to the floor, turned and began the check-in process.

Marc knew she wasn't going to turn around again. He also knew that she was hoping he would leave, but he felt obligated to look after her for as long as he could see her. When she was out of sight he started for home.

As promised, Marc opened Mel's note in the privacy of his own apartment.

My Dearest Marc,

You are an amazing man whom I am proud and honored to call my friend. And please don't think because I'm not in New York I'm out of your life. I'll always be here for you, just like you've always been for me. I'm only a phone call or an email or text away. I see some wonderful things in your future, so please, keep your eyes open so you'll be able to see them, too! Thank you for everything. Be happy!

Love

Mel

New York hadn't been the same for Marc since 9/11. With Mel gone the city was now an emptier and lonelier place.

Thankfully he would be back at LaGuardia in a few weeks, where he would be heading for his next regional theater gig… in Kansas City.

Kansas. It could only be an improvement.

Chapter Ten

New York/Kansas City

2006-2007

Andy Synch had been in New York early in August to find a few more actors for the 2006-2007 season of the Brewery Theater in Kansas City, Missouri. His last New York appointment was for an actor named Marc Guiro. Marc's agent had called to say he was running late due to another audition that had run long, a common occurrence for working actors. This was not a problem for him as long as this last actor arrived in the next half hour. He had been seeing actors back to back for two days and appreciated a few minutes of downtime. Aside from grabbing a soda, Andy took time to review this last resume before the actor arrived.

Marc Guiro had excellent training. He had solid credits having worked in New York, several regional theaters in addition to television and film roles. When he flipped the resume over he studied the picture. Andy liked Marc's look and prayed that Marc, in person, would look like his photograph. That's when Marc arrived.

"I'm so sorry but I got held up on the other side of town. He walked to Andy his hand extended. "I'm Marc Guiro."

"I'm Andy Synch. And please don't mention it. It's the nature of the beast and I often found myself in the same situation when I was working in New York, so believe me I understand."

Marc thought this man had a New York aura, not to mention a great name.

Andy laughed. "I get that a lot. "Synch" is what the officials at Ellis Island shortened the original Eastern European name to when my family first arrived in this country a few generations ago. The original name was fifteen or sixteen letters long and virtually unpronounceable."

Andy had noticed Marc's accent. "Where are you from originally?"

"Montreal, Quebec, Canada, but I've been in the States for years. I went to NYU."

Andy flipped Marc's photo over and looked at the resume again. "I saw that. You have a good resume. How long did you work with ACT?"

Marc found this a surprising choice of credits to discuss. "I'm still working with ACT in different capacities. I've directed productions for the touring company, or companies now. I've trained several of their company managers and still do educational seminars in the city when my schedule allows."

"ACT does excellent work. When they're in Kansas City, I always try to catch a performance. They've brought a new standard to children's theater. I think the last thing I saw was an adaptation of *Taming of the Shrew*, maybe two years ago. It was a good production."

Marc smiled proudly. "Thank you. I directed that production."

Andy took a look at Marc. He reminded him of someone, but for the life of him he couldn't say who.

Marc did his two contrasting monologues, with Andy noticing that he'd chosen to do one piece with a standard American accent, which he didn't even notice until Marc was finishing the piece.

At this point the monologues were a formality. Andy hired actors with his gut. He liked Marc. He just needed to decide where he'd be using him.

Andy told Marc a bit about the theater and that most shows required a two month commitment between rehearsals and performances. He asked Marc if he had any additional questions.

Marc had just one. "How did a New York actor end up in Kansas?"

Andy was amused, but he had answered this question many times before. "I had a pretty good career going in New York, but at one point I realized that's all I had-a career. And I wanted more. I wanted a life, *but* I wanted to keep the career."

Marc had been feeling this way himself for quite some time. He gave Andy his undivided attention.

"Just about everyone I knew said it was impossible to do both, you know, having a fulfilling artistic career as well as a full personal life. I've enjoyed proving them wrong. I'm the artistic director of an Equity Theater, which does very good work if I do say so myself. I teach acting at the University, which is giving me all sorts of benefits personally and for the theater. My wife was also a New York actor and has been able to keep working. We have three children who make us see what life's really about."

He realized he'd gone on a bit. "Marc, the short answer to your question would be that I moved to Kansas City to have it all!"

Marc was impressed, and started to wonder if he, too, could have it all someplace else.

After Marc left, Andy realized that Marc reminded him, of *himself*, at about the time he was considering leaving New York City.

***

Marc's trip to Kansas was in two legs, the first being New York to Chicago, where the plane's passengers looked very New York urban. Many fit the New Yorker stereotype: slender, wearing a lot of black and radiating a no-nonsense New York persona.

The second leg was Chicago to Kansas City, Kansas. The passengers on this leg of the flight were more average in size, wearing a variety of colors and prints and had a distinct easygoing Midwestern quality that Marc had not experienced lately.

His gigs in regional theater had taken him to major cities like Washington D.C., Hartford, Boston and Philadelphia. Cincinnati had been a surprise when he realized it was a modern city with a Tony Award-winning state-of-the-art theater. But he truly didn't know what to expect from Kansas City, and halfway expected the theater to be in the middle of a cornfield. But since he was finding living in New York unpleasant and extremely stressful, he welcomed the change-whatever that might be.

He wondered if a rolling stairway would be brought up to the plane for unloading passengers right onto the tarmac, but there was a jet way just like you would find in any other major American airport. The jet way took him into a state of the art terminal that boasted free Wi-Fi.

Andy Synch was waiting for him in baggage claim.

"Marc, welcome to Kansas City! Now tell me the truth. Your preconceived ideas of Kansas are already being proved wrong." Andy had been through the *Kansas is so civilized* scenario with New York actors many times.

"You're right. I got off the plane looking for Dorothy, Toto and amber waves of grain."

Andy took one of Marc's bags. "Well, it's November so on the way into town you'll only see remnants of amber waves and a lot of big open spaces, but we'll be in the city soon enough."

They made their way through the parking lot to Andy's Jeep Cherokee and before long they were on Interstate 35 heading into Kansas City, Missouri. Marc was surprised to see a skyline with high rise-buildings.

Andy asked Marc if he wanted to grab a quick sandwich. The two had barbeque at a place that was no more than a shack located between two modern high rise buildings downtown. Marc had the best pulled pork sandwich he'd ever had in his life.

Next, Andy took Marc to the Brewery Theater for a mini tour. The Brewery was a modern and comfortable four-hundred-seat theater that had actually been a brewery at one time.

Andy proudly showed off the new lighting board he had purchased from the Guthrie Theater in Minneapolis when they upgraded their main board the year before. "It may be used, but the Guthrie only had it for two years and it serves our purposes well. This is still the best lighting board in the area."

After a quick stop at a grocery store for a few staples, Andy took Marc to the apartment where he would be staying for the next two months. It was a good-sized one bedroom unit in a building that housed several graduate students at the University.

Andy helped Marc get his groceries inside the apartment and showed him a folder that listed different businesses and services in the area.

"I'll let you settle in, but if you're up for it would you like to come to the house for dinner? Don't worry, we'll make it an early night."

Marc accepted.

Andy picked Marc up just after six-thirty and drove him to his home that was in a beautiful neighborhood. It had a huge front yard with several trees surrounding the property.

Once inside, Andy was greeted by three excited children. Andrew was eight and full of energy. There was Heather, who was a very mature six-year-old. She reminded Marc of Marie-Christine with her curly dark hair and sparkling dark eyes. And finally there was four-year-old Mason who had just celebrated a birthday and was still telling everybody just in case there were any additional gifts to be received.

Andy made introductions, hung up Marc's jacket and took Marc into the large open family room/kitchen area where Andy's wife, Helena, was busy with dinner. Andy greeted his wife with a big kiss and brought her over to meet Marc.

"Helena, this is Marc Guiro who'll be playing Bob Cratchit in *A Christmas Carol* this year."

Helena had an hourglass figure and long curly dark hair. Marc had no problem imagining either one of them working as actors in New York. She quickly wiped her hands on a towel before extending a hand to Marc.

"Welcome to Kansas, Marc. Is it everything you expected?" She glanced at her husband smiling. They had played this game before.

"Actually it's not what I expected at all. You've all been keeping this city a secret from the rest of us. I'm impressed with what I've seen so far."

She motioned for Marc to take a seat.

"Well we hope you'll enjoy your time here. Have a seat and Andy will get you something to drink."

A few minutes later Marc was enjoying a beer and talking about the upcoming production with the Synchs.

Marc learned that Helena would be playing the Ghost of Christmas Present in the production. Most of the leads in this production were coming in from out of town. The actor playing Scrooge was from Chicago, while the Ghost of Christmas Past was also a New Yorker who would be arriving the next morning. Most of the supporting cast was made up of local talent.

"We do *A Christmas Carol* every other year. It's become sort of a tradition and we usually play to full houses. I try to use as much local talent as I can. There are a few professional actors in the area who are mostly working with me at the university. And if there are any grad students who can confidently do roles I try to cast them. There are two this year playing the roles of Fred, Scrooge's nephew, and Belle, Scrooge's girlfriend in the Christmas past sequence."

Marc couldn't help but be surprised. "I just never imagined that you could earn an acting degree in this part of the country."

Andy and Helena had also heard this as well.

"Well, it's possible. We may not have the reputation of a Julliard or Emerson, or even an NYU, but I'd like to think that our students leave with a solid foundation. To be honest, most of our students stay close to home. They end up teaching drama in high schools, or running community theaters, which is great and necessary. A few have gone to other places, and some have returned to work with me at The Brewery. Now there are the exceptions that go to New York, Chicago or even Los Angeles and have decent careers in the industry. Our Belle, Elizabeth, is a very good actor who could be competitive in a large city. She's a first-year grad student."

Helena suddenly remembered something. "Andy, Glenn Perkins is also a New Yorker!"

"Yes, he is. Marc, Glenn is doing our Artist in Residence program this year. He's doing a role in The Brewery's current production and will be playing Jacob Marley in your production. He'll be sticking around for the winter quarter to work with the students."

Helena explained the program. "About four years ago, Andy thought it would be great to have a professional actor from one of the major acting markets here to give expertise, and to give these impressionable students a realistic look at the industry. The *artist* designs their own program. It's been a successful addition to the drama program."

To Marc, this program sounded interesting and innovative.

Just then the three kids ran into the room as Andy tried to corral them. "Kids, we have a guest so please pretend to be human beings!"

The next thing Marc knew, Andy was on the floor roughhousing with the kids. Marc found himself enjoying every moment of this evening at home with a family. It was what most would think of as *normal*...but in a very good way.

Helena served chicken and rice with fresh vegetables from a nearby farmers market. For dessert she baked an apple pie made with apples her daughter picked herself during a recent school field trip to an area orchard.

After dessert Marc was back in the Cherokee with Andy heading back to his Kansas City apartment. He had been in Kansas City for less than twelve hours and was already enjoying the comfortable energy of the city. He felt relaxed for the first time in months.

As he was getting out of the car, he thanked his host for making him feel so at home. "I enjoyed meeting Helena and your kids. I envy you."

Andy didn't understand. "Why would you envy me?"

"You've found a way to have it all." Marc replied. "I guess it really *is* possible, after all."

Andy smiled to himself. "I won't deny it; I'm a very lucky man."

Andy told Marc that someone would pick him up for the first rehearsal the next day, then said goodnight.

As Marc walked into his apartment, he found himself wondering if he could ever leave New York City…permanently.

***

The rehearsal period passed quickly, and now the run of *A Christmas Carol* was almost over. There was no performance on Christmas Eve, because that was the night Andy wanted to share with his theatrical family. He and Helena opened their home to the cast and crew of the show. There was plenty of good food, spirits, music and joy that Marc hadn't experienced in a very long time.

Marc had been thoroughly seduced by the heartland with its warm kind people, clean air, good food, and an environment that was quiet and virtually stress free. Kansas City had been good for him, so good that he was becoming anxious about returning to New York in just over a week.

At one point during the evening, Andy discreetly asked him to join him in his study. He poured a brandy for both of them and asked Marc to sit down for a few minutes.

"I hope you've enjoyed your time here in KC. We've loved having you here. I think my daughter's going to miss you something horribly after you've gone."

Little Heather had developed a crush on Marc.

Marc was somewhat embarrassed. "Please tell Heather I'm going to miss her too, but she could probably do a lot better than me."

Both men laughed.

"Andy, I had no idea what to expect before I arrived, but being in Kansas City has been a wonderful experience and one I wouldn't trade for anything. You've been great and I've enjoyed…no. I've loved working at The Brewery! Time has gone so fast and I can't believe I leave for New York next week."

Andy heard exactly what he was hoping to hear. "So, you'd consider coming back to Kansas in the future?"

Marc sat forward, curious. "Of course I'd consider returning. Do you have something in mind?"

Andy was about to present Marc with an incredible opportunity.

"Our first play for next season is *The Glass Menagerie*, and I can easily see you as Tom Wingfield. Helena agrees that you'd be perfect. Right now I'd just like to see if you're interested."

This was a role that Marc had always wanted to play. "Of course I'd be interested. Thank you, Andy."

Andy was going to sweeten the pot. "And then what would you say to staying in town to take the Artist in Residence position next year. You're more than qualified and I think you'd be a good fit."

Marc was stunned. "I don't know what to say."

Andy understood. "I don't want you to say anything for now. Go home and think about this. We'll talk in June to see what's going on in your life and career. I know how fast things can change for actors. If you land the big Broadway show or film role, of course, you're going to take it and never think of us again, and I get that. But before I post the position, we'll talk. If you're still interested and available, the role and position are yours. Feel free to look at the show and the position at the University as two separate things.

The play is a two-month commitment. If you do both the show and Artist in Residence program, you'll be here from September through March with December off. It's a long time to be away from New York, so please give it some serious thought."

Andy felt he'd given Marc plenty to think about. "Merry Christmas, Marc." He raised his glass to Marc who in turn raised his own glass.

"Andy, Merry Christmas. And thank you."

They returned to the party with Marc feeling that he had just received the best Christmas gift of all time!

***

Marc accepted the role and the residency, and in September of 2007 returned to Kansas City.

When he told Mel he was heading back to Kansas City for six months, Mel didn't hesitate. "So what's her name?"

Marc didn't blame Mel for asking, but he was truly making an effort to put the bad-boy Casanova persona behind him. Marc was starting to think about a life beyond his career.

"Mel you probably won't believe me but there's no woman involved. I really enjoyed Kansas City and I'm looking forward to going back."

And Marc had told Mel the truth; there had been no woman in Kansas City. But now, Marc was finally ready to look beyond his career, and consider the possibility of allowing another person-a woman into his life.

Andy picked Marc up at the airport and took him directly to the apartment where he would be staying for the next six months. This was a larger and nicer apartment than the one where he'd stayed the year before. This was just to drop off Marc's bags, because a few minutes later they were heading to Andy's house for dinner where the Synch family greeted him as if he were a favorite relative whom they had not seen in years.

A few days before Marc left New York he had started to feel anxious about the trip for the first and only time. But once inside the Synch household, his anxiety vanished.

Marc was in Kansas City to play a role that he'd dreamed of playing, and "hopefully" to experience more soothing domestic tranquility.

He had brought gifts for the three Synch children. Little Heather, now seven, was thrilled with the sparkly purple scarf that he brought her. She thanked him with a big hug.

Now he remembered why he'd wanted to come back to Kansas. Things were simpler and moved at a slower pace where he could enjoy life's individual moments.

After dinner and the kids were sent to bed, Andy and Helena began to tell Marc about the other cast members in *The Glass Menagerie.*

Amanda Wingfield was being played by Dori Evers, who was born and raised in Kansas City, but had been a working New York actor for over thirty years. Helena described her as sixty-three inches of dynamite and a sheer force of nature. She had the perfect bigger-than-life personality required for the role of Amanda, Tom and Laura Wingfield's overbearing ex-Southern belle mother.

In the role of Jim O'Conner, Laura's gentleman caller, was Owen Crawford, a Chicago based actor with a solid theater background. Owen possessed an everyman quality and a natural charm that made him instantly likable.

Helena couldn't wait to tell Marc about their choice for Laura: a second-year grad student Elizabeth Pryor "You might remember her from last year's production of *A Christmas Carol* where she played Belle."

Marc thought back to the year before. "She was very good as I remember. She did a lot with a role that could have been overlooked. She had a nice ethereal quality as I remember."

Andy brought Marc a beer. "Exactly! That's what I saw when she auditioned. I was considering two New York actors, but I kept coming back to Liz. She has a softness about her that I think will translate into Laura's fragility. Could you do me a favor and make sure that Dori doesn't overwhelm her. I love Dori but I can see how she could be intimidating to someone like Elizabeth. Dori couldn't understand why I hadn't hired someone with more experience. I politely told her that when she directs her own production of *Glass Menagerie*, she can hire whoever she wants."

Marc grimaced. "In that case, I hope she doesn't intimidate me!"

Andy shook his head. "No offense, but I'm not worried about you. Three of the understudies are grad students, and one of our professors will be covering Amanda. The understudies will be doing performances for school groups in the afternoon. So far we have three of these performances scheduled. And then, of course, if any of you can't go on..."

Marc stopped him. "That will never happen."

Andy and Helena laughed.

"Good! That's what I want to hear."

Marc was very happy he had returned to Kansas City.

***

The next afternoon Marc entered the Brewery Theater and made his way to the rehearsal space located in the backstage area. Just as he entered the rehearsal hall he heard boisterous female laughter. Dori Evers had arrived.

Marc knew who she was before Andy introduced her. Dori was a very small woman, but her huge personality made her appear larger than she was in reality. She was five foot three with dark auburn hair. She wore a floral print dress that showed off a good figure. This was a woman who took care of herself. Marc had no idea how old she was, though he guessed she had to be in her early sixties.

Dori approached Marc and gave him a quick tight hug before looking to Andy.

"Thank you Andy! Thank you for a good-looking Tom."

She then turned back to Marc. "It's a pleasure. Andy tells me that you're also a New Yorker." She was quite the charmer.

"Yes, for quite some time now."

Dori's eyes grew huge. "My God, that's a sexy accent! Where are you from originally?"

Marc still didn't understand the fascination that Americans had with accents, but for Dori he exaggerated the accent. "Montreal, Quebec, Canada."

Dori's mouth dropped wide open. "Andy, I may not be able to control myself."

Andy looked toward Marc almost apologetically. "Dori, first off, Marc will be doing the role of Tom with a New Orleans accent. And secondly, please, remember he's playing your son."

Dori shot Andy a dirty look. "I'm perfectly aware of that, but remember that no one in their right mind is going to believe I could possibly have a son this old."

Marc chose this moment to introduce himself to Owen Crawford, the actor playing the gentlemen caller. Marc learned that Owen was living and working in Chicago, but had spent a few years in New York.

Owen explained. "I was doing really well in Chicago, but I guess part of me felt that if I wanted to be a *real* actor, I had to go to either New York or LA, and I'm a theater person, so my wife and I moved to New York. This was in 2002, probably not the best time to make a major move to New York. The city was still in recovery from 9/11, and I don't think things were ever really the same after the commercial strike back in 2000. I worked, but not like I had in Chicago. My wife never fully adjusted to life in New York, though she tried and would have stayed longer if I'd wanted. She's always supported my career. After a few years I decided the best move for the both of us was coming back to Chicago. I've never looked back."

Marc was curious. "Did you work?"

Owen nodded. "Sure, I did a few commercials, some low budget theater, and I worked on a few of the soaps."

Marc had to ask. "Which soaps Owen?" This man could easily play a Southerner, so he had a feeling he had worked on Mel's show.

"Guiding Light, One Life to Live and *Clayton's crossing."*

Marc couldn't help smiling. "One of my best friends was the head writer on *Clayton's crossing* the last few years it was on the air. I worked on the show several years ago myself. It was a good couple of months."

Dori joined the conversation. "I'm also an alumnus of *Clayton's Crossing*! Your friend must be Mel Holden."

Marc smiled. "You know Mel?"

Dori's next statement made Marc smile with pride and make a mental note to text Mel later.

"She was one of the hardest-working people in daytime. She and her staff knew how to write for actors. Sure it was a soap opera, but the dialogue was anything but soapy, which is part of the reason we all enjoyed working on her show! I had a recurring role as a judge there for years. It was a soap opera, so someone was always getting into trouble and I could always count on being called in several times a year. I even showed up at a gala or wedding every once in a while. *Crossing* was one of the friendliest places for an actor to work. I miss it, I really do."

Dori turned serious. "About twenty years ago there were somewhere between thirteen and fifteen daytime dramas on network television, and now there are just a few left, and only two are done in New York while the others, I think maybe four or five, are done in LA. The soaps had been a major employer for actors, not to mention an excellent training ground for newer actors. The industry has changed drastically over a short period of time!"

Marc and Owen agreed and began to talk about the changes they had seen and experienced. They had been going on for quite some time when Andy interrupted them.

"Dori…guys, I'd like for you to meet Elizabeth Pryor, our Laura."

Elizabeth was very thin and blonde with big expressive brown eyes. At this first rehearsal she appeared very shy, just like her character in the play, barely managing a smile as Andy introduced her to the rest of the cast.

Dori was on her best behavior and reeled in her huge personality. She did not want to say or do anything that would cause Andy to apologize to Elizabeth later.

Owen was the perfect gentleman, standing and shaking her hand only when she offered hers.

And when she was introduced to Marc, he could have sworn he saw her blush slightly. It had to be the accent, again.

They exchanged pleasantries and complimented each other's work on *A Christmas Carol.*

Dori was happy to hear that she could speak, which she had questioned about a minute before. She had also questioned Andy's choice of a semi-professional actor and grad student coming into the cast of a challenging play with a group of solid professional stage actors. But Andy believed in her so she would have to keep her opinions to herself-for now anyway.

Jesse, the stage manager, got everyone's attention. "Alright, ladies and gentlemen, why doesn't everybody get settled and we'll start the table read in five minutes. Thank you."

Marc looked toward Liz and saw a hint of anxiousness cross her face. He made sure that when the table reading started she was safely seated between Owen and himself, just in case Dori reverted back into her overbearing self.

***

The first few days of rehearsal went smoothly with Andy blocking his actors (giving his actors direction as to where and when to go onstage in each scene) on the taped outline of the stage in the rehearsal hall. While the actors were familiarizing themselves with the script and their characters, the real in-depth scene work wouldn't begin until later in the week.

Liz seemed to be relaxing into the rehearsal process. Marc, Andy and Owen were treating her just like any other actor, while Dori was politely professional, though she continued to watch her closely.

Marc was concerned that Liz was still feeling like the new kid in school. He invited her to join him for coffee one day after rehearsal.

He took her to a place that had become a regular hangout for him the year before, a small coffee shop with a Bohemian vibe and overstuffed chairs that seemed straight out of the sixties. They served good coffee and made artisan sandwiches and homemade soups. Marc and Liz ordered drinks and took a seat at a table near the window.

He asked her how things were going.

"Well…" She wasn't sure if she could be completely honest with him. "To tell you the truth it's been kind of intense for me."

Marc seemed surprised. "Really? I was thinking that things are pretty mellow so far."

She ripped open a sugar packet. "Not the rehearsals themselves, but for me this is a pretty intense working environment. When I did *Christmas Carol* last year it was different. There were a few other people like me-grad students who had supporting roles in a play that had a fairly large cast. I knew a lot of people and it made my first professional experience positive. But now I have a role in a four character play-and a classic at that. I can't hide. All of you have been doing this for years, and I have to admit it's all a little overwhelming."

Marc tried to put her at ease. "Andy never would have brought you onboard if he didn't think you could handle the role. He could have easily hired someone from New York, but he hired you and that says something. He trusts you, so now you have to trust yourself and your instincts. And from what I've seen, your instincts are excellent."

She stared into her coffee. "Thank you. I guess I needed to hear that."

She looked up and got even more serious than she had been. "When I came to the rehearsal hall on the first day I heard all of you talking about soap operas and commercials-and life in New York. And I recognized Dori from TV or somewhere. That's when it hit me: This is happening and it's for real! I swear, somewhere deep inside I started to panic. I probably would have still been listening at the door if Andy hadn't brought me into the room and introduced me."

She seemed relieved that she had gotten this off her chest. "Marc... did you have any anxiety when you did your first job?"

He thought for a moment. "No, not one bit."

This was bullshit-and she knew it. They shared a hearty laugh.

"I was twenty-two years old and working a lot of special events primarily as a juggler, a skill that came in handy early in my career. I answered an ad in one of the trades and went to an audition for an Actor's Equity show. I wasn't a member of the union, but the ad called for someone French-speaking, so I went anyway. I was seen after all of the AEA actors. They had read several French speaking actors that were in the union but apparently none of them found the humor in the script-which was important since this was a comedy. They hired me as an Equity apprentice for the amazing salary of $150 a week. I don't even know if that program exists anymore, but at least I was on my way to earning my Actor's Equity card, so it didn't matter."

"So what was your first day like?" She asked.

He thought back to an event that had happened about twenty years before. "The play was called *European Package Deal,* and was about two Midwestern couples going on a whirlwind trip through Europe. I was cast as a French waiter/artist who attempts to seduce one of the women, who considers being seduced by a sexy young Frenchman part of her European experience. In a twist, it's actually the American tourist that seduces, or at least tries to seduce the Frenchmen. The American woman ends up scaring the hell out of the Frenchman."

Liz couldn't help but giggle.

Marc was glad to see Liz relaxing and continued. "So on my first day of rehearsal I arrive at the rehearsal space and see a guy who's the current spokesperson for one of the big car companies. Then I see this woman who had a role in the latest Woody Allen film I'd seen two weeks before. I go on to learn that most of my fellow cast members have had roles on television and in films and in commercials and the theater. In other words, they're actors. At this point

I'm not seeing myself as an actor. I juggle and I work at kid's birthday parties. I'm starting to feel horribly out of place when I meet the woman who plays the Midwestern woman I'll be seducing. She's very friendly, attractive and we start talking. I'm thinking that she looks familiar but I can't place her. So finally I ask where I may have seen her, and she looks at me closely and asks how old I am. I tell her I'm twenty-five, which for some reason sounded better than my real age of twenty-two. Then she asks me if I've ever seen a film called *Sword Quest*. This was a low budget medieval fantasy film with knights, witches, sorcerers and fairies. I'd seen the film many times when I was twelve or thirteen, so about ten years before."

This puzzled Liz. "Many times? Was the film really that good?"

Marc laughed under his breath. "It was horrible-except for one thing. It featured scantily clad women which made it a masterpiece in the minds of many teenaged boys, myself included."

Liz started laughing. "And let me guess? This woman was one of the scantily clad women?"

Marc smiled almost wickedly. "She was a fairy princess and the guardian of this enchanted sword everyone was questing over. And when I say fairy princess, think the *extreme* opposite of Disney. Scantily clad would be describing her wardrobe generously, because she was pretty close to naked. She made her entrance in slow motion through a thick fog with a sword raised above her head."

Liz clasped her hand over her mouth as she tried to stifle a laugh.

"Talk about subtle imagery. She was topless and wore what I can only describe as the skimpiest bikini bottom I've ever seen, made of flowers that matched the flowers in her hair."

Liz was no longer trying to suppress her laughter. "I'm surprised you noticed her hair!"

Marc lowered his eyes as Liz laughed even harder. "Well, as I said, I saw the film many times and eventually began to notice the subtleties. As a young filmgoer and teenaged boy, I thought this was cinematic genius. I'd seen *Playboy* magazine, but she was my first *live action* naked woman!"

Liz looked at Marc shaking her head. "When did you realize…"

Marc was starting to laugh again. "As soon as she said the name of the film I recognized her face and refused to look below her nose. That really threw me and I was uncomfortable for the first two days of rehearsal. I mean I couldn't help thinking about what she looked like naked. As a teenager I thought she looked fantastic, but now as a twenty-two-year-old adult I was going to have to kiss her eventually. And she was a married mother of two, which really caused me to have issues."

Liz tried to stop laughing. "So how did you deal with it?"

Marc smiled as he remembered. "The actress was very sweet and patient, and had a pretty good idea what I was going through. She pulled me aside early on and told me that everyone had a first job, and she suspected that this play was mine. She reminded me that I'd earned the right to be there just like everyone else in the cast. She told me there was no reason to be uncomfortable around her, but if I was, to use the feelings onstage. It ended up being a great experience. I did have to go to my bartending gig after every performance, but I was a bartender who was also a professional actor working in a play in New York City."

Liz enjoyed the story. "That's a nice memory. I hope I can feel the same way after this experience."

He asked her for her backstory.

"Well there's not much to tell." She said. "I'm from the middle of nowhere in Oklahoma. I always liked theater, and I was named after Elizabeth Taylor, but then I came from a family that didn't understand that people can actually make a living acting, so I got a degree in education and started teaching. But a few years ago I wanted to try-well, I wanted to act. I'd always wanted to act. I'd taken a few classes and done community theater, and then I learned about Andy's program here. So I left my job and moved here to study, and it's been the greatest thing I've ever done for myself. I'm so happy that I'm here and doing what I really love."

Her honesty made Marc stare. "You should be happy, Liz. Very happy, because not only do you possess the passion, you've got the talent."

She became quiet and introspective. "I'm happy, but I wonder if I'm doing the right thing by pursuing a career in the arts. My family is convinced I'm on my way to becoming a prostitute and a drug addict. I'm almost twenty-seven, and they're saying I'm too old to start something like this."

Marc had heard similar scenarios from so many other actors, not to mention the issues with his own family.

"Liz, who's to say you're too young or old to stop or start anything? Isn't this your life and your decision? So many of us have families that just don't get us or our career choices. It takes time. I've finally started to try to make things right with my own family after more than twenty years of misunderstanding."

This alarmed Liz. "That's a long time. I don't know if I could be on the outs with my family for that long. Didn't anyone in your family support your career?"

"My younger sister, Marie-Christine, has always supported me, and I am grateful." Marc was detecting sadness from her. "Liz, it doesn't have to be all bad. Look at Owen. It seems that he and his wife support each other. I have some friends in California, Gary and Natalie, who have always supported each other, and have always had the support of both of their families."

Liz was suddenly curious. "What about you. Have you ever been married?" For a moment she regretted asking that, but Marc put her at ease.

"I was married once several years ago, for less than a year. She never completely understood what I did for a living, which didn't help matters, but that was the least of our problems."

Lauren's image quickly flashed through Marc's mind.

Marc and Liz finished their drinks.

They finished their drinks and headed home to work on lines and prepare for the next day's rehearsal.

Marc observed that this woman was not afraid of working hard, a quality he admired in any actor. He also admired her passion for the profession, and her honesty.

And then Marc realized he admired Liz, not only for her abilities as a performer... but as a woman.

Marc did not have a personal life. He often remembered Mel's words from years before when he told her about another causal relationship, and saying it was nothing serious.

Mel had laughed. "Of course it's nothing serious. It never is with you!"

She had said this in a lighthearted manner, but the truth of her words stung.

That afternoon over coffee with Liz, real or imagined that's when his attraction to her began. Real or imagined, Marc was beginning to feel emotions that he had not allowed himself to feel for anyone in a very long time.

Marc was over forty and had never had a successful adult relationship when Liz entered his life.

Truth be told, it could have been anyone.

***

The rehearsal process was entering week three and Andy had invited the cast to his home for dinner. Liz, Owen and Marc were present, while Dori was nursing a cold and had stayed home.

As soon as Marc arrived, little Heather wearing her sparkly purple scarf greeted Marc with a big hug which Marc had come to expect and even look forward to.

Andy and Owen were playing some sort of video game with the boys and Marc was going to join them until he saw that Liz had already arrived and was helping Helena in the kitchen.

As soon as Helena saw Marc she greeted him and asked him to open a tight lidded jar. Once he'd completed his task Liz gave him a quick hug, sat him down and handed him a beer. He watched Liz as she chopped vegetables and then tossed them into a salad.

Then Marc asked Helena if he could help with anything else.

"Well, if you and Liz could set the table that would be great!"

So together, Marc and Liz worked in close proximity placing plates, silverware and glasses on the table.

Helena asked her daughter to bring napkins to the table. Once in the dining room Heather saw that Marc was paying too much attention to this Liz girl and she didn't like it one bit, though she didn't understand why. She ran back into the kitchen and hovered near her mother looking sad.

In the dining room, Marc caught sight of a reflection in a mirror in front of him. He saw himself with Liz in this peaceful domestic setting. He looked relaxed and happy. Maybe for the first time he consciously started to think of her as someone who could be more than a cast mate before he stopped himself, momentarily forgetting what he was doing at the table.

She noticed and was concerned. "Marc, are you alright?" He forced himself to come back from the strange and wonderful place where his imagination had just taken him.

"Yeah, I'm fine. My mind just wandered for a moment, that's all."

She was now pouring water in glasses. "I'd love to know where you were just now because you looked mighty happy."

But he was not going to say anything. Not yet. For the next several weeks Liz was still playing his sister. For him to even think of anything beyond a professional relationship could be detrimental to the play and both of their performances. For the first time in a long while he wanted more than a quick affair that would only last for the run of the show.

A few nights away from the play's opening Andy gave Marc an interesting note after rehearsal. Marc had asked Andy to pay attention to his several monologues that are delivered throughout the play. Andy's note, or observation, had to do with Tom's final speech.

"You captured something in the last speech I'd never seen. Some have said that part of Tom's resentment and frustration with his sister comes from the fact that he's attracted to her and morally can't do anything about his attraction."

Marc sat straight up. "What are you talking about?"

Andy calmed him down. "No Marc, believe me, whatever you're doing is working beautifully considering that the final speech has so many ambiguous layers. We never know if Tom finds the adventure he's looking for, though he travels a great deal. I've always thought that Tennessee Williams writes the final words about Laura as if he's talking about the loss of a lover as opposed to the loss of a sister. Several critics have thought that, too. Tonight I just saw something different that I liked a lot. From when you began the section where you talk about *being pursued by something,* through the end of the speech was really quite powerful! Wherever you went, don't be afraid to go there again. "

He was unsettled as he listened to his director's note. While he had been thinking about pursuing a romantic relationship with Liz, his thoughts often turned to Lauren as new feelings toward someone else released buried memories from years before.

Just as Tom Wingfield's memory of his sister Laura could creep up on him when he least expected, Marc's memories of Lauren lurked in the recesses of his mind, every once in a while making themselves known and taking him by surprise. This usually occurred when he allowed himself to be emotionally vulnerable.

"Thanks, but I don't think Kansas City is ready for an incestuous version of *The Glass Menagerie,* but thanks for the note just the same." Marc resolved to keep focused.

***

Right before the show opened the cast and director started doing publicity for the play in the form of appearances and interviews for the local media. Dori did at least fifty percent of the interviews, since she was a local celebrity-she had made it in New York, but still returned to Kansas City to perform. People were still talking about her Mama Rose in *Gypsy* that she performed in KC two years before.

Liz also received a lot of media attention. She expected to be interviewed by the University paper and radio station- that made sense. But several local television stations wanted to do a story from the angle of a promising newcomer getting her big break. Liz found that ridiculous, but talked to the stations anyway.

The show opened to excellent reviews, and the theater was filled most nights and at the two weekly matinees. After the first week the show began to run itself and the cast and crew settled into a more relaxed routine.

Marc began putting the finishing touches on his program that he was designing for his Artist in Residence program that would begin in January. During his residency he would direct an undergraduate production.

Owen flew back to Chicago twice during the run after the Sunday matinee to spend his off days with his wife. He would fly back into KC on Wednesday morning in plenty of time for the evening's performance.

Dori was enjoying being home in Kansas City and playing the diva, though she did miss two performances of the show due to an unexpected booking in New York. Her understudy went on and was wonderful. While Dori had finally come to see that Liz was more than qualified to be in this production, Liz felt at ease working with the understudy, another former New York City actor who had joined the staff of the University in Kansas when she was ready for a life change. While her Amanda was different from Dori's, she gave an excellent performance. Besides, Liz liked working with an actor who didn't have a diva's attitude.

The closing performance of *The Glass Menagerie* was the matinee held on the second Sunday of November. Part of Marc was sorry that the role of Tom was ending; he hoped that one day he'd be able to play Tom again before he outgrew the role. But because the show was ending, he would no longer have to keep his feelings for Liz to himself, though he was unsure of how to approach her. He wondered how she would respond when she learned that his interest in her was more than professional.

Marc had always brought his leading ladies roses on closing night and had already ordered a dozen for Liz. Marc usually selected yellow or pink roses, but for Liz he chose red. Perhaps they could say what he couldn't. Instead of having them delivered to her dressing room, he would deliver them to her himself, after the performance and before the cast party. That's as far as he'd planned. If the time was right to say anything, he would. Then again, if saying anything was inappropriate, he'd still be in Kansas City for a few more weeks before he left for New York and Montreal at Christmastime.

At this point, he had no idea what he would say to Liz whenever he decided to talk to her. He resented the fact that he was feeling like an inexperienced teenager trying to ask the popular girl to the big dance. He was too old be putting himself through unnecessary stress.

On the Saturday night before the play closed the cast went out for drinks so they could have a quiet celebration before the large party the next night. Andy and Helena joined them along with Owen's wife, Beverly, who had flown in from Chicago to join her husband for his closing weekend. It was a bittersweet gathering with the cast remembering the process and all the little things that had gone into making the production a success.

Dori was rather quiet, as if she had checked her personality at the door. She sincerely told the cast that she had enjoyed working with all of them, and that she would miss them after she returned to New York on Monday.

She looked at Liz and told her she had a promising career ahead of her. All she had to do was to want it badly enough, and to aggressively go after it. She added that it had been a pleasure to work with her on one of her first professional jobs.

This surprised everyone at the table, especially Andy. He had rarely seen this side of Dori.

"Dori you're absolutely right about Liz and a career if she wants it. We've talked about her going to Chicago or New York to pursue a career after she graduates this spring."

Owen was quick to sing the praises of Chicago. "Liz, Chicago is a great place for new actors. It's a smaller community and it will be easier for you to learn the business of the business. There's a lot of work-everything from theater to film and commercials and industrial work. And more and more television shows are coming into Chicago nowadays."

Now Marc spoke up, amused. "But certainly not as many as there are in New York. Sure it's a bigger city, but the opportunities are endless! There's everything that Owen mentioned, and so much more. You've also got some of the best workshops and teachers in New York. All you have to do is find your niche. And, you're already a pro, so you're a step up on most new arrivals. I think you'd really enjoy living and working in New York." He had said it and meant it.

Liz was speechless as Owen and Marc talked about living and working in these big cities and industry centers. It was Dori who became the voice of reason.

"Liz, whatever you decide to do, make sure the decision is yours, and yours alone. Have a plan, and above all, make sure you're focused on your goals. So many factors can cause you to veer away from the path you're laying for yourself. It may be your family, or a man that can cause you to lose focus."

Marc sank down slightly in his chair. He would never let Liz lose sight of her artistic goals. He continued to listen to Dori.

"Then again, you might find your fulfillment in the profession away from one of the large centers like so many people have. It doesn't mean that they're less talented. It's just that they've chosen a different path."

Andy wanted to hug Dori.

"Dori is absolutely right. Helena and I were both in New York for years, but wanted to start a family and frankly couldn't afford the life we wanted in New York. An opportunity presented itself here and it's turned out to be the best decision for the two of us. I still have a few friends in New York who can't believe we're still here."

Andy looked to Marc. "When I first met Marc last year, the only question he had for me was how a New York actor like me ended up in the middle of nowhere."

Marc spoke up. "I didn't put it that way!"

Andy jumped right back. "But that's what you meant! Helena and I are used to that way of thinking, believe me. But you came here and worked last year, and more importantly you came back this year, and you'll be here for another three or four months! If someone told you you'd be living and working in Kansas City for an extended period of time two years ago, you never would have believed it."

Of course, Andy was right.

"I imagined myself going into the middle of a cornfield to do theater, but I was proved wrong." Said Marc. I love being in KC and working at The Brewery, and I am looking forward to working with you at the University."

Andy smiled at Helena before looking back at Liz.

"So, see, there are a lot of possible scenarios to having a career in this industry. Even big city actors can see that it's possible to practice their craft in a smaller city like KC."

Liz shook her head clearly overwhelmed by the conversation. "But, Andy, to me Kansas City *is* the big city! I'm really nothing more than a simple country girl from Moreland, Oklahoma, a place with a population of less than two thousand people. Kansas City is the furthest I've ever been away from home, and it was a big deal for me to travel so far away from my family who have no idea of what I'm trying to achieve by considering a career in play acting-that's what my father calls it. I've never been on an airplane, and haven't been exposed to many of the things I'm sure most of you take for granted. But I've already learned so much, and there's so much more I want to learn. Andy, I can't thank you enough for giving me the opportunity to work in your theater. I keep pinching myself to make sure all of this is really happening!"

She looked down and quickly wiped something out of her eyes. All at the table were touched by her passion, honesty and innocence. Andy put his hand on hers.

"Liz, your wonderful talent is what got me to notice you and bring you to the Brewery. But your talent, along with luck and sheer determination, can take you wherever you want to go. Please remember that." He squeezed her hand until he saw her smile.

Then Owen proposed a toast to Andy. "Through his wisdom and guidance, we were able to bring an American classic to the good people of Kansas City. Thank you for bringing all of us onboard. To Andy!"

All raised their glasses and toasted their director.

After the group left the bar, Liz offered to give Marc a ride home since she was going in his direction. Marc was happy to spend a few minutes alone with her.

"Liz, are you sorry to see the show come to an end?"

She thought for a moment or two. "Yes. I really am. But an ending can also be a beginning."

Liz smiled a smile that Marc could not read.

A few minutes later she pulled in front of his building.

Marc grabbed his bag and started to leave but stopped himself. "Liz, I really think you'd enjoy living... and working in New York."

She looked to him, her hands still on the steering wheel. "Marc, right now none of this seems real... I don't know."

She looked so beautiful in her confusion.

"Liz it will be alright. I know because I'll be there to help you." He reached over and kissed her cheek, then stepped out of her car and watched her drive out of sight.

Maybe with Liz at his side, New York might once again become a bearable place to live.

***

The next day, before the final performance of *The Glass Menagerie*, Marc delivered three yellow roses to Dori's dressing room.

She seemed touched yet underwhelmed by the gesture.

"Dori, I've loved working with you and I hope we have the opportunity to work together in the future. I know you're leaving for home tomorrow, so you'll find the rest of your roses waiting for you in New York so you can enjoy them. I just wanted to put something in your hands today."

Dori turned on the charm, and pulled him into her arms. "Marc I've loved working with you too, and I'd gladly welcome the opportunity to work with you again." She took a hard look at him. "If I were only twenty years younger! Good looking and a sexy accent on top of that."

Marc found himself blushing. "Dori, I don't think anything as insignificant as age would stop you from doing anything, which is why I'm going to leave you to get ready for our last performance. I'd hate for them to have to hold the curtain simply because you had no self-restraint and couldn't keep your hands off your onstage son!"

Dori loved Marc's sense of humor. "You're right! You better get out of here before I have you seeing stars!"

He left wondering if she had been serious. With Dori, you never knew.

He made his way to Owen's dressing room to give him some cigars.

"Marc, these are Cuban! How did you manage to score these?"

Marc was happy Owen had appreciated the effort. "Owen, my sister sent these to me from Canada, where there's no embargo. I hoped you'd enjoy them."

Owen was still marveling that he had these illegal cigars in his hands. "I'd just hate for you to get deported."

Marc feigned fear. "Then please destroy the evidence by smoking and enjoying them. Owen I'll see you later, but I just wanted to make sure that I told you it's been great working with you. Thanks for everything."

Marc only had one more cast member to thank, but he would wait until after the performance.

The stage manager called "thirty minutes," and Marc began his transformation into Tom Wingfield for the last time.

Three hours later the performance was over and the audience was on its feet applauding enthusiastically. All of the actors and their director agreed that this had been an exceptionally good show, as so many final performances are.

The party was to begin at 6:00 in the ballroom of an old Kansas City hotel. The party was part celebration for the success of the first show of the season, and part business. In addition to the show's cast and crew, the staff and board of the theater would be in attendance as well as many of the theater's patrons and supporters. Several other members of Kansas City's artistic community had also been invited.

Marc quickly got dressed, and packed up the rest of his belongings since he would be leaving his dressing room for the last time. Time was of the essence, especially since he hoped to spend a few minutes with Liz before they left the theater. He knew he didn't have to be at the party right at 6:00, but he didn't want to arrive any later than 6:15 or 6:20.

Fifteen minutes after he left the stage, he crossed the hall to Liz's dressing room hoping that she had changed and prayed she was alone. He knocked, and heard her say to come in.

Marc stepped into her room, the vase of red roses in hand. She had changed for the party and looked amazing. She was wearing a silky burgundy cocktail dress, strappy heels and a small pair of diamond stud earrings. He had only seen her wear her hair back in a ponytail or up, but tonight she let her long blonde hair cascade over her shoulders. Marc had never seen her like this. For a moment he was speechless before he finally said, "You look amazing!"

He remembered the roses. "These are for you."

She blushed as she took the vase of roses from him while he closed the door behind him.

He then remembered what he had planned to say. "Liz, you were a wonderful Laura. I can't tell you how much I've enjoyed working with you. I think you have a wonderful future ahead of you."

She put the roses down on the makeup table and smiled the same unreadable smile she had smiled the night before.

"They're beautiful. This is the first time anyone has ever brought me flowers after a show. Now I feel like a real actress. Thank you for that, Marc. Thank you for everything."

Then she crossed to Marc and put her arms around him. He returned her embrace and felt Liz pulling him even closer. Then with purpose, she kissed him firmly on the mouth, taking Marc completely off guard.

After several moments Liz took a step away from Marc. "Do you know how long I've wanted to do that?"

All of the feelings Marc had been holding back were released as he took Liz in his arms and eagerly kissed her back.

Marc wasn't sure how much time had passed before he pulled away from her. They were both out of breath.

"Marc, I'm not your sister anymore." She stepped toward him while resting her hands on his chest, but this time *he* stepped away from her.

"I know, but Liz, we really need to get to the party."

She understood and dropped her hands. "You're right. Would you like a ride?"

Marc wasn't exactly sure what had just happened. "Yes, I could use a ride…thank you."

And to think that Marc had no idea what to say to Liz. As it turned out words were completely unnecessary.

The party was wonderful, with good food and drink. Marc met several people in the artistic community and made a few more contacts he hoped to use during his time in Kansas City. Andy and Helena made sure that the community knew Marc would be staying in town for the University's winter semester.

Dori was the belle of the ball, enjoying her last night in her home town.

Marc spent some time with Owen and his wife Beverly, a graphic artist. They would be headed back to Chicago first thing in the morning because Owen had an audition the next afternoon. Such is the life of a working actor.

Liz made sure she stayed a good distance away from Marc for most of the evening. That practically drove Marc insane.

The theater's photographer took several pictures of the cast and other partygoers. The only time during the party that Marc was anywhere near Liz was during a cast photograph that would appear in the next day's *Kansas City Star*. Marc held onto Liz long enough for the photographer to take a photo of just the two of them before she disappeared again.

The party continued until just after nine.

Andy assured Dori he would be taking her to the airport in the morning. Marc admired the way Andy looked after his actors. Owen and Beverly had rented a car, so their transportation to the airport was set.

Andy and Marc confirmed their one o'clock lunch at the University where Marc would be meeting a few more members of the drama department and take his official tour of the University campus.

Andy and Helena asked Marc if they could give him a ride home. That's when Liz suddenly appeared, saying that his belongings were already in her car and she'd be going in his direction, so she had no problem dropping him off.

After a final goodbye to their fellow cast members they headed to her car.

Marc and Liz were silent as she drove the nine minutes to his apartment building. But instead of just stopping to let Marc out, she pulled into a space, parked and turned off the engine. They sat in silence for at least a full minute before Marc finally spoke.

"Liz, would you like to come inside?"

She paused as if in thought before saying yes, enjoying the game. He helped her out of the car and took her inside.

Once inside Marc made tea while the two talked for a short time about nothing in particular. Then the conversation stopped altogether as they began kissing. Marc was hesitant to move too fast, so it was Liz who suggested they move to his bedroom. Marc didn't argue.

For the first time in a very, very long time, Marc was genuinely allowing himself to care about a woman. For Marc it was an intense mix of emotions, the most prominent being fear.

When Marc and Liz were not working they were inseparable. He enjoyed the normalcy of an adult relationship. They cooked together, watched movies, and

Liz showed Marc potions of KC that he never knew existed. He never imagined Kansas City had an active jazz district.

Marc would be beginning his Artist in Residence program in January. Shortly after *The Glass Menagerie* closed, Marc submitted his program to Andy Synch.

Marc was excited as he presented his plan. "In addition to the piece I'll be directing I'd like to do a series of workshops on Surviving the Business, with one workshop dedicated to technology. I'd also like to do an audition workshop that may have to be limited to upper classmen and grad students since this could be very popular."

Andy nodded his head in agreement. "I'd hate to do that, but it may be the only fair way to offer the seminar...unless you wanted to do some sort of a lottery."

Marc liked the idea. "What if we opened this to only the upperclassmen and offered, say twenty spots. I could handle that. Then we do a lottery for underclassmen for an additional three to four spots? That's a lot of people, but I'm willing to do it."

Andy liked Marc's enthusiasm. "That's a lot of people, so let me give it some thought. Is there anything else?"

Marc turned to the last page of his plan. "I'd like to host three to four open discussions on issues and elements of the business from a working actor's perspective. Some of the topics I've chosen are the unions, paying to work, family issues, the realities of living in a big city, that type of thing. I want the students to have a realistic idea of what they're in for in the real world. I can only speak from my experience, but my hope is, they'll be able to take away something from my experiences. These discussions would be informal and open to everyone."

Andy seemed interested in the last part of the proposal. "We've never done anything like that, and you're right. A working actor's opinion on elements not normally discussed in an academic setting could scrape some of the stardust from these kid's eyes. I'm meeting with the board at the end of the week, so hopefully I'll have good news for you next week."

The business part of the meeting was over and both men relaxed. "Marc when are you heading back East?"

Marc turned to the calendar on his phone. "I leave for New York on December 1 where I'll be until the 21st. Then I'll head to Montreal for Christmas, and return to Kansas on January 3 or 4. You were going to try to schedule auditions for my production on the first two days of the semester."

Andy was marking his own calendar. "Those auditions are already set so don't worry about that. You'll be here for Thanksgiving, so if you don't have plans Helena and I would love for you to join us."

Marc looked like he was going to accept the invitation before he hesitated. "Andy, Liz and I are seeing each other."

This caught Andy by surprise. He saw that Marc looked anxious.

"We've probably been more discreet than we need to be."

Andy understood what Marc was not saying. "Marc, it's okay. There's no conflict, if that's what you're worried about. You're both adults, and even if she were to participate in any of your programs at the University there's no grading involved so your position would never affect her standing. The play that you're directing is for underclassmen so there's no conflict involved there, either."

Marc started to relax.

Andy smiled. "Liz is a very nice woman and there's no reason for the two of you not to see each other. We'd love to have both of you over for Thanksgiving dinner. I know Helena will be pleased. And it's a good thing you're seeing someone new. I hate to break it to you but Heather has a new boyfriend. She's dumped you for a younger guy. Marc, he's eight."

Both men enjoyed a good laugh.

Chapter Eleven
New York, December 2007

On December 1, Liz took Marc to the Kansas City Airport. While they had been together for just a few weeks, their parting was difficult. She would be back to pick him up on January 3 2008.

Marc spent Christmas at home in Montreal where his parents looked forward to his arrival. It would be the first time in years that all three Guiro children were home to celebrate the holiday.

Marc and his family had made great strides in repairing the rift between Marc and his father. The healing between father and son began the year before when Marc went to Montreal to be with his sister after her surgery.

Before returning to his family, however, he had a few professional commitments, including a film in New York. He had been offered the role earlier in the year, just before he left for Kansas City. Fortunately, the director arranged the shoot so that Marc's scenes would be among the last shot in December after Marc returned to New York.

In addition, ACT booked Marc for several school seminars which he enjoyed, plus he ran an orientation session for three new company managers. The company was expanding and the ACT board wanted to have people trained and ready to step in to the position if necessary.

Marc also took time to reconnect with his agents and several of his other industry contacts. Marc's few weeks in the city were very productive. For the first time in years he was enjoying New York.

The highlight of Marc's trip to The Big Apple was seeing Mel. She'd flown back east to visit her family on Long Island, and made a trip into Manhattan specifically to see him. Her husband, Eric, wouldn't be arriving until after Marc left for Montreal.

The two met at a small bistro near his apartment. Marc greeted her in his usual way of kissing her forehead and hugging so her tightly that her feet came off the ground. They took a seat at a table near a window.

"I'm beginning to wonder if this husband of yours exists!"

Mel looked like she wanted to hit him, but Marc diffused what he'd just said. "Lighten up! I look at you and I see how happy you are! I know he's real, and I'm very happy for both of you. Maybe one of these years I'll get to meet him."

Mel had missed Marc. "Don't worry. I'll make it my mission to introduce the two of you."

She didn't know if she wanted to even bring up the subject, but decided to ask anyway. "What about you? Have you found any interesting prospects in the heartland?"

Marc's strange smile and uncharacteristic silence gave him away.

"Oh no! Don't tell me you've finally met someone?"

Marc couldn't contain himself. "Her name is Elizabeth-Liz. She's from Oklahoma and she's the most incredible actor. I mean she has a natural gift." An idea came to him. "Mel, when will your condo be available for rent again?" Mel's condo would be the perfect place for Liz and himself when she came to New York.

"Possibly June. Don't tell me that you're actually thinking about…"

Marc completed her thought. "Having her come to New York to be with me? That's exactly what I'm thinking. She completes her master's in May and I'm praying that she'll want to start a career in New York. She has the talent, and I'll be right here by her side supporting and guiding her. I'm hoping that she'll want that too!" He couldn't believe what he was saying.

Mel had not remembered Marc ever being excited about starting a life with a woman, and her curiosity was piqued. She hardly knew where to begin. "So… do you have a picture?"

Marc took out his phone, found a photograph and passed his phone to Mel.

"I took that at the Kansas City Airport the morning I left for New York."

Mel saw a photograph of a slight blonde woman smashing her lips into Marc's cheek. Her reaction was restrained. "Cute."

Marc quickly took the phone back. "Let me find a picture where you can really see her."

It only took him a few seconds before he passed the phone back to Mel. "That was taken on Thanksgiving Day at the Synch's house."

Mel took the phone and saw the couple in front of fireplace in a shot that she found disturbingly domestic and very unlike Marc.

She studied Liz. If her actor's headshot would have come across her desk when she was doing *Clayton's Crossing,* Mel would have classified her as *Midwestern pretty with a salt of the earth quality.* In other words, exactly the opposite type of woman Marc was usually attracted to.

Mel had known Marc for years and remembered that he was usually attracted to women with dark hair, dark eyes and a few curves somewhere. Liz was very fair, had blonde hair (that she was wearing pulled back in a tight bun in both of the photographs that Marc had shown her), light brown eyes and was rail thin.

Mel was looking at the picture so intently that Marc started to get uncomfortable. He asked what she was thinking."

"Nothing, really. I just thought you preferred your women more… complicated."

Marc didn't like the remark which Mel saw immediately. "Sorry, that didn't come out right."

"Mel it all happened so fast!"

"How long have you known each other?

Marc talked it out. "I met her last year but didn't get to know her until this year…September. She was Laura in *Glass Menagerie.* I was attracted to her, but didn't pursue her until after the play closed in November."

"So you've only been together for maybe five or six weeks, and you've been in New York for at least three of those weeks." Mel sounded cautious.

"Something like that, but we're in contact every day. I've never met anyone like her. Mel, she's... wonderful!"

"I'm sure she is. So how old is she?"

Marc didn't like being interrogated. "She's twenty-seven...which would make for an age difference of more than ten years if that's what you're getting at."

Actually Mel thought it was more like a twenty year gap. But knowing how sensitive Marc could be, kept it to herself.

"Marc, please calm down."

He seemed momentarily embarrassed by his sudden burst of emotion and relaxed as Mel expressed her concerns to Marc.

"Marc, I love you. You're the bratty little brother I never had, remember? And like it or not I am always going to be looking out for your best interests."

It took Marc a moment, but he finally calmed down.

"It sounds like you're serious about this woman...Liz, and I'm thrilled for you." Mel continued. "But you said it yourself, that this all happened quickly. I've known you for years... and I *know* your history."

"Mel, I'm actually thinking of a future with Liz. Doesn't that say something?"

Mel made an observation. "Marc...you haven't once said that you love her. Doesn't *that* say something?"

Marc looked away from Mel knowing she was right.

Mel continued carefully. "Marc, unless you've been keeping something from me, I can only think of one other time in your life when you really, truly loved someone. I also remember how hurt you were when …whatever it was at the time, ended so suddenly. I was worried about you then, and I'll worry about you now. I don't want to play therapist, but I think that one relationship, such as it was and despite how many years it's been, has affected *every* relationship you've ever had!"

Marc had calmed down and seemed to go to a place deep inside of himself. After more than a few awkward moments of silence, he asked two questions. "So…how is she? How's Lauren?"

While Marc had thought about Lauren over the years, he was finding himself thinking about her more than usual. Tennessee Williams dialogue in *The Glass Menagerie* triggered some of these thoughts. As he was trying to get closer to Liz he found himself comparing what he was feeling for her to something he had felt years ago with Lauren; there was no comparison. Since arriving in New York a few weeks before, familiar places sparked long forgotten memories of Lauren.

Mel was hardly surprised by Marc's question. "After all these years you still want to know how Lauren's doing."

Marc shifted uncomfortably. "I know. It's been years since I've seen her. Do you think I'm strange for wanting to know about her? "

Mel gave him a supportive smile. "No, why should I. You were in love with Lauren and it's obvious you still care about her."

Their eyes met as he slowly returned her smile; she was right.

Mel had always suspected that Marc had never completely gotten over Lauren. Now her suspicions were confirmed. It was evident he still thought about Lauren and maybe she still had a place in his heart.

Mel had never lost contact with Lauren and knew of all of her ups and downs. There had been several downs over the past few years but things were finally starting to turn around for her.

"Marc, Lauren's fine."

She could see that even the smallest piece of insignificant information affected him in some way.

Marc and Lauren's story was befitting a modern-day soap opera, or as Natalie Connelly had said more than once, a classic Shakespearean tragedy. Mel asked the question she had wanted to ask him for years.

"Marc…have you ever thought about getting in touch with Lauren?"

He started to say something but she stopped him.

"Just listen to me for a moment. Whatever happened between the two of you happened a very long time ago when you were both very young. Don't you think that it's time for you to get some closure? Or should I say for *both* of you to get closure?"

Marc said nothing as Mel continued to speak her mind. "In 1989 when Lauren left it would have taken some effort to find her. But today with very little effort and basic technology you could probably find her in a minute or two…if you really wanted to." She saw Marc start to come back from wherever his mind had taken him.

"Or I could just ask you how to get in touch with her…or you could take out your phone and call her right now."

Neither spoke for a few moments, but she sensed his apprehension. "Sure, you could ask me, and with her permission, I'd tell you how to contact her. I might even consider calling her. But after all these years, you're still not ready, are you?"

Mel imagined being able to give Marc a phone number or an email address if he asked and if Lauren agreed. And if Marc really wanted her to call Lauren, she would make the call in what might be considered a Christmas miracle of sorts.

But after a few moments Marc looked back to Mel. He could have given Mel a short answer, saying that despite the passage of time, he was still afraid of reaching out to Lauren. She had rejected him once and the thought of her rejecting him again all these years later terrified him. But Marc gave her a much longer and brutally honest answer.

"Mel, thank you, but you're right. It has been a very long time since I've seen Lauren, and we're probably very different people now. I'm sure she has a life of her own and the last thing I want to do is to interrupt her life again. Remember, she was the one who put three thousand miles between us. And if you remember correctly, we may have had feelings for one another, but we only acted on them once and a few days later she was gone. Then for whatever reason I got married, and you remember how well that worked out. It's been so hard for me to find a relationship that goes beyond the physical. Several years ago you told me that you were worried about me, and you should have been. I resented it when you called me Casanova, but the name fit my actions. But now with Liz… it's been so long since I've allowed myself to genuinely care about someone. I loved Lauren… but I was never with her…and I just don't mean physically. We were never together as a couple, and

I've regretted not pursuing her for years-but I'm afraid it's too late."

Marc paused for a moment. "Mel, at the end of *Glass Menagerie*, Tom Wingfield says, *Time is the longest distance between two places*. Tennessee Williams was a very wise man. So much time has passed and Lauren is so far away... maybe its best that I leave her in my past."

Mel knew Marc too well to believe this was true. But again she decided not to go there. "But do you think Liz could be the real thing?"

Marc tried to smile as he thought of her. "Maybe. Since 9/11 I've never felt comfortable in New York, but thinking about Liz with me in New York has me looking at things differently." He was thinking that he would no longer be alone.

Mel did her best to be supportive. "Whatever you do, please don't rush into anything."

Then she answered his initial question. "Marc, Lauren is fine. In fact, she's doing very well. Some great opportunities have come her way over the past few months. She's happy, Marc."

Marc smiled sadly, relieved that Lauren was doing well. "Thank you for telling me."

What she didn't tell him was that Lauren had been in New York in the spring for a high profile job with an A-list director."

They enjoyed the rest of their visit, talking about mutual friends and family.

Marc asked her if she had any idea where he could find an antique broach for his sister. Mel had the name of a place that specialized in estate jewelry and was reasonable priced.

Three hours later, it was time to go, though she found it hard for her to leave her good friend. Marc kissed her goodbye and put her into a cab to take her to Penn Station, where she would catch a train to Long Island.

While he'd been happy to see Mel, he was now disturbed that she had made him talk and think about Lauren. Or maybe Marc had wanted to talk about Lauren. He had been thinking of her often lately.

Marc hoped he had successfully banished Lauren's memory to the outer recesses of his mind, but now realized he had been fooling himself. Maybe he had tried to replace his thoughts and memories of Lauren with Liz, and maybe it had worked until now. After his conversation about Lauren with Mel, Marc felt that a part of him was missing.

He called Liz and felt better for the brief time they spoke. His feelings for Liz were just as clear as they were confusing. But several hours later, the sad and empty feeling that had come over him earlier returned and refused to leave him. He found his mind wandering back to another time, and another woman.

***

Bronte's Vintage Jewelry was in an area where Marc hadn't been in years. It was in the Village close to the old movie revival house. He quickly found the shop and once inside found an amethyst broach that was exactly his sister's taste. After a minimal amount of haggling, Marc left with his last Christmas gift in hand.

As he started to walk he was hit with a distinct aroma of garlic. While it had been years, he knew he was near Isabella's Italian Restaurant. He followed the scent of the garlic and soon found himself at a table in a restaurant that hadn't changed since the last time he had been there, years before.

The smiling waitress offered him a menu, but he waved it away.

"I remember you used to have the best Fettuccini Alfredo."

The waitress smiled. "And we still do. Can I bring you an order?"

"How about a half order, with a dinner salad and a glass of Pinot Grigio." The waitress wrote the order down.

"Will do. I'll be right back with your wine and salad."

As the waitress left, Marc remembered the last time he ate here. He was with Lauren, sharing the same meal he had just ordered. And then the very next night, she had walked out of his life forever.

The next thing he knew the waitress was back and placing a salad and a glass of wine in front of him.

"Miss, thank you, but could I get the pasta to go please? I need to leave sooner than I expected."

He picked at the salad and quickly finished his wine before paying the check and heading home.

Discussing Lauren caused him to be bombarded with memories of her. He vividly remembered the night she left him. He had never forgiven himself for hurting her.

Marc found himself looking forward to leaving for Montreal the next day where he would hopefully escape his past.

Chapter Twelve
Kansas City, winter 2008

Marc had an enjoyable Christmas and New Year's in Montreal. He continued to reconnect with his family over home-cooked meals, through shared memories and stories. The rift between Marc and his father was now buried in the past. Marc and his father, Charles often spoke until the wee hours of the morning as they got to know each other again. When his two week visit was over, he experienced an unexpected sadness.

On January 3 2008, Marc boarded a flight departing Montreal for Chicago, while the next leg of the trip took him into Kansas City where Liz was eagerly waiting for him in baggage claim.

He couldn't wait to get his arms around her. He kissed her as if he were leaving her forever instead of just having returned to her.

There were several inches of snow on the ground which made Liz drive cautiously and slowly into the city. That drove Marc crazy, since he only wanted to get her home and into bed.

After what seemed like hours, though it had only been around thirty-five minutes, Liz pulled into parking lot of Marc's apartment building. She had been busy here over the last few days. They were going to have a belated Christmas celebration and she had decorated the apartment with a small tree and many small lights. The space was warm and inviting. He smelled a roasting turkey and baking chocolate. He turned to her looking stunned.

"Merry Christmas!"

He took her in his arms again, determined to get her to the bedroom, but she advised against it since she was about to remove the turkey from the oven, and suggested he take a shower.

"It will be a cold shower, Liz. Thanks."

By the time Marc had returned from the shower dinner was on the table. They enjoyed a leisurely meal before cleaning the kitchen together.

Afterwards they exchanged gifts. Liz gave Marc an umbrella and a thick cable knit sweater. Since he planned to rent a car for this part of his stay she also got him a Kansas City street guide.

Marc gave Liz a slip. It was the same shade of burgundy as the dress she wore to the closing night party of *The Glass Menagerie* a few weeks earlier. She had never had anything this exquisitely feminine and sexy.

"This is something a movie star would wear!"

He smiled a naughty smile. "I was told that this is for sleeping...or not sleeping."

She saw Marc leering at her. "Wait...did you get this for me, or did you get it for yourself?"

He never answered her.

Then she opened her next gift. Marc had gotten her several books, guides and pamphlets for New York actors that covered a range of subjects from photographers and headshots, to teachers and coaches to set and theater etiquette. She looked at them unsure of what to make of them. "Marc?"

He sat beside her. "I want you to seriously consider coming to New York with me-after you get your degree, of course. You'll love it there, and I'd love having you there with me. I'll help you get started by helping you network and introducing you to my contacts. I really think you have a future in New York-that is, if that's what you want."

She nervously began to look at some of the literature, leafing through pages and reading liner notes. But then she suddenly excused herself.

Marc wondered if he'd offended her. He sat alone by the warm light of the Christmas tree wondering if he'd made a mistake.

Then he felt her hands on his shoulders and turned around. She was wearing the burgundy slip. It fit her perfectly and grazed over her body. He was speechless.

"So…do I look like a movie star?"

His answer had no words as he lifted her into his arms and took her into his bedroom. She had worn her new slip for no more than three minutes before it wound up on a heap on the floor.

***

Marc wasn't sure how much time had passed when he awoke after a deep sleep.

Liz was next to him smiling. "I guess you really missed me! And I am glad you missed me! You should go away more often!"

"Oh, I don't plan on leaving anytime soon!" He rolled over and wrapped himself around her while laying his head on her chest and holding her close. They stayed like this for a few minutes before Marc realized she was quietly laughing.

"Liz, what's so funny?"

She rubbed his shoulders. "You'll have one more Christmas gift coming from me sooner than later."

He held her tighter. "I've got everything I want right here."

But she begged to differ. "Oh no, not quite! You see, my final gift to you will be a few sessions with a licensed psychologist!"

All of a sudden Marc was sitting up amused as Liz giggled. "A psychologist? What for? Liz, what have I done to make you think I'm crazy?"

Liz thought what Marc had done was funny in a weird way. "Well, first of all let me say that you were extremely passionate this evening. Incredibly, intensely passionate, to the point where I practically passed out."

Marc was enjoying the compliments. "Well, pushing you over the edge...that's a good thing, right?"

Liz collapsed back against the pillows. "You were amazing...and I'm not complaining. But, in the heat of the moment... you called me Laura!"

Liz laughed, but Marc sat up startled, not knowing what to say and feeling guilty.

"Don't tell me you're still thinking of me as your sister in *The Glass Menagerie?*"

He looked at her mortified.

"*That's* why I think you need therapy!"

Marc was ashamed and couldn't even look at Liz. "I'm so sorry. That was… inappropriate."

Liz couldn't understand why he couldn't see the humor in the situation.

"You know I'm joking! For weeks I was Laura to you so it only makes sense that you'd call me Laura… especially when *you're* going over the edge!"

He pretended to accept her theory by kissing her on the forehead. "I guess you're right, but I promise I won't do it again."

She kissed him back and slid down beside him. A few minutes later she was fast asleep.

Marc looked at Liz sleeping peacefully by his side and longing for peace himself. He knew the name he called wasn't Laura, but Lauren or possibly Laurie. He was grateful that Liz had heard Laura and had a plausible explanation for what she thought she heard.

Maybe Liz had been right. Maybe he did need therapy.

Marc had recently left New York, trying to escape painful memories from his past, but now he wondered if his memories had followed him to Kansas City, lingering when he was most vulnerable.

***

The students at the University loved Marc. His workshops were well attended. His discussions had to be moved to a larger space because there was so much interest. He prayed that at least a few students would turn out to audition for his production, never imagining that more than eighty percent of the underclassman enrolled in the drama program would audition. He had chosen to do a series of three short one act plays by a favorite author and had fifteen roles to offer. Casting would be more difficult than he imagined.

Marc was also receiving a lot of attention from female students. Marc told Liz it was just the accent, but she knew better. Marc was attractive, charming and exuded an intensity that many women, herself included, found appealing and downright sexy.

She warned him. "If I see any girl older than Heather Synch making advances toward you, she's dead!"

Marc was flattered by her pretend jealousy. At least he hoped she was pretending. Liz had nothing to worry about. During non-working hours they were always together. Liz's own apartment was now an oversized closet because she had all but moved in with Marc.

Most of the time Marc and Liz's relationship was good. But as the weeks passed Marc was projecting his wishes of a perfect life in New York City onto Liz, which sometimes confused her and caused awkward moments between them.

Liz enjoyed being with Marc but still had several important decisions to make about her own life. While she enjoyed hearing Marc talk about New York, it sometimes sounded as if he was talking about a fairytale kingdom in a place that didn't really exist. This was a place where he expected them both to live happily ever after. She sometimes detected a desperation in him that made her suspicious of his intentions.

As January turned to February, Marc talked more and more to Liz about moving to New York. He even went as far as creating a timeline and moving plan that would have her in New York by mid-June.

Marc had never asked Liz to leave Kansas, a fact that Liz noticed immediately and told her a great deal about this man. While she had obviously been attracted to Marc, she never saw their relationship as anything permanent. From the beginning she always knew that Marc would return to New York in the spring, just as she was beginning the next phase of her life when she finished graduate school. While she was unsure of her future, she was positive it did not include a move to New York, or a man who wanted to be both her mentor and lover.

In mid-February a huge snowstorm closed Kansas City. There were no classes, no work and Marc and Liz were happily snowed in together. Together they put together a pot of chili and settled back to watch a few movies.

That was until Marc started to talk about New York again.

But this time Liz stopped him. "Marc, please stop! I have enough on my mind trying to graduate this spring. To be honest, I don't know if New York would be a good fit for me."

This seemed to surprise Marc. "Please don't say that! New York is an amazing city where you can create your own path as an artist. I know this because I've lived there for several years, and I've met actors from all over the country-from all over the world really, who call New York home. And Liz, you actually have talent! The city can be your oyster. And I'll be by your side every step of the way!"

"Why do you think I belong in New York?"

For Marc it had always been a given that Liz belonged with him in New York. Maybe she could take away some of the pain and loneliness that had become a constant in his life.

Marc paused before answering Liz. It was clear she had doubts about leaving Kansas. He now wondered if the world he had created with Liz was real or an elaborate illusion fabricated in his mind.

Marc took a deep breath. "There was this one little eighteen-year-old girl from a place called Middleton-no, Middle*town* Ohio. She was easily mistaken for a child, she looked so young. All she had was a dream… and talent. Originally she had someone in her life, another performer who was going to help her get started, but fate dealt her a cruel hand and took this person away from her. He died and she was in the city alone, blending into the woodwork."

Liz shook her head not understanding where Marc was going. "This doesn't sound very uplifting or encouraging."

Marc agreed. "No, it doesn't, but while it was hard sometimes, she continued to believe in herself and even to believe that the person who was going to help her was still with her in some way. Suddenly she was being led to people who could help her, and guide her toward her dream; a dream that eventually became a reality."

Liz noticed Marc had become very serious and seemed to be talking from a dark place inside of himself.

For a moment she wondered if he was even aware of her presence.

"Who was this girl to you?"

Not wanting to reveal more than he had to, Marc struggled with his response and told a familiar lie. "She was… my… best friend." He felt a pain in his gut.

He wanted to stop, but found himself talking more. "By the time I met her, everything she touched turned to gold! And while I'm not proud to admit this, I may have been jealous of her and may have even resented her at one time. But I soon saw she was a hard worker, and generous, and beautiful inside and out. I guess, in some ways, she inspired me to work harder."

He had never said this aloud and paused for a few moments as his words reverberated in his head. Lauren had inspired him to work harder to become a better artist, a better performer and maybe a better person.

He turned back to Liz less confident now. "Her talent was just one of her exceptional qualities."

He tried to make the conversation about Liz again. "I can see those qualities in you, too. I know what's possible out there and I want you to have that opportunity… if that's what you want."

Liz had never seen Marc's vulnerable side before. She suspected his *best friend* may have been someone who was much more to him. Marc had put up walls preventing her from being able to read him. Despite the fact he was sitting right next to her, he seemed so far away.

She continued cautiously. "Where is she now… your friend?"

That sounded strange coming from someone who didn't know the story. He wasn't sure why he had even mentioned Lauren at all and was now uncomfortable discussing her with Liz. He felt he was being unfaithful to Lauren's memory though that made no sense at all.

"She moved to Los Angeles several years ago. Last I heard, she was doing well."

To Liz it appeared that Marc went even deeper inside himself, and for a moment she didn't know what to say. She moved closer to him resting her hand on his leg. Intuitively she sensed there was much more to this story, and whatever those unsaid details were had caused him a great deal of pain.

"Marc, I think you have pretty high expectations for me in New York, and I don't know if I can live up to them. Your friend in LA sounds like the exception to the rule."

He turned to her. "No, that's not true. I told you one story, but I could have told you one of several stories. There are so many possibilities! I want you to be happy. And if you come to New York, I'll do anything and everything in my power to make you happy. And, Liz, if you came to New York…you'd make me happy! "

So there it was. Marc wanted her in his life, but Liz was beginning to question the reasons why. Maybe Marc wanted her to replace someone else. Maybe she had always been in competition with a memory.

She put her head on his shoulder. "Marc, please let me think about all of this… and please stop pressuring me. You've been working at your career for a long time and there are things you've learned that maybe I have to learn for myself. Thank you for everything you've done for me, and everything you want to do for me. You're an amazing man." She meant every word.

He took her in his arms and kissed her with the intention of telling her he loved her, but couldn't say the words. Marc wanted to be in love with Liz-at least he thought he did. But as he tried to get closer to Liz emotionally his memories of a true love from long ago always stopped him.

Later that night, as he laid in bed with Liz, he was acutely aware of his past. It had been more than twenty years since he had seen Lauren, but her effect on him had been life altering. No matter how hard he tried, it was impossible to forget her.

***

In the first week of March the one- act plays Marc directed were performed and well received. His audition workshops received praise from the students and faculty members, while his open discussions were standing room only. Marc's residency had been more successful than he had ever imagined.

Andy Synch, who had selected Marc in the first place, was thrilled with the success of the program. He was now preparing to say goodbye.

The University drama department held a reception for Marc the week before he left Kansas City. He was overwhelmed by the turnout. He was asked to say a few words and was doing fine until he started to talk about what being a working actor in Kansas City had meant to him. He started to choke up. Marc would remember this night as one of the best nights of his professional life.

The semester ended and the students went off to spring break. Liz helped Marc pack up the last six months of his life in preparation for his return to New York in early April.

It was time to go home-long past time. As much as Marc hated to admit it, he was getting restless as Kansas City was suddenly small and claustrophobic. Without a nearby ocean he felt landlocked and was finding it difficult to breathe. Or perhaps this was simply anxiety.

For a brief time Marc toyed with the idea of staying in Kansas City, but deep down knew he didn't belong. Maybe Andy Synch had *found it all* in Kansas City, but Marc was going to have to keep looking.

Liz would not be joining Marc in New York.

Marc was with her when she received the call. He heard the excited tone of her voice as he listened to her end of the conversation, deducing that she had been offered and was now accepting an offer of employment. Somehow he managed to stay composed and conceal his hurt as he sadly realized Liz never planned on joining him in New York.

"So I guess congratulations are in order, Liz. When did you interview for this position?"

She had never mentioned anything about interviewing for anything in Kansas City. Now that she had been caught, she was embarrassed. "I had my first interview just over a month ago."

In Marc's mind her silence on this issue was just short of a betrayal, but for some reason he wasn't disappointed and knew this was probably the best move for both of them.

Marc tried to be positive, reminding her that the best part of her staying in Kansas City was that she would be able to continue to act professionally at The Brewery if she desired. He knew Andy had already spoken to her about a few roles he could see her doing the following season and told her auditions would begin in July.

Liz then confessed she was not ready for a career in New York, or ready to begin a life with Marc-or any other man. For Marc, this was just as well.

He held her, telling her that they both were going to be just fine, though he was not sure about that himself.

While Liz genuinely cared about Marc, she knew they came from two different worlds and were at different times in their lives and anything permanent between them was unlikely. And intuitively Liz knew she could never be the person that Marc wanted, or needed her to be.

Perhaps one day Liz would make it to New York, but it would be a decision she would come to on her own. For the time being, Kansas City was exactly where she wanted to be. Strangely enough they both understood this as they prepared to say goodbye.

Liz originally planned to drive Marc to the airport herself, but as the time approached she called Andy Synch to ask him if he could take Marc instead. She wanted to avoid any potential scenes at the airport. Andy understood.

They were both waiting for Andy in front of the apartment building when he arrived. Andy put Marc's luggage into the back of the Cherokee and got back into the car to allow Marc and Liz to have a final goodbye.

They had already said everything that needed to be said before they left the apartment. There were no regrets or bad feelings. They kissed one last time before Marc got into the passenger side of the car.

After one last wave Andy began the drive to Interstate 35 and the Kansas City Airport.

Liz stood on the sidewalk waiting for her tears to come. They never did.

When Marc left Kansas City and Liz, he left behind the idyllic domestic fantasy he had imagined for himself over the past several months. The perfect wife, kids and house were Andy Synch's reality, not his.

Also gone was the dream of a picture-perfect life in New York City with Liz.

If anything, Marc's experiences in Kansas City showed him he wanted so much more out of his life, though he still had no idea what that meant.

Stranger, still, was the fact that the first time Marc had thought about seriously pursuing a future with a woman since his divorce, Lauren began to uncontrollably fill his thoughts. He hated to admit it, but his memories of her were just a part of him.

Marc realized in many ways, he was very much like the character of Tom Wingfield in *The Glass Menagerie*. Towards the end of the play, Tom's mother Amanda accuses Tom of manufacturing illusions. Marc could easily be accused of doing the exact same thing.

A few hours later, any of Marc's remaining illusions from the heartland faded away completely as his plane touched down in a very real New York City.

Chapter Thirteen
American Northwest/ West Coast,
Spring 2008

New York City was cold and rainy during the second week of April. This was in direct contrast to the warm spring like weather Marc had experienced in Kansas City. The darker skies reflected his mood.

Marc had been home for less than a week and was going through the motions of trying to reestablish himself in the New York acting community. So far the only appointment on his calendar was a meeting with Ben Stewart, the managing director of ACT, the next week. Marc guessed he probably wanted to talk to him about directing a production for the next season.

Marc knew he should concentrate on auditioning again, focusing on theater in the city. But he felt uninspired.

And then there was Liz. Marc knew beyond certainty their relationship beyond Kansa City would not have been viable. The relationship had run its course and they parted amicably with neither harboring any bad feelings toward the other. But Marc was still depressed. He had allowed himself to genuinely care about a woman for the first time in years. Now that Liz was out of his life he felt vulnerable, alone and to some extent, injured.

For the first time in his life, Marc found himself toying with the idea of leaving the industry altogether. Now that he had healed the relationship with his family, he was continually assured there was a place for him in his family's business. But the thought left him empty.

He was going to have to make his peace with New York at some point, though for now he still felt miserable, out of place and unmotivated. Marc found himself craving more from life, but unsure of what he wanted.

Meanwhile, on the other side of the country, Brian Dunn, the company manager for the ACT Company currently touring the American Northwest, was admitted to the hospital complaining of severe abdominal pain.

This single and seemingly random incident would set off a chain of events that would bring Marc the answer he sought.

***

Four days after his arrival in New York, Marc received a phone call just after 11:00PM. It was Ben Stewart from ACT.

"Marc I'm sorry to call you so late but we have a company emergency. Brian Dunn our CM for the company in Washington State just had an appendectomy and won't be able to finish the tour."

Marc had trained Brian.

"Ben, what can I do?" Marc heard papers rustling on the other end of the phone.

Ben wanted Marc to help him choose a replacement since he knew and trained the individuals he was considering. It never occurred to him to ask Marc himself.

Marc cut him off. "Ben, what about me?"

Ben didn't believe what he was hearing. "Marc, I need someone who can leave immediately! Like now! You just got back in town and I can't ask you to…"

Again, Marc cut him off. "Ben, you didn't ask me, but I'm telling you I'm available. The only firm appointment I have in the next few weeks is a meeting with you next Tuesday. Just go ahead and book the flight and I'll be on it!"

Marc didn't realize it, but he was actually doing Ben a favor. He'd certainly sleep better at night with Marc managing the company.

Ben jumped before Marc could change his mind. "Marc is all of your information on file up to date for your ticket?"

Marc breathed a sigh of relief. Ben was going to let him take the job, meaning he wouldn't have to face New York for a few more weeks.

Less than twelve hours later Marc's plane was landing at Seattle-Tacoma International Airport. He had no idea that he would remain on the West Coast…indefinitely.

***

Marc began his assignment as ACT's company manager as soon as he arrived in Seattle. He grabbed his bag then took a cab downtown to theVirginia Mason Medical Center where Brian Dunn was recovering.

Marc casually strolled into Brian's hospital room. His presence was unexpected.

Brian was very groggy due to pain killers. "Marc? Really? They sent you? Whoa… either you're really here… or I'm getting some really good drugs."

Marc sat beside him. "Brian, you know if you wanted to leave the tour early you probably could have just called the New York office and skipped the histrionics. I mean abdominal surgery is a bit much, don't you think?"

Brian began to laugh but forced himself to stop. "Man, please don't make me laugh…it still hurts. But I appreciate the effort." He was very glad to see Marc.

"Seriously Brian, how are you feeling?" He could see Brian was slightly embarrassed.

"Well, *today*, I'm doing okay."

He then explained that the day before he woke up with what he thought was a bad stomach ache that he thought would go away. It only got worse. By lunchtime he realized he couldn't continue to work. Kit, the company stage manager took charge of the company. Her first task was getting Brian got to a hospital. He was in too much pain to argue. Less than ninety minutes later he was being wheeled into surgery.

As Marc listened, he could also see himself working through pain to fulfill his company obligation.

Brian changed the subject. "You got out here mighty fast! I didn't even think you were in town."

Marc wasn't going to go into the entire story. "I got back to New York a few days ago. What can I say? Timing is everything. Before I tire you out, is there anything I should know about, company wise?

Brian shook his head no. "They're all pros and a good group of people. You taught me how to do a good log, so all my information will be right in front of you. You'll have no problems stepping in. Kit pulled double duty today as stage and company manager, so I know she'll be glad to see you."

Marc had read the logs on his laptop during his flight to Seattle. Gone were the days of handwritten logs.

"When are you out of here?"

Brian smiled. "Hopefully tomorrow. The appendix was removed before it ruptured, so the surgery wasn't as invasive as it could have been."

This was good news. "Brian, as soon as you get your clearance, call Ben so he can finalize your travel arrangements. He's been working with the host theater and they've assured us they'll get you to the airport. Ben plans on meeting you at the gate in New York himself, so please don't worry about anything, just concentrate on getting better. Is there anything else you need, or that I can do for you?"

Brian hated to be a bother. "Thanks Marc, I'm good, and I can't wait to get home. The company is probably in the process of breaking down since you'll be leaving town in the morning." Even when heavily medicated, his focus was still on his company.

He spent the next thirty minutes working out details, then he let Brian rest.

Marc left Brian and headed to the motel to meet the company.

***

Early the next morning Marc was in a van heading to a community south of Seattle for two shows at a high school, before breaking down, travelling south, checking into another motel and starting over the next day.

As the company made its way down the West Coast, Marc found himself enjoying the scenery, having forgotten the West Coast's beauty. He was amazed at the emerald green hills that stretched as far as the eye could see. The clean air seemed to have a therapeutic effect on him. He was calm and relaxed despite the very long hours and constant travelling.

In San Francisco the company had a bit of downtime, and Marc was able to see an old friend from New York, Crimson Wells. They met at her gallery and headed to a small neighborhood bistro for dinner.

Crimson was doing very well. She no longer looked like the hippie chick he remembered from New York, but was happy to learn she had never compromised her artistic integrity. Of all the artists Marc knew, Crimson had the best business savvy.

In addition to running a successful art gallery, Crimson was a successful award-winning poetess. To date she had published two volumes, the most successful being the first, *everything*. She hoped to have a third volume of poetry ready for publication by 2010.

Marc congratulated her. "I remember when *everything* was published and the accolades you received. I was very happy for you. I remember seeing you perform *everything* years ago. I mean… how could I *possibly* forget that poem?" He smiled appreciatively.

Crimson laughed. "Marc it's okay. I know you referred to that piece as the *naked* poem, and you weren't the only one." This did not seem to bother her in the least.

Marc was curious. "Why did you perform the piece nude? While I honestly had no problem with your choice to bare your body-I mean you looked amazing-but why such a bold choice?"

Crimson took a sip of wine. "That's a fair question, and I have two answers. The answer I gave to the press all those years ago was that the poem was a piece about baring one's soul and becoming naked emotionally. I felt that I could reach a deeper level of emotional nakedness by also being physically naked. This left me totally exposed and vulnerable, making for truly honest performances."

Marc nodded. "Okay, I get it. So what's the second answer?"

Crimson shrugged. "Being naked on stage for less than a minute a night was a guaranteed way to sell out my shows every night and get a lot of press-and it worked! I performed *everything* in my show *FEEL,* which was a success in New York, and also here in San Francisco. I performed *FEEL* here shortly after my move and the show's reputation preceded me. I'm sure some bought tickets to see me naked, but the work was solid and helped me establish myself on the West Coast. After I did *FEEL* that first time in San Francisco, I never felt the need to take off my clothes again. Tell me the truth. Do you remember anything about *everything,* other than the fact I was naked?"

Marc did remember this particular poem. "I do remember thinking that the poem was beautiful and moving. But I have to admit that I didn't totally understand what you were saying. I mean, a love that becomes *everything*…I just didn't get it. I don't know if I'd get it now."

Crimson smiled. "You didn't understand the poem because when you heard it all those years ago, you'd never experienced that type of love, right?"

Marc shifted uncomfortably.

Crimson took a deep breath, closed her eyes and began to recite a stanza from a poem she had written several years ago. Her voice became lilting and lyrical.

You are. You are and I am.

I see, breathe and feel.

You are.

My joy, pain, and angst.

You are euphoria.

You are balance, serenity...peace.

I am, because you are.

Everything.

Crimson opened her eyes and smiled as she realized her words had Marc transfixed. "Now, be honest. Didn't those words effect you just now?"

Marc exhaled deeply. "Of course, they affected me because they're powerful words spoken beautifully." He briefly thought of Liz though she hardly fit the description in the poem. "But that still doesn't mean I fully understand the poem." He took a sip of his drink.

That's when Crimson finally asked what she had been wondering for years. "Marc, whatever happened to Lauren?"

This caught Marc off guard. "Crimson that was a very long time ago. I know she's in LA and seems to be doing fine, according to Mel."

Crimson smiled sadly. "Okay... I'd just hoped that the two of you had gotten together at some point. There was so much between you that I seriously thought you were destined to be together."

Marc remembered that Crimson had seen the connection between Lauren and himself before anyone else. She knew long before he did.

Marc changed the subject and asked about his former roommate. "Crimson, how's Wes?"

Crimson brightened suddenly. "Why don't you ask him yourself?"

Crimson's gaze went over Marc's shoulder, and as Marc turned around he saw Wes coming toward the table. He stood to greet his old friend.

The three of them spent the next two hours together catching up and reminiscing.

For a while, Marc felt like his old self, temporarily forgetting about Kansas City.

He had said goodbye to Liz less than ten days ago, though in light of recent events it felt like much more time had passed. Marc could honestly say he was moving forward and held no ill feelings toward her.

In a short period of time she had taught him that it was possible for him to care about someone else. In some ways Marc had become a better person because of her.

The trip and his duties as an ACT company manager were helping him deal with the pain of saying goodbye to Liz, and he found himself thinking about her less as he began to heal emotionally.

If being able to meet with Crimson and Wes was the highpoint of this trip, then the entire trip was worth three weeks in a van. Marc was feeling peace and contentment for the first time in months.

The important thing, was that Marc, was feeling.

***

The ACT tour was quickly coming to a close, and Marc was starting to review the travel plans for the company. There were three vehicles with two drivers each that would be heading back cross country in a caravan. Any company members who wanted to ride in the caravan were welcome to make the seven-to-eight-day trek across the country, but in the past several years most company members were saving time by flying back to New York from Southern California. ACT provided a one-way ticket to New York City. This year, most company members were booked on a 10:30 AM flight out of LAX on Wednesday, May 7. Some company members chose to extend their stays in Los Angeles at their own expense. They would be responsible for making their own travel arrangements.

A week before the tour ended Marc was coordinating the logistics of departure day. The tour was ending in Irvine, California in Orange County, a city close to Disneyland. Once the vans delivered the cast to LAX they'd rendezvous and head to Interstate 10 and begin their drive to New York.

Usually the company manager rode back with the vans and truck. But due to the special circumstances involved in Marc's case, he was given the option to fly. The company's stage manager, Kit, would handle the caravan as it returned to New York City.

Marc had not booked himself on the 10:30 flight to New York. He had been meaning to do this for two weeks, but kept procrastinating since he was in no hurry to return to

New York. He was in Southern California, and who knows when he'd get back again. He was in absolutely in no hurry to get back to New York and saw no problem extending his stay for a few more days.

He dialed Gary Connelly in Culver City, California.

This call was a welcome surprise.

"Marc, my God! We're great! How are you? And where are you?"

Marc couldn't remember the name of the small town. "I'm up near Sacramento with ACT. The CM had to have surgery a few weeks ago and I came out to finish the tour which ends next week."

Gary sat at his desk in his home office disbelieving that Marc Guiro was in California. "Marc, where is the tour ending this year?"

Marc had to consult his paperwork. "Irvine. Do you know it?"

Gary laughed knowingly. "Irvine really isn't that far from Los Angeles. It's down in Orange County not too far from Disneyland. I know Irvine well because Natalie and Sabrina have a favorite mall down that way. If they could live in that mall I'm sure they'd pack up and leave me here alone."

Marc laughed. "Gary I can't believe Sabrina is old enough to have a favorite mall!"

Gary stopped laughing and turned very serious. "Marc, I have the bills to prove it. Trust me, she has several favorite malls. You know she's a teenager now. She turned fourteen last fall."

Marc hadn't seen Sabrina since she was eight years old and had come to New York with her parents.

"That's unbelievable, Gary!"

Then Marc got to the purpose of his call. "You know I'd love to see all of you. It's been way too long, and I'm here, or at least I will be. Is there any chance I'll be able to see you next week? Maybe we could do dinner?"

Gary mouthed a silent *"thank you"* to the heavens. "Marc, when are you due back in New York?" Gary crossed his fingers.

"I have no plans beyond the end of the tour next week."

For Gary, this call was getting better and better! "Then Marc just plan on staying with us for a few days. We have a guest room and I even have some free time next week. I know that Natalie and Sabrina will want to spend some real time with you too! What do you think?"

This was more than Marc had hoped.

"Gary, I'd love to spend a few days with you and the family. I'll be taking the company van to LAX to drop off the company members, and should be finishing up no later than ten o'clock in the morning. Are you sure this won't be an imposition?"

Gary talked fast. "Of course not! So it's settled. You'll do what you need to do, and then you'll call me and I'll pick you up. We're not that far away from LAX and I could be there in thirty minutes or less depending on traffic. What day are we talking about?" Gary was beside himself.

"That would be next Wednesday, May 7."

Next Wednesday couldn't come fast enough for Gary. He made Marc promise to call on Tuesday to confirm.

I'll plan on picking you up on Wednesday morning. Marc, it will be so good to see you!"

"And you, too, Gary. Please give my love to Natalie and Sabrina."

Marc hung up thinking that this unexpected trip west was the best decision he had made in a very long time.

Quite possibly, this would be one of the most important decisions Marc would ever make.

***

The Epicenter Theater had been Gary Connelly's dream for most of his professional life. He and Natalie moved to Los Angeles to open this theater a few years before. The theater would open in two stages with an educational wing coming first since Gary felt he could obtain more funding for an educational endeavor. The second phase would be an artistic wing, a professional theater that specialized in new works from new and established authors. In Gary's mind he also saw a resident company of actors, a touring company and space that would include a main stage theater, a smaller workshop space for small productions and classes, as well as space for administrative offices all under one roof. He had found the perfect building, but needed someone to underwrite the project. In a time when funding for the arts was limited, Gary didn't see his dream coming to fruition anytime soon.

The Epicenter was working out of another theater and renting space. Gary held smaller productions and readings in his rental space, and had a small company that toured schools in the Greater Los Angeles area. It had been tough getting started, but things were moving forward.

Then the miracle happened. Gary went to pitch the project to another corporation, something he seemed to be doing often. Two months after Gary's initial presentation, he was asked to come back to discuss the project further. They were very interested and asked if he had a space in mind. Gary gave them the address of a building in West Los Angeles. One thing led to another and eventually the abandoned building was purchased by the corporation. Next Gary found himself in a series of meetings with lawyers as the specifics of the new venture were finalized. The Epicenter was going to become a reality. A short time later Gary was authorized to begin assembling a team to turn the abandoned building into a theatrical center.

Gary was suddenly working very long hours between the current Epicenter and the New Epicenter that would stage its first production in 2010.

He needed help; someone who shared his unique vision and had an understanding of both educational and artistic productions. Ideally he was looking for someone with a creative and educational background who also had a good head for business. He was looking for someone who he could rein him in when need be, and above all someone who he could trust to make important decisions. He had been searching for the right candidate for months. Now he was sure he'd found the right person.

He called his wife.

As Natalie joined her husband in his office she could see he was excited.

"Nat, I've made my decision for the Creative Director position at The Epicenter!"

No wonder he was excited. He had been having trouble finding the right person to work with him. The last time they had spoken about this matter, Gary had narrowed his choices down to two people.

"That's great! You were trying to decide between that guys from USC…"

Gary threw out a name. "Paul Hudson."

Natalie nodded. "And my favorite…the guy from Berkley…Ron Rubio! So Gary, don't keep me in suspense. Who gets the job?"

Gary sat Natalie down in the big leather chair in the corner of his office and paused dramatically before saying the name. "Marc Guiro!"

Natalie's face went from looking happy and excited to looking confused. "Gary? Marc Guiro? You mean *our* Marc Guiro from New York?"

Gary made a joke. "Well, if things go my way, not for long! Nat, Marc's a perfect fit, can't you see? Marc has the background, the knowledge and the know-how."

Natalie was starting to understand her husband's thinking. "And he also knows all of your quirks and idiosyncrasies. You may have gotten this one right! Gary, I didn't even know you had approached him. Has he accepted?"

Gary began to laugh. "Natalie… he doesn't know anything about the position." Gary brought her up to speed as he told her about Marc's unexpected phone call.

Natalie understood completely. "So, when are you going to call him to discuss the position?"

Gary was smiling again. "There's no need to call him since he'll be here next Wednesday! He'll be staying with us for a few days. And Natalie I'll need you! I need you, and I'll probably need Sabrina too! Together we've got to convince Marc that he needs to move to LA."

Natalie was up for the challenge. She had always had a soft spot for Marc, not to mention she was always looking out for her husband's best interests. She knew that Marc stepping in as the Creative Director at The Epicenter was a brilliant and inspired idea. Now all she and her husband had to do was to convince Marc.

Chapter Fourteen

Los Angeles, CA 2008

Marc stood outside of Terminal Five at LAX, waiting for Gary to arrive. The day had started off cold and drizzly, but shortly after the company members headed to TSA check in, the sun had come out, burning off the marine layer and revealing a brilliant blue sky. It was going to be a warm and beautiful day in Los Angeles.

Marc heard the honking of a car horn and looked to see Gary who quickly double parked and popped the trunk of his Honda Accord before getting out of the car to embrace his friend. "Welcome to Los Angeles!" There was a much deeper meaning behind this statement.

"Thanks. I'm happy to be here!"

Gary thought this was a good start. "And we're glad to have you. You have no idea!"

Both men got into the car as Gary smiled knowingly. Marc Guiro belonged in California. He just didn't know it yet.

***

It was just before ten as Gary exited LAX. He asked Marc how early his day started. He'd been up since

5:00AM, so Gary suggested grabbing breakfast at a small restaurant on Abbott-Kinney Boulevard in Venice. Natalie recommended the place both for its food and ambience. They also had outdoor seating which would allow the California air and smell of the ocean to begin to work their calming magic. The environment was relaxing and one hundred percent stress free.

After the coffee was poured, Gary asked about the tour. "How have things changed since we toured years ago?"

Marc sat back sipping his coffee. "Computers have made things easier on the road for one thing. It's great to be able to email the daily logs to New York at the end of the day. Things have gotten more corporate and uniform, which isn't necessarily a bad thing. But the big thing is that the company members have gotten younger. It's kind of frightening because I don't ever remember being that young!"

Gary agreed nodding his head. "How the hell did that happen? It seems like it was just yesterday when we were bringing quality theater to the children of America. And we enjoyed ourselves for the most part, as I remember. How was this last trip for you?"

Marc thought about it for a moment. "To tell you the truth, the three weeks were fine. I really don't know if I could have lasted much longer. I'd forgotten how grueling touring like that can be. It was an emergency situation and I was available so I was glad to help out. The fact that I got to leave New York again didn't hurt, either. Anyway I'd forgotten how much I like the West Coast."

Gary listened attentively. "When was the last time you were out of the city?"

He told him that he'd just returned from a gig in Kansas City when he was summoned west. Perhaps it was exhaustion speaking, but for a moment he wasn't sure if he'd made the right decision. "Ben called to get a recommendation for a company manager to leave for Seattle ASAP, and I told him I was available. In retrospect, maybe it was selfish of me to take a job away from someone else."

Gary felt he had to jump in. "Or maybe you were supposed to take over the company at that specific point in time, *and you're right where you're supposed to be.*"

Marc considered Gary's theory. Gary firmly believed the Universe often placed you where you needed to be. Marc remembered talking to Gary on the morning of the 9/11 attacks, and Gary saying that he was exactly where he was supposed to be; safe in Philadelphia instead of in harm's way in New York at Ground Zero. "Maybe you're right."

He told him about his experience in the heartland. Then Gary asked him about New York.

Marc shook his head. "For me it's never been the same after 9/11. I left one New York and came back to another. The resilience of the city is amazing and New York's come back stronger than ever, but not for me. Things seem dirtier, more crowded and stressful. Everything moves faster. Whenever I'm in the city I find myself constantly racing from one place to another and I'm not enjoying it like I used to. But I honestly can't imagine calling anyplace else home. Once a New Yorker, always a New Yorker. What can I say?"

Gary sighed intensely. For a moment he doubted whether or not he should bring up the creative director position. But then the Universe stepped in, in the form of Jay Steiner.

Jay Steiner was television royalty and a comedic genius. He was credited with creating the modern day sitcom. Several of his shows produced from the sixties through the eighties aired daily throughout the world.

Steiner took a seat at a table behind theirs. "Gary I know this might sound silly, but I've admired that man since I was a kid." He leaned in closer. "In a way I guess he's always been one of my influences... or heroes!"

Gary took Steiner's sighting as a message that told him Marc was definitely meant to be in Los Angeles. There's something about the star power of Hollywood that captivates everyone, even a hardened New Yorker. Gary was now more determined than ever to convince Marc to join him at his theater.

After breakfast Gary told Marc he was going to take him to the house to let him get settled before Natalie and Sabrina came home, but he wanted to show him something first. The two men walked down the west side of the street to a small pathway. They walked for about a minute before Gary heard Marc catch his breath at the sight of the Pacific Ocean.

"Now *that's* beautiful!"

Gary's move had been calculated. "So Marc, that's the Pacific Ocean, and you're right, it is beautiful. It's one of the reasons so many of us enjoy living out here." He suggested they head to the house. He wanted to make sure Marc was well rested before he showed him what else LA could offer him.

***

Gary and Marc were on the patio where Gary was preparing the grill when Natalie and Sabrina returned home.

As soon as Sabrina saw Marc she ran to him and threw her arms around his neck. Marc gave her a big hug in return before stepping back. He could not help staring.

The last time Marc had seen Sabrina she was eight and had visited New York with her parents. He had spent a day with her while her parents attended a theater conference. He remembered her in a New York T shirt, rolled up jeans and high top sneakers. Her hair was worn in two high braids. She had her mother's eyes, her father's personality and had to be the coolest kid he had ever met.

He smiled as he remembered taking Sabrina to Radio City Music Hall, then to lunch at one of his favorite hole in the wall pizza places, and then to the observation deck of the Empire State Building before rejoining her parent's for dinner. By the end of the day he no longer thought of Sabrina as a child, but as a mini adult.

But the girl he saw in front of him was hardly the child he had met six years ago. Sabrina was now a beautiful young woman who looked just like her mother.

Sabrina flashed Marc a bright smile. "I remember the last time I saw you. Mom and Dad went to some sort of meeting and you took me to Radio City Music Hall." She remembered that day fondly, too, especially since Marc had always treated her like an adult. "Welcome to LA, and I'm glad you're here."

Heather Synch had not been the only little girl to have had a crush on Marc.

Sabrina stepped aside so her mother could greet Marc properly. Natalie put her arms around Marc but was suddenly overcome with emotion and could hardly speak.

Marc hugged her gently. "Natalie, thank you for having me."

Natalie spoke softly. "I am so happy to see you... and I'm glad you're here, too!"

She looked toward her daughter. "Sabrina, I only pray that one day you'll be lucky enough to have a friend like Marc in your life. Those early days in New York weren't always easy for your father and me, but we could always depend on Marc."

She looked back to Marc. "And thank you for that." She kissed his cheek. "And forget what I said about you being a friend, because as far as I'm concerned you're family. Welcome home Marc!"

Marc now embraced Natalie tightly.

At that moment Gary found himself very much in awe of his wife, because she had done nothing but simply state the truth as she predicted Marc's future.

***

The next morning Gary took Marc to the current Epicenter Theater. Gary took him into the theater and showed off the ninety-nine seat house. "It's an intimate space and very easy to work in. Our actors enjoy working here."

Gary spoke about the founding principles of the theater. "You know I've always wanted to have a theater with an education and artistic arm. We have a touring company that tours schools in the greater Los Angeles area. ACT hasn't come to LA since we started up a few years ago. I don't know if we've taken the market or if it's out of respect. We seem to be growing every year!"

Gary led him back into the theater's lobby, where Marc looked at the photos of the current company on the wall. He thought they looked like *LA* actors, being *prettier* as opposed to *grittier* like New York actors.

Gary continued to talk about his company. "Now our artistic arm has a resident company of actors, while our productions are newer works. But I can easily see putting a new twist on a classic from time to time. The show running right now was written by a man who has never had anything produced. The response and houses have been very good."

Marc was enjoying Gary's excitement.

Then Gary mentioned another new play. "This fall we're doing a production called *Couched*. It's a comedy about a couple in marital counseling and their therapist. The play was written by a woman who's known for her television writing."

Marc seemed interested so Gary continued. "We also do a regular play reading series which is open to the public, similar to what you did in New York at the library. The theater is attracting a lot of good people, and we're doing some good work, if I do say so myself."

Marc had no idea The Epicenter had evolved so quickly.

Gary then explained that one day he planned to have a space that could accommodate one large stage as well as a smaller stage for smaller productions, workshops, readings and classes. He wanted a welcoming lobby, state of the art dressing rooms and space for administrative offices. But that was the future. For now Gary was happy The Epicenter was actively producing theater and asked Marc if he'd like to see the current production while he was in town.

When they left The Epicenter, Gary took Marc to lunch at a Hollywood establishment, El Coyote Mexican Café on Beverly Boulevard near CBS's Television City in Hollywood. He told Marc about the restaurant's notorious history.

"This was where Sharon Tate and her friends had dinner before they went back to her house and met up with the Manson Family."

Marc cringed, but Gary told him to relax and order a House Margarita and he'd be fine. Marc's experience with Mexican food had been Taco Bell, so Gary helped him order and Marc left an enthusiastic fan.

Gary had one more stop he wanted to make with Marc that afternoon. Gary had driven to West Los Angeles and stopped his car in front of an old industrial looking brick building with an art deco façade that appeared to be empty.

The men left the car and as they approached the building, Gary pulled a set of keys from his pocket and opened the padlocked gate and walked Marc around to a side entrance. There he unlocked a large iron door. The men stepped into an open space that was dimly lit by sun that struggled to shine through windows that were missing or hadn't been cleaned in years.

Gary began the tour. "So this old building was a rather large bakery that was built back in the thirties and was active until the eighties. Its solid brick, has a good foundation and has survived more than a few earthquakes."

Gary led him through a door into an even larger space. Marc was surprised at the enormity of the room and its high ceilings.

"Gary this is impressive! It looks small from the outside, but inside it just seems to go on forever. How long has this building been empty?"

Gary proceeded slowly, wanting Marc to have a full understanding of what he was about to tell him.

"The bakery closed in 1984 and the building has been empty ever since. There have been several organizations that have tried to secure the building to no avail, and of course there have been developers who wanted to tear the building down to build luxury apartments, but luckily the building is protected by a historical trust, primarily because of the façade that was designed by a significant architect whose work seems to be disappearing. The good news is that the building won't be empty for much longer. It was recently purchased by a large corporate group, who'll be funding the renovation of the building."

Gary took a deep breath. "Marc, *this* is the new home of The Epicenter; *The Epicenter Theater Complex*. If the renovation goes as scheduled, the first production here will open sometime in 2010. And when it does, I'd like for you to be here with me."

"This is fantastic, Gary…and congratulations! Sure, just let me know when and I'll be here for your opening."

Gary grasped his friend's arm. "Marc you don't understand. I don't want you to be here for the opening. I want you to come to LA…*now*! I'm offering you a job!"

Marc's eyes widened as he stood stunned and silent. He wasn't expecting that.

Gary released Marc's arm. He decided it would be best to discuss the creative director position over a drink. Frankly, Marc looked like he could use one.

Two hours later Gary and Marc were at a table in the bar of a small restaurant near the future home of The Epicenter Theater Complex.

Marc nursed a Scotch on the rocks while Gary's beer sat virtually untouched as he pitched the creative director position of The Epicenter to Marc. Gary had been talking for almost a solid hour.

"Marc, you have been a working performer for over twenty years and have been directing for at least ten. You've had a great deal of experience in educational theater, and have worked in some of the best regional theaters in the country. You've managed and done PR. You helped to develop the seminar program at ACT, and have taught classes for young people all over New York City. I was very impressed with the program you developed for the University in Kansas City. Add to that your people skills and the fact that you can talk to and charm anybody. Marc, you're a great fit!"

Marc slowly took another sip of his drink. "Gary I don't know what to say. I mean… Gary, why me?

Gary thought carefully and then explained. "When I realized The New Epicenter was finally going to become a reality, I knew I needed someone to work with me. I immediately started interviewing candidates and met with some incredibly talented people with credentials like you wouldn't believe! And I liked several of them. It's hard to explain, but all of them were missing something. Some unknown X Factor, if you will. I've been looking for months and had finally decided to go ahead and make a decision and hire someone simply because things are going to start moving forward very soon. I'd narrowed it down to two candidates. I was driving my wife insane because I've been talking about nothing else for weeks, and I still couldn't make a decision between the last two people. And then last week *you* called, and I knew! There was no question that *you* were the person I wanted to hire! Your timing couldn't have been more perfect!"

At the mention of the word timing Marc took another swig of his drink. "You can't possibly be talking about me because my timing has always been awful."

Gary was suddenly very serious. "So maybe your timing just got better."

Gary signaled the waitress to bring Marc another drink. "Maybe this position is an opportunity that will take your career to a new level! Look, when you told me you were in California last week, something clicked. You have that quality that all of the other candidates were missing."

Marc raised an eyebrow. "Gary, what quality is that?"

Gary paused momentarily. "Damn if I know, but whatever it is, you have it! I know it! Natalie knows it…"

Marc was amused. "Your wife is aware you're courting me for this position?"

Now Gary was amused. "Of course, she knows I want you working with me. Natalie is my rock. She knows me better than anybody! As soon as I mentioned I wanted you as my creative director, she said that I'd finally gotten it right. She was surprised that your name hadn't come up earlier."

Marc was intrigued, but tried to keep his expression neutral. "You're presenting me with a life changing opportunity. It's an incredible offer, but there are so many things to consider, in addition to starting over in a new city that I don't know at all."

Gary tried another approach. "Marc can't you see the possibilities? I'm offering you an imagination factory at The Epicenter. You'll still be able to perform and direct, plus you're in the middle of Hollywood with the film and television industry, so you'll have even more opportunities available to you if that's what you want!"

The waitress put down Marc's fresh drink.

"I'd like a scotch as well. Thanks." Gary was suddenly feeling he needed something stronger than beer. While Gary was talking and Marc was clearly listening, Gary could not read Marc.

"Gary, this is…well I'm flattered for one thing, but you're talking about a major life change. I've been in New York since I was nineteen years old! I've built a good solid career in the city. New York is home!"

Gary recalled a recent conversation. "Marc honestly, how's the city treating you? Are you enjoying your life in the city or are you looking for another excuse to leave? You said yourself that New York hasn't been the same for you since 9/11, and that has been how many years ago?"

Marc's New York was a distant memory.

Gary wasn't going to give up. "Marc, take the leap. I know you'll enjoy living…and working in Los Angeles! Please tell me you'll at least consider my offer?"

In Gary's mind and all Marc had to do was to say yes.

"Gary you've given me a lot to think about. Can I sleep on this?"

Okay, so at least he was going to give the offer some thought. "Yes, of course. You need to consider everything. I'm sorry, but I'm only seeing things from my perspective. That is, I think together we could really do something good…and even important. I'm forgetting I'm asking you to leave your home and move across the country. I'm being rude and I apologize."

Gary took an envelope from his pocket. "If you're considering factors, then you might as well consider the money, too."

The last thing on Marc's mind was compensation, but he opened the envelope and found the proposed salary more than acceptable.

"That figure is not set in stone, so please feel free to negotiate. I have a good business manager already in place who will be taking care of salaries and contracts if you'd like to meet with her."

Marc slipped the envelope into his own pocket. "Thanks, and I'll be considering everything. Gary, this is really an amazing offer."

"The offer only becomes amazing if you accept it."

The waitress appeared with Gary's drink.

"We don't need to talk about this anymore today, just promise me that you'll give the offer some serious thought. And if you're up for it, come see the show at the theater tonight just to give you an idea of the caliber of work we're doing. I think you'll be impressed."

Marc nodded. "I'd like that, thank you."

"I think it's time to change the subject, because you're driving me to drink."

Gary took a drink feeling confident that he may have gotten through to Marc.

***

As Gary and Natalie prepared for bed that night, Gary recapped his conversation with Marc earlier that afternoon. He then told her that Marc enjoyed and had been impressed with the evening's performance at The Epicenter.

Natalie seemed pleased that Marc was at least thinking about accepting the position as Creative Director of the Epicenter.

Gary was busy the next day and Natalie offered to show Marc the city before meeting up with Gary later in the day for dinner.

Natalie was looking forward to spending time with Marc. "Now Gary, please understand that I don't plan on bringing up the position unless he asks. I'm not into the hard sell."

Gary was crawling into bed. "And you've made the reservation at Pacifica." This was their favorite seaside restaurant.

"Gary, I made the reservation last week. Six tomorrow night, and I've requested a table with an ocean view so we can watch the sunset."

Gary laughed at his wife. "Oh yeah, I can certainly see that you're not into the hard sell!" Every once in a while he remembered why he married this woman.

Something else had been on Natalie's mind. "Gary...has Marc asked about..."

Gary shook his head. "I suggest we don't mention Lauren or her association with The Epicenter until we've closed the deal."

Natalie snuggled up beside her husband. "I understand perfectly, and there's no need to give him anything else to think about. Not yet, anyway. For now let's hope we can get Marc to say yes to your offer so you can start paying attention to me again."

Gary reached over and turned off the light and showed Natalie that he hadn't forgotten her.

Marc had a rough night thinking about Gary's offer. Up until a few hours ago he was planning on going back to New York and getting back into the New York actor's pool, which meant staying in New York, a city he had not enjoyed in years though he still considered it home.

Marc had *never* thought of leaving New York permanently. But now Gary's unbelievable offer would not only provide steady employment in a new theater, but access to the entertainment capital of the world. This was in addition to beautiful weather and sunshine. He would have the chance to grow as a director and producer in addition to any performing. The positives of leaving New York far outweighed the negatives, yet he still could not decide.

The major reason preventing Marc from making a decision was fear- fear of the unknown. Sure, Gary's theater sounded great, but there was no guarantee that the project would be successful-and if it failed, where would that leave Marc? However, if the Epicenter was a success the rewards and opportunities could be amazing.

Marc would eventually fall asleep without making a final decision. He felt he needed more time.

By the time Marc woke up on Friday morning, Gary had already taken Sabrina to school and was off to the theater to prepare for a meeting with his investors. He had enjoyed the last two days with Marc, but today he would get back to work and let Natalie perform her magic.

As Marc entered the Connelly kitchen, he said good morning and poured himself a cup of coffee. Natalie smiled seeing that Marc looked more relaxed than he had the night before. When Gary really wanted something he could come on strong, and right now Gary wanted Marc to rip up his New York roots and move across the country to work with him on the project that had been his lifelong dream.

Knowing that Gary had an intense pitch session with Marc the day before, she decided to simply spend time with an old friend.

"So how did you sleep, Marc?"

Marc had too much on his mind to have a restful sleep. He had not slept most of the night because he was thinking about Gary's unbelievable offer, and when he did manage to sleep he was dreaming that he was in the middle of a large city, but he didn't know if it was New York or LA which caused him to wake up anxious.

"Well, let's just say your husband gave me a lot to consider yesterday, so I spent most of last night thinking about his offer as it played over and over on an endless loop."

Natalie smiled sympathetically. "You know my husband. When he gets focused on something there is no letting go, and right now he's focused on you and bringing you to LA. But please remember that in the end it's ultimately your decision... no matter how much we'd enjoy having you here.

"That's nice of you, Natalie. Thank you."

Natalie was determined not to talk business.

"Marc, I know you want to go to Amoeba Music in Hollywood, and I'll take you this morning if you like."

Gary had been talking about this amazing music store for years.

"I'd like that very much. Thank you!"

Natalie shook her head when she thought of how focused her husband was on business. "I think it's criminal that Gary has showed you so little of the city, so I thought we'd take the scenic route through the city. Take your time, but I'm ready to leave when you are."

A half hour later Natalie was heading east down Santa Monica Blvd showing off West Los Angeles, Century City, Beverly Hills and West Hollywood. At one point she turned north and eventually turned onto Sunset Boulevard so he could see the Sunset Strip and notable places like the Troubadour and The Comedy Store.

This day was a typical day in Southern California. The sky was a bright brilliant blue as the sun shone brightly while gently warming the city.

Natalie noticed that Marc had completely relaxed and was looking and sounding like the Marc she had known years before. Not only that, he was taking an unusual interest in his surroundings and asking a lot of questions.

Then Natalie told him they were entering Hollywood. To Marc, Hollywood looked like any other Los Angeles neighborhood. Natalie practically held her breath as she passed through the area where Lauren was currently living.

A few minutes later she pulled into the underground parking facility at the Hollywood and Highland Center.

"I'm going to let you play tourist for a few minutes. I can't let you come all this way without seeing the Hollywood Sign and the Walk of Fame. Amoeba doesn't open for another forty minutes so let's make the best use of our time."

In a few minutes Marc had the best line of the day. As Natalie was showing him the Kodak Theater where the Academy Awards are held, he saw stores like The Gap,

Express, and Victoria's Secret. He looked to Natalie appearing disturbed. "Natalie, you mean to tell me the Academy Awards are held in a shopping mall?"

Natalie had never looked at it this way, but when she considered their surroundings she had to agree.

A short time later they were entering Amoeba Music, a cavernous facility on Sunset Boulevard that carried just about every type of music available. Gary had been talking about this place for years and Marc was finally getting his chance to browse the aisles of this enormous store. He was careful not to take advantage of Natalie's time and was ready to leave in less than an hour, though he could have spent several hours combing through every stack of DVDs and vinyl. He limited his purchases at Amoeba that morning, but could have easily spent a small fortune. There was a possibility that he would be back here in the future.

Natalie showed Marc where she and Gary had their first Hollywood apartment on a street called Beachwood Canyon. She drove down the narrow road then stopped in front of a Spanish-style apartment building. She pointed up to show Marc they were underneath the Hollywood sign. "We loved waking up to that every morning."

She drove a few blocks further into a small village area that contained several small businesses including a coffee shop, dry cleaner and post office. It was very quiet and pretty. "See Marc, LA is very much like New York in that it's really a series of neighborhoods-connected by freeways."

Marc was looking at the iconic Hollywood sign through the palm trees.

"Natalie, I guess I see why so many people fall in love with California. It's pretty close to perfect."

Natalie considered this comment. "I've often thought that myself."

She drove to the 101 and into North Hollywood, or Noho, to show him the Arts District. "Gary's first directing job in LA was at this theater. He directed *The Woman in Black* and has been working ever since."

As Natalie began to drive down Lankershim Boulevard, she suggested that they grab a light lunch since they'd be having dinner with Gary later. Marc agreed only if it was his treat.

"Thanks. And I think I know the perfect place not too far from here.

Less than ten minutes later they arrived at Zach's Italian Café, a small neighborhood restaurant that the locals kept to themselves. The atmosphere was very casual and laid back while the food was exceptional and reasonably priced. Marc followed Natalie's lead and ordered soup and salad in anticipation of a big dinner later in the day. Unfortunately both of them had two garlic cheese rolls, a house specialty. Natalie called them addictive and Marc soon agreed.

The conversation flowed easily as Marc told her about his experiences in Kansas City. "Natalie, on the one hand Kansas City was one of the best professional experiences I've ever had in my life. But personally it was another failure."

While Marc tried not to dwell, he told Natalie about Liz. "I think one of our problems was that we were at different points in our individual lives. I wanted her in New York with me, but she didn't want to be in New York, period. As time passes I feel bad about pressuring her to move to New York, especially since I haven't enjoyed living in New York myself lately. Thankfully Liz was much smarter than I was. She may have sensed that I was trying to turn her into something…or someone else… I don't know."

To Natalie's surprise, Marc turned the conversation to business. "I feel bad for putting the pressure on Liz to make a major move, but now I know how it feels. Your husband is a driven man, and yesterday he made quite the case for me to come to California. He was on a mission and wouldn't let up."

He leaned into the table to get closer to Natalie. "Is it your turn to pitch now?"

Natalie sat back and away from Marc. "Marc. I will leave any pitching to Gary. I'm just enjoying spending time with an old friend."

Marc had forgotten how much he had also enjoyed spending time with Natalie. He may have teased her mercilessly in the past, but he had a great deal of admiration and respect for her.

"Thank you, and I am also enjoying this time with you. But Natalie, I'd really like to hear what you have to say. Hypothetically, if you were to make a pitch to me, what would you say to win me over?"

Natalie was hesitant to say anything.

Marc reached across the table and put his hand on top of hers. "Natalie, please…"

Natalie took a deep breath and spoke in concise bullet points. "I think you're the best person for this position. I know it, Gary knows it…and I think deep down you know it, too! We both know that Gary wants you in this position and so do I. Personally I'd love having you here in LA, and I think you'd like living in California."

Then she leaned in closer. "And…for *once* in your life could you please be honest with yourself? Are you happy in New York? Maybe a change of location could be good for you. Marc, *change* can be good!"

She exhaled deeply and sat back in her chair and resolved herself to say nothing more. "That's probably what I'd say Marc…hypothetically speaking, of course." She thought she noticed a change in his eyes.

Marc squeezed her hand, knowing everything she said was true. "Of course… and thank you Natalie."

That afternoon nothing more was said about Gary's offer as two old friends enjoyed each other's company.

***

The trio arrived at Pacifica at exactly six o'clock and was escorted to a booth facing the Pacific Ocean.

"This is incredible! I don't think I could ever get tired of looking at this." Marc exclaimed.

Gary chimed in immediately. "Marc, this is one of the reasons we live in California. While this may be something you see every single day, it never gets old. While it's the same ocean, it's never the same."

Marc and Natalie were surprised by Gary's sudden poetic assessment of the Pacific Ocean.

Marc contemplated the remark. "Gary, that's really beautiful, and somewhat romantic."

All Natalie could see was her husband trying too hard.

"Marc, how much longer will you be in California?" She was hoping that her relaxed tone and manner would influence Gary to do the same.

"I've loved being here, but maybe I should think about heading back to New York this weekend; there's a redeye tomorrow night. I was hoping to spend a little time with Sabrina. Where is she tonight?"

Gary loved talking about his daughter, but he had more pressing matters to deal with this evening. Not letting Marc get away from him was number one on the list.

Natalie remained casual. "Tonight is her mall/movie/sleepover night, which beats dinner with the old folks any day, but I'm sure she'll want a proper visit with you before you leave, maybe over breakfast tomorrow? And, Marc, we've loved having you. We've really missed you!"

Gary was starting to sweat. "Now Marc, have you thought anymore…"

That's when their waitress appeared.

"Good evening everyone, and welcome to Pacifica. I'm Zoe and I'll be your server this evening. Can I start anyone off with a drink, or appetizers?" Marc and Gary each ordered a Scotch while Natalie ordered a glass of red wine.

As the waitress walked away Marc watched her appreciatively.

"Gary, I've decided that *all* of the women in California are beautiful!" He glanced at Natalie. "But then you married a California girl, so you know what I'm talking about!"

Natalie laughed out loud. "Marc, I knew there was something I missed about you! You can charm anyone."

Marc smiled and excused himself from the table and headed off in the same direction as their waitress. Natalie made sure that Marc was a safe distance away before she looked to her husband.

"Gary, please…don't act so desperate! Let Marc come to his own decision in his own time. And Gary, be prepared that he may *not* accept your offer."

Gary looked straight ahead at the ocean. "You're right. You're always right about these things. But can't he see that this position would be perfect for him?"

Natalie knew her husband was stubborn but he had to see both sides. "And for you too! But in the end it's *his* decision, and you have to respect that no matter what he decides."

Gary heard his wife, but that didn't mean he had to like what she had to say no matter how right she was. "You were with him today. Do you have any idea which way he's leaning?" He wasn't going to let this go.

"I don't have a crystal ball, but I can tell you that he's been giving your offer some serious thought, and at this point that's the most important thing you can ask of him. So please… relax! Whatever is meant to happen will happen!"

Natalie saw Marc returning and lowered her voice. "Let's just try to have a nice dinner."

As Marc sat down Natalie noticed her husband shift his position in an attempt to get comfortable which seemed to work, for a moment.

But Gary couldn't help himself. "So, Marc…no pressure, but have you thought anymore about my offer?"

Natalie gave her husband an exasperated look.

"It's alright," said Marc. "I understand how important this is to Gary and he deserves to know where I am in my decision process."

Gary and Natalie looked to one another.

"If I had seen you first thing this morning I would have told you that I had decided to return to New York as planned and take a few days to weigh the pros and cons of accepting the Creative Director position. I wanted to make a final decision away from the great weather, the ocean…" He looked at Natalie and smiled. "…and the beautiful women. Gary, I know The Epicenter has been your dream ever since I've known you, which has to be over twenty years now. And to see how far you've come is amazing. And to think you want me to become involved in the next phase of The Epicenter in such a major way is staggering, and I'm extremely flattered."

Gary started to relax a bit more. "Well, what can I say? I think you're the best person for the position and I'd really like to work with you again."

Natalie sat back and again looked toward her husband, silently pleading with him to back off.

"Marc, I don't know what else I can do to sweeten my offer. Except maybe offer you a role in our fall production."

Natalie had not even heard about this part of the offer.

"I told you about the comedy *Couched?* I've told the author about you and she would like to meet you. The role of the therapist reads like it was written for you. It would be a good showcase and introduction to the LA acting community for you. I have so many ideas that include you directing and producing. If it's the money, maybe we could work on that."

Marc assured him that money was not an issue. Then he continued. "Look… I've been based in New York for my entire professional life. I've lived there since I was nineteen years old and have never considered leaving. I know I've left town to do regional theater and go on tour, but in the end I always come back because I'm a New York actor. The thought of leaving the city scares me because I've never known anything else. I know New York, and even though I've had issues with the city for the last several years, it's still home."

Gary nodded, seeming to hear Marc for the first time. He also remembered being a New York actor.

The mood at the table had changed somehow.

Marc took a deep breath and continued. "For every reason I came up with to stay in New York, there were three or four reasons to move to LA. And then I came to the realization that there was really only one reason I had for staying in New York: the *fear* of leaving New York! I have nothing holding me in the city, and the position you've offered me seems tailor-made for me-and yes, I realized that almost immediately. But still, I wanted to go about this the right way and come to a decision properly and logically, because a major decision involving a major life change can't be entered into lightly."

Gary sighed. By now he had had resigned himself to the fact that Marc hadn't made a decision either way. But Marc had more to say. "Yes of course I'm right! But then something happened today. I had lunch with an extraordinary woman who said something that changed everything for me." He looked at Natalie and smiled. "She told me that *change can be good.* And then…I can't explain it, but the idea of moving to LA didn't sound so frightening anymore."

Natalie was smiling confidently as she grabbed Marc's hand, squeezing it for a few moments before leaning over and kissing his cheek.

Gary was trying to make sense out of what Marc had said when a popping sound got his attention.

A few moments later Zoe was placing three champagne flutes on the table as Gary tried to stop her since they had not ordered champagne.

But Marc motioned to Zoe to continue. "Gary, I ordered the champagne.

Marc raised his glass to Gary. "I would like very much to accept the position as your Creative Director at the Epicenter Theater." As he spoke a huge weight seemed to lift from his shoulders.

Gary looked at Natalie and breathed a sigh of relief. His dream was coming true.

"Gary, thanks for your trust, and for giving me this… amazing opportunity. It's going to be great working with you again, especially on this level. I just hope I can live up to your expectations."

Gary was beside himself. "Marc, I don't know what else to say. It's going to be great working with you again too! Thank you for coming on board! I see some wonderful things in our future."

Natalie raised her glass and made a toast. "To The Epicenter!" The trio toasted the theater, each other and their new professional relationship.

Marc would spent another full week in Los Angeles, hammering out the details of his contract with The Epicenter, and preparing for his relocation.

He returned to New York on the return ticket from ACT, closed out his life in New York, and then left New York City permanently on July 4, 2008. He arrived in Los Angeles in time for the Connelly's holiday barbeque and fireworks.

Marc would always remember the day he left New York; he was excited, anxious and terrified all at the same time. But July 4, 2008 not only marked the day he left New York. For whatever reason, Marc felt that this was the day he came home.

Marc's first LA apartment was in Venice, CA, not too far from the beach. He considered buying a Jeep Cherokee because he had enjoyed driving Andy Synch's Cherokee in Kansas City. Gary and Natalie convinced him to get something more practical and gas efficient, which led to the purchase of a Toyota Prius. Marc was originally fascinated with the car's technology before he found himself liking the look of the car, especially in the Magnetic Gray color. Marc loved the car's *cool* factor, and found it suited his needs perfectly.

July and August were spent networking, finding an agent, and beginning to work with Gary at the Epicenter. Before the year was over he produced and directed two play readings, including *A Private Matter* by Charlie Simmons.

Charlie had made his name in television, first working with television legend Jay Steiner in the seventies. He had gone on to produce several successful television shows of his own. He had written several plays but none had been produced since the late nineties.

The Epicenter's Play Reading series was an integral part of the Epicenter's regular season. In 2006 an innovative producer brought attention to the series when she assembled a strong cast which included a star from a successful television show, which insured the reading would receive the right publicity. Her marketing plan was ambitious but successful. As a result the theater received a great deal of attention and interest, not to mention a packed house for the reading itself. Since then the program had become an integral part of the Epicenter's mission to find new plays and authors.

In September, Marc found himself back in the business of being a working actor as the rehearsals for the new comedy *Couched* began. Gary Connelly had been correct. It was as if the role had been written specifically for him.

It was not long until Marc found his new normal.

Marc directed The Epicenter's first main stage production for 2009. Casting and rehearsals began in January. He was also looking into the future as he considered the possibility of adding a bilingual touring company to the Epicenter's educational arm within the next two years.

Within a month of Marc's arrival he knew his decision to move to LA had been the right move at the right time and confidently began to call Los Angeles home. Marc's life was finally moving forward and in a positive direction.

***

A few months after Marc arrived in Los Angeles, Natalie asked if he had thought about contacting Lauren.

Marc immediately thought of Tom Wingfield's line from his final monologue in *The Glass Menagerie*.

Time is the longest distance between two places.

Marc may have been in the same city as Lauren, but she may as well have been a million miles away.

"Sure, I've thought about contacting her, but I don't think the time is right."

The truth was, Marc was afraid. Fear is a strong, paralyzing and debilitating emotion. As easy as it was to settle into his new present, Marc was still unable to confront his past.

***

Life continued on everywhere else, including Kansas City where Andy Synch was looking to finalize his casts for his 2008-2009 Season at The Brewery Theater. He auditioned actors in person in Kansas City, New York and Chicago. But this year he had also interviewed and auditioned actors in Los Angeles via live streaming and found some good people. He even asked Marc Guiro about doing a role in the first show of the season, but Marc unfortunately was committed elsewhere. Such is the nature of the business.

A few months later in September, Andy was still thinking about Marc as he walked into baggage claim at the Kansas City Airport to pick up an actor he had booked out of LA. He felt Marc and this woman would have had great chemistry. Andy had a gut instinct about these things, but he also had complete confidence in the actor he had hired for the role he had wanted to give to Marc.

Whenever possible, Andy tried to meet his visiting actors upon their arrival at the Kansas City Airport. Experience had shown that this created a good first impression. His new actor's plane had landed minutes before and he knew she should be arriving in baggage claim at any moment. That's when a large group of people came down the escalator. He spotted her immediately. Andy moved toward the escalator calling to her. "Lauren…Lauren Dey!"

***

The new Epicenter Theater Complex would open in July of 2010 with the premiere of the comedy *A Private Family Matter.*

This play would be a fully produced version of the same play that was first presented as a staged reading in 2008.

When Gary, the artistic Director of The Epicenter Theater approached Charlie Simmons about doing a full production of *A Private Family Matter* as the first show in the new theater, he was ecstatic. So was Marc who had discovered the play and began to develop it shortly after his arrival in LA.

As previews and the show's opening night loomed closer, Marc was feeling the stress of technical week. Things were coming together, but much slower than he had hoped. He found himself spending very long hours at the theater.

In the middle of technical week chaos, Gary asked Marc if he would please do him a favor by going out on a commercial audition. The commercial for a new all-inclusive resort chain called for a professional juggler, though Gary had no idea what this had to do with an upscale resort. Gary would have sent someone else, but Marc was the only juggler he knew. Luckily, Marc had kept up this unique skill, and as far as Gary was concerned, Marc fit the description:

Juggler: Not your typical kid's birthday party performer. He can be sexy or an interesting character type with an edge. Must be skilled in all basic juggling equipment. Fire skills a plus. Looking for a strong actor with good comedic timing.

At first Marc refused to go, saying the description made no sense. But when Gary refused to take no for an answer, he relented and agreed. Besides, it might be good to get away from the theater for a few hours.

The next day he regretted the decision to leave the theater as he found himself heading to a casting studio on Sunset Boulevard in the middle of Hollywood.

Marc was extremely irritated to find the casting session was running more than thirty minutes behind schedule. There was no telling when he would get back to the theater. At one point he became so frustrated he almost left the casting studio without auditioning. Thankfully, Gary convinced Marc to stay. Marc's audition appointment was scheduled for 3:20 but he would not be seen until almost 4:00 while finishing his audition just before 4:15.

Marc's timing was *perfect*. He was in the lobby at Salon Casting on Sunset Boulevard in Hollywood California at 4:15; the correct time and location.

Marc had no way of knowing he was right on time for an *unscheduled* appointment....with his past.

Finally, it was time for the next act of Marc Adrien Guiro's life to begin.

Thank you so much for reading

Fall Again: Lost Boy

I've enjoyed sharing Marc & Lauren's story.

If you enjoyed this novel, please consider leaving a review here:

https://www.amazon.com/review/create-review?ie=UTF8&asin=1517108845&ref_=dpx_acr_wr_link#

Marc and Lauren's story is hardly over!

Thank you.

www.fallagainseries.com

Late one cold winter night, Lauren Phillips told Marc Guiro she loved him. Minutes later, he broke her heart. Feeling she had no other choice, Lauren left her beloved New York City...permanently.

*All the leaves are brown
and the sky is grey
I've been for a walk
on a winter's day
I'd be safe and warm
if I was in L.A...*

Michelle Gilliam, John Edmund Andrew Phillips

California Dreamin'

Coming Soon…

Fall Again: California Girl

Lauren: The Interim Years 1989-2010

Donna Figueroa

The Fall Again Series

Donna Figueroa

Fall Again: Beginnings

An Unrealized Romance

Fall Again: Lost Boy

Marc: The Interim Years 1989-2010

Coming Soon

Fall Again: California Girl

Lauren: The Interim Years 1989-2010

Fall Again: Reunion

A Romance Realized

www.fallagainseries.com

About the Author

Donna Figueroa is an actor and writer living and working in Los Angeles, CA. She has worked on stage and on the big and small screens. Her credits include appearances on several daytime dramas, voiceovers for animation, commercials and industrial projects, and several television commercials.

She is a producer and storyteller at The Story Salon, Los Angeles's longest running storytelling venue where she has written, performed and developed three one-person shows.

Donna considers herself an athletic shopper always in search of the ultimate bargain.

She lives in Hollywood with her husband writer/comedian Tony Figueroa, and three neurotic cats.